GW00716590

About the Author

Robin Porecky is of Polish origin but was born and brought up in England. For over twenty-five years he has worked in Sweden as a writer and knife-maker. This is his seventh novel, following 'A Pathless Land', 'Fool's Island', 'Come Into My Arms', 'The Devil's Field', 'Finished' and 'RaRa's Last Fan Dance'. It is the fifth and final book in the Magnus Trygg Swedish crime series.

Dedication

To all those who have made my life as a writer so happy and fulfilling. I have never forgotten the thrill, at the age of twenty, of seeing my first story in print. That excitement is still just as intense now, with the publication of this final Magnus Trygg novel so many years later.

Robin Porecky

BENIN BRONZE

AUSTIN MACAULEY
PUBLISHERS LTD.

A CIP catalogue record for this title is available from the British
Library.

Royalties from the sale of this novel go to the registered charity
The Camphill Village Trust Ltd.

ISBN 9781849636469 (Paperback)
ISBN 9781849636476 (eBook)

www.austinmacauley.com

First Published (2016)
Austin Macauley Publishers Ltd.
25 Canada Square
Canary Wharf
London
E14 5LQ

Acknowledgements

Special thanks to all those at Austin Macauley who helped me along the seven novel journey, notably Frances Moldaschi, Brett Sanderson, Gemma Cox, Melissa Ward, Lily Ryan and Vinh Tran.

Gratitude to Gustav Winberg, Co-founder of Readly Books AB of Stockholm, who read my novels and then, even though they were in English, added them to his list and streamed them to tablets and iPhones within Sweden, the country that has in so many different ways played an important part in my life.

None of these books would have been possible without the encouragement of my life companion who has given me such a long and loving marriage as well as finding me a log cabin in Sweden where I could write.

ALSO BY ROBIN PORECKY

A PATHLESS LAND (2009)

978-1-90560-958-1

In 1897 Martin Janow sets out to rescue Tempest, a mad
evangelist, from the wilds of Swedish Lapland. His motive is not
entirely unselfish, for Mary Warmouth has promised herself to him
if he succeeds.

But why is she so eager to save the priest, and is Tempest really
mad? On the increasingly frightening journey homeward the layers
of truth are gradually peeled back and Janow must fight for his
own sanity and his survival.

CRITICAL ACCLAIM

"The plot resembles both Conrad's *Heart of Darkness* and Henry
James' *The Ambassadors,* but is none the worse for it. The scenes
in Lapland are superbly eerie; and what Janow finds at the end of
his voyage of discovery suitably disturbing."

Alexander Lucie-Smith, The Tablet

"A gripping, erudite and highly original journey into the heart of
Nordic Darkness. Porecky explores issues of spirituality, culture
and fanaticism with the flair of a born storyteller."

Liz Jensen, author of 'The Ninth Life of Louis Drax'

"There are echoes of the great Australian novelist Patrick White's
'Voss': the same epic feel and sense of inevitability. I felt plunged
into a powerful place... and was swept along."

Piers Plowright, Triple Prix Italia winner and Radio 4's 'Saturday

review' critic

LONGLISTED FOR THE AUTHORS' CLUB BEST FIRST
NOVEL AWARD 2010

FOOL'S ISLAND (2011)

978-1-84963-075-7

In 1759 the young and wilful Franulka leaves her castle home for Warsaw, where she attracts the attentions of the King's son. Eighteen months later, with her Fool and maid, she vanishes. A closed carriage in the early morning, with an armed outrider, suggests disgrace and exile.

But nothing is as it seems. Caught up in a deadly conspiracy, only the Fool can save her. But is the price too high?

Shifting between Poland, Russia, Venice and an Adriatic island, this is a gripping historical mystery, a passionate love story and a moving study of the painful growth of self-awareness.

"Here's a novel that grabs you by the ear and eye and plunges you into the life of 18th century Poland: court intrigues, love sacred and profane, jealousy, rage, adventure, comedy and danger. And your guide is that wisest of men, a professional 'fool'. The journey to his island is a thrilling one."

Piers Plowright, Broadcaster and Critic

"A born storyteller."

Liz Jensen, author of 'The Rapture'

"Powerfully written, impeccably researched."

Elizabeth Carter-Jones, Reviewer

COME INTO MY ARMS (2012)

978-1-84963-166-2

Magnus Trygg is a happy man. He loves his Swedish wife, his two young children and his home in the sparsely populated northern county of Jämtland. He is proud of his job as a junior policeman in the local force and, though half-Thai, he has always thought of himself as fully Swedish.

Then a young Kurdish girl is found in the forest, tied to a stake and shot. Magnus, waiting with the body throughout the long summer night until an Inspector is available, discovers the murder weapon. It suggests an honour killing, and he is ordered to bring in the father. But Magnus knows Hashmet Nazif, likes him, and is reluctant to believe he would harm his daughter. Unsettled by the sudden explosion of anti-immigrant feeling, he decides to use his local knowledge to uncover anything that may suggest a different truth. It is a very dangerous decision.

"Tremendous pace, a lot of tension and a thoroughly gripping climax."

Piers Plowright, Critic and Broadcaster

"A good and surprising read."

Bernard Krichefski, Television Drama Producer

THE DEVIL'S FIELD (2013)

978-1-84963-167-9

Magnus Trygg, temporarily in charge of the High Coast district, is called out to a body with a knife in its back. August Frisk, who alerted him, insists he's never seen the man before, and the others living there agree. The only suspect is Paulus, a Sami reindeer herder who flees to the White Sea where the Russian authorities prove uncooperative. Inspector Amrén suggests the case might be suspended until he can be questioned.

But Magnus, eager to prove himself, carries on probing. He's sensed hidden tensions at Frisk's and, his own marriage in crisis, he's powerfully drawn to August's daughter-in-law, Hanna. But putting pressure on already vulnerable people reveals other secrets, which have unwanted consequences for them all.

Set in northern Sweden, Poland and the crime-ridden Russian enclave of Kaliningrad in 2004, this is the second book in the Magnus Trygg series.

"A splendid piece of work."

Brendan Walsh, Literary Editor 'The Tablet'

"A powerful tale, grippingly told. I salute the author's energy and skill."

Piers Plowright, Critic and Broadcaster

FINISHED (2014)

978-1-84963-642-1

In the Swedish town of Sundsvall the female owner of a basement flea market is killed by a single hammer blow. Magnus Trygg is away on an Inspector's course and so the case is reluctantly given to his rival for the post of Head of Homicide, Lennart Havendal. An unlucky man, struggling to cope with the death of his wife, he does uncover one vital clue: although the murder weapon is beside the body, another hammer has been removed from a display unit.

Unable to make more progress with the first murder, he is soon investigating a second. Magnus, when he returns, volunteers to act as protection officer for the woman Lennart believes will be the next victim. Magnus has his doubts, but another hammer is missing and time is not on their side.

Set in northern Sweden and England in 2005, this is the third book in the Magnus Trygg series.

"The best yet. A cracking opening, highly page-turning, full of tension, and, ultimately, rather touching."

Piers Plowright, Broadcaster and Critic

RARA'S LAST FAN DANCE (2015)

978 1 84963 644 5

Thrust into the limelight when he is tipped for future stardom as Sweden's Chief of Police, Ragnar Amrén is persuaded to perform his special fan dance at a private dinner during the County Commissioners Conference. Shortly afterwards, visited by an elderly doctor he has never met before, Amrén disappears and his visitor's dead body is discovered hanging above a road. Scandal threatens to engulf the force, and Magnus Trygg, Amrén's closest colleague, is secretly ordered to find the fugitive and take 'appropriate action' to safeguard the reputation of the police.

Set in Sweden and Poland in 2006, this is the fourth Magnus Trygg novel.

"I was on the edge of my seat and page-turning like mad. The author has given us two memorable characters in Magnus and Amrén and I'm full of admiration for the skill and storytelling which seem to me to develop with each novel."

Piers Plowright, Critic and Broadcaster

PART I

WEST AFRICA 1953 – 1954

ONE

By the time he was nineteen Johnny had managed to expunge many of his unhappy childhood memories. But as he prepared to leave England he was careful to pack three letters that were especially precious to him. The first was a thin blue air mail from North Africa, written by his father in 1942, stamped by the Military Censor and addressed to Master John Callin, the first personal mail the six-year-old had ever received. In it his father described how he had procured a one-man Africa Korps camouflage tent, adding, to Johnny's acute excitement, that he was keeping it as a present for him. Illustrating the episode was an ink drawing of a moustached infantry officer, clearly intended to be his father, peering down at the tent, revolver in hand, with a bubble coming from his mouth saying, "What a hero I'll be if Rommel is asleep inside and I capture him as well as the tent!"

Although the Desert Fox was not to be caught like that, his father, shortly afterwards, did in fact become a hero for his bravery at El Alamein; but neither the tent nor his father survived the battle.

Johnny put the folded letter in a leather pouch and carried it with him around his neck. Sometimes he missed the tent almost as much as his father, but at the age of ten the memory of something he'd never actually owned was edged aside by a neighbour's offer to him, at a price his mother could afford, of a silver Raleigh drop-handlebar racing bike with 24-inch wheels. Scarcely believing that it might soon be his, he took it for a trial spin. With the wind in his ears, he pedalled rapturously along the almost empty country roads, stopping after a mile or so to watch some German rocket-propelled doodlebugs passing low and noisily overhead on their way to attack London. Since his father's death he'd been obsessed with the details of tanks, aeroplanes and weapons. He had a secret black notebook in which he recorded technical details culled from newspapers, magazines and pamphlets. So he knew about this new German secret weapon, that about a hundred were launched each day and that the danger moment was when they ran out of fuel and the engine fell silent. Then a ton of explosive would glide down at ever increasing speed towards the ground. Mostly they reached the battered capital, but occasionally, if something was wrong with the fuel measurement, they fell early. One newspaper he'd seen claimed some had fallen on Kent, and even on Sussex, where he lived.

As if that very thought caused it to happen, the propulsion unit of the tail-end Charlie, just at that moment passing over his head, did stutter several times and then the sky was suddenly empty of sound. By then he was on his bike and racing desperately home, pedalling faster than he ever had before. But the flying bomb easily outpaced him, rushing down towards their house and exploding within his hearing.

Numbly he clutched the bike beside the rubble and watched the air-raid wardens carry the stretcher away, a blanket covering his mother's face so he had no last sight of her. The kindly neighbour attempted to distract him by telling him he could keep the bicycle. But when he was sent to live with his only surviving relative Uncle Alan, a Croydon antique dealer he'd never met, he proved to be a tight-fisted bachelor who immediately sold the bike to cover the expense of another mouth to feed.

There were so many other children orphaned by the war that Johnny did not feel exceptional in his suffering. In 1946 the second special letter arrived, this time from King George V1, addressed to all schoolchildren under a facsimile signature. "For you have shared in the hardships and dangers of a total war" he wrote, "and you have shared no less in the triumph of the Allied nations." Though Johnny could not remember ever sharing in any triumph, he liked the King for openly referring to hardships and dangers when everybody else avoided the subject in front of a child, especially his uncle who was responsible for his worst hardships.

The third memorable letter, a document on parchment, dated 1953 and specifically addressed to him, was from Queen Elizabeth II and had only recently arrived. In it, she greeted him as "Our Trusty and well-beloved John Frederick Callin" before adding, "We, reposing especial Trust and Confidence in your Loyalty, Courage, and good Conduct, do by these Presents Constitute and Appoint you to be an Officer in our Land Forces." Proud of becoming a commissioned infantryman like his father, he felt especially honoured

19

by the Queen's words. His only regret was that the experiences of the past years had made him bitter, old for his years, and so he'd already decided his forthcoming military career in Nigeria would bypass Loyalty and good Conduct altogether, though it would certainly require Courage.

***

The British Army's target, to get its soldiers to West Africa in one day instead of two, depended on the new four-engine Hermes. Johnny, who'd left London by coach at 17.15 hours, was in as much a hurry as the War Office. England held only bad memories for him: and, with no family remaining since the sudden death of his uncle, he could not wait to see the back of it. He'd never flown before, he'd never been abroad before; but he was impatient for fresh experiences and a great adventure. Flying out of Blackbushe Aerodrome that night was the start of a new life that would, he hoped, obliterate the past nine years.

He ate his meal by himself, avoiding those few subalterns he knew while he continued to shed his skin in preparation for the new persona he would gradually reveal. Then he joined the other sixty-five passengers passing through Customs and boarded the Airwork plane. All of them were military personnel: officers, NCO's and a scattering of families. In fairly cramped conditions, in high-backed seats facing the tail, they flew up into the night sky; and every second of the take-off, the climb to ten thousand feet, the gradual disappearance of the lights below, the levelling out into the empty heavens, filled him with relief. He'd plotted his path and now he was beginning to grasp his reward.

In the early hours of the morning they landed in Malta to refuel, and he allowed himself a moment's enjoyment of a country entirely new to him: the sultry air, the lapping of the Mediterranean, the inhalation of strange scents. Then he shaved, changed into tropical kit, picked up a sandwich and went outside again to watch the dawn lighten the sky. The whole island beneath was covered by a purple haze, heralding, he was sure now, his new life.

They reached Benito outside Tripoli at 1000 hours, the final stop before they crossed the Sahara. Then they were in the air once more, Johnny touching the single golden pip on each shoulder of his bush jacket, and stroking the gilt blue-backed palm trees in his pocket which would adorn the lapels of his white mess jacket. Commissioned into The Royal Sussex Regiment, seconded to The Royal West African Frontier Force, he would be attached, on reaching Lagos, to The Nigeria Regiment. It was an achievement that might have made him proud if his eyes had not been fixed on a very different ambition which was not military at all.

The plane did not behave well over the Sahara. It soared on the thermals, dropped without restraint, shuddered, and then rose again. Johnny felt queasy, many were sick, but by 16.30 he sensed the nose had dipped and the plane was losing height. Suddenly white buildings, mud huts and desert landscape appeared in the window, gratifyingly alien. It was Kano, in the north of Nigeria, their last stop before Lagos. He stared down, powerfully drawn to the barren terrain. He'd considered volunteering for The Somaliland Scouts, dreaming of

21

solitary camel patrols through empty areas, but finally the special pull of Nigeria had been too strong.

After the briefest of stops, they were flying again; and that evening the beautiful cloud formations below began to thin, allowing him glimpses of a land of rolling greenery. Behind him, Jack Chilfer was talking test match cricket, pleased that Morris was out, though it was unfortunate rain had stopped play. Johnny was as close to him as he was to anybody, and there was much he liked about him. He was tall, long-legged, at ease with his body in a way Johnny never had been; he had the straight floppy hair, piercing blue eyes, relaxed manner and confident laugh of someone educated at a real public school. Yet he didn't seem to have learnt much there, and had none of Johnny's curiosity about the world. He looked exactly as an officer and a gentleman should; an outsider would easily see in him a future diplomat or even an explorer, scanning far horizons with his vivid gaze. But he seemed to notice very little with those fine eyes, carried no strong ambition in his manly frame, and was content to drift genially, assured of wealthy ease and unconcerned about much beyond sport. Yet Johnny, aware of his own more serious and carefully hidden failings, was glad to have him as a friend and envied him his lack of demons.

As he stepped from the plane at Lagos, in the early hours of the morning, he was conscious of the damp heat of the rainy season, the shrill whirr of crickets and his own elation. He was close to where his real interest lay, a mere 370 miles to the east, the site of the ancient kingdom of Benin.

TWO

A rickety truck took five of them, all subalterns who'd trained together at Eaton Hall, to the Officers Mess at HQ Lagos. An elderly boy showed them to their rooms, and Johnny collapsed into bed, remembering just in time to tuck the bottom of the mosquito net firmly under his mattress. There was so much for him to do and there wouldn't be time enough if malaria laid him low. So it was with the determination to take no risks with illness that he fell into an exhausted sleep.

The first day was a round of visiting various listed officers. Some simply noted any useful skills he might have, especially in the sporting line; others gave him information about uniform requirements, mosquito precautions and acclimatization problems. But the most rewarding interview was with a major who told him that he and Jack Chilfer were posted to the 3rd Battalion at Abeokuta. He nodded, hiding his pleasure, for although it was not in the north, it was a small town, isolated and unpopular, so it would suit him very well.

"It's not the greatest posting," the major conceded. "No polo because of the tsetse fly, and no river bathing as the water's full of bilharzias. Abeokuta itself is a dead and alive hole, just tin shacks with no entertainment and not really the place for Europeans, which is why there are only about thirty in civilian posts outside the barracks. There aren't any better towns within striking distance either, though you may be lucky and be sent on detachment to Lagos. But militarily it's considered the best of the five battalions, perhaps because there's nothing to do except concentrate on training the men and increasing your own experience of army life. I see you were an under officer at Eaton Hall, which is no mean achievement, so you, Callin, should appreciate that. Of course there's a pool on the battalion site, tennis and squash courts, and you'll get some hockey and cricket."

As the day progressed he was increasingly fascinated by the world within a world that was military life in Nigeria and perhaps all colonial postings. The currency remained pounds, shillings and pence, and in the mess on that first day they ate fish for lunch, then steak and kidney pie for dinner. All the boys spoke English, though their lilting pronunciation was initially hard to understand, and he could not help noticing that though the locals seemed a fine race, the conditions of their life, as seen in nearby housing, roads and shops, were pretty squalid. It was as though his existence, as a white man and an officer, was to be within a protective bubble that kept out any contaminating African influences, enabling all of them to remain exactly as they always had been, English and proud of it. It did not seem to occur to anyone that he, and possibly a few others, might want to be contaminated, that he was fascinated by Nigerian culture and wanted to immerse himself in it and so expand his horizons way beyond the England he had known and hated.

It took him two days of headaches and stomach upsets to become acclimatized. He'd been constantly drilled in the basic anti-malaria precautions, the daily Paludrine tablet which he'd started taking a week before he'd flown out, the six o'clock evening change of uniform from short-sleeved bush jacket and Sam Browne, starched khaki shorts, knee-length socks and shoes, to long-sleeved shirt and tie, cotton slacks with a webbing belt and suede mosquito boots. With both uniforms, the head was always protected by a broad-brimmed felt bush hat; but despite all this he'd been bitten by a mosquito on the hand and it had swollen painfully.

After those two days in central Lagos he was transferred to the 3rd Battalion detachment just outside the city. It was livelier than HQ and that first afternoon he and Jack joined a group going off to swim. They clambered into canoes, each poled by two Nigerians, and eventually they reached the only decent bathing beach in the vicinity. Although the water was dirty brown and the currents fairly strong, they had an enjoyable swim and dried themselves lying on the hot sand.

It was on their return from this, by launch, that Johnny met the senior detachment officer, Captain Scott, and the drinking began. He was a personable man, ex-Indian Army as so many senior officers here seemed to be; but Johnny was surprised that a man of his experience and obvious intelligence was not a major at the least. But whereas Johnny sipped his one gin and tonic slowly, anxious not to get too much on his mess bill at this early stage, Scott drank whisky with steady deliberation, the bar boy refilling his glass without needing to be told.

"I tried civvy street for a while after Indian Independence," he explained, "but I couldn't get on with it. So I signed on again, this time for Nigeria, and I liked it well enough, though it was nothing like India. I went after one more civilian job back home when the opportunity came up, but that didn't suit me either. Now I'll be here until 1960 when Independence will be handed to these poor bastards too."

"What will you do then?" Johnny asked.

"I've high hopes of getting an advisory post. They're just not ready for independence, they're not long enough down from the trees and they're bound to make a mess of it. If I'm any sort of prophet, they'll need us for years or each tribe will simply go its own way, there'll be bloodshed just as there was in India, and possibly civil war. So it should see me out all right."

He pointed to the glass of whisky and winked; and Johnny liked him for his realism about his drinking problem. Later that night Scott, who had clearly enjoyed a fresh young audience, invited Jack and Johnny to join him on a trip to a place he knew in Lagos where women were available, but both politely declined, saying they were still suffering from acclimatization problems. Scott looked even worse when they saw him the next morning and he ignored them, steadily drinking himself into a stupor by lunchtime.

That afternoon Johnny was driven out into the sun by the puerile antics of two visiting subalterns whose idea of a joke was to summon the bar boy, point to the ocean several miles away through the mess window and ask if he could see it.

"Yes, sah."

"Well, don't just stand there, go and jump in it!"

They then collapsed into beer-fuelled laughter, and, delighted with themselves, repeated the trick a few minutes later. By the third time, Johnny walked out, nodding to the boy whose impassive dignity had impressed him.

The heat struck his head and so he walked into the detachment garden to get some shade. A trader, in a long white robe with a matching round cotton cap on his head, both spotlessly clean, was seated on a colourful woven mat beneath a tree, his goods spread out on a cloth before him. He rose to his feet as Johnny approached, not as a demonstration of servility but with well-mannered dignity.

"I am Kano Brass, the trader," he said, and he put his long fingers together, close to his breast, and bowed.

"Johnny Callin."

"Will you sit and look?" the trader asked, offering him a stool.

Johnny sat and cast his eyes over the ebony carvings, the bone trinkets, the beads and the brass figures.

"You do not wish to buy, I think," the trader said, smiling slightly. He had watchful eyes and Johnny thought he might be a Hausa from the Muslim north.

"Not that sort of stuff," he replied. "I do want to buy. I came to West Africa to buy. But I'm only interested in the old and the best."

"What is the old and the best?" the trader asked him courteously.

"Sixteenth or seventeenth century Benin bronzes."

The trader pursed his lips, then briefly rolled his eyes. "You must have much money," he said reflectively. "Eighteenth century work is fine, too, even if just outside the Golden Ages, but that also is rare and expensive. Perhaps you should consider more modern Benin work, even from this century, or Ashanti Kingdom pieces from The Gold Coast?"

"Late Benin pieces would be inferior copies of earlier work, Ashanti items are likely to be nineteenth century cast brass gold-weights, and neither would interest me. Have I passed the test?"

The trader acknowledged the hit with an inclination of his head. "You have the knowledge and I believe you are serious. I am still concerned about the money."

"I'll find a way to get the money if you can get a Benin bronze."

The trader thought for a while. "It will not be easy. Your countrymen looted Benin City when they attacked it fifty-six years ago, and everything of value was removed to Europe."

"That's true, and it was shameful," Johnny admitted. "But I happen to know that three years ago the Curator of the British Museum, Hermann Braunholtz, decided to sell back to Nigeria, over a number of years, thirty pieces that he felt were virtual duplicates, and so of lesser interest. I remember thinking at the time that the low prices might indicate an uneasy conscience."

Kano Brass stiffened. "You keep your ear remarkably close to the ground, Mr Callin. But this arrangement was at government level, so why would you feel it might increase the chances of such pieces becoming available?"

"Some shipments have still to arrive," said Johnny thoughtfully. "It occurred to me that with such old and fragile works of art it would not be surprising if one happened to get damaged and the smaller broken pieces might be sold off. Regrettable though it would be, one complete plaque might even be lost in transit. And then there's always the possibility that a few pieces were hidden from the British at the time of the raid, and so never went to England."

Kano Brass considered this, and finally he nodded. "I will talk to people, and then I will come to you in Abeokuta. But I fear you may be unable to afford anything I find."

"How did you know I was posted to Abeokuta?"

The trader smiled gently. "We are naturally interested in our masters, where they will be, what they will do. It is also important that we understand your individual characters so that we do not make mistakes."

"What will I be doing in Abeokuta? Do you know?"

"You will probably be given many jobs because you will do them well. But it is likely your main task will be to take charge of the Mortar Platoon."

"And what is my character?"

"You walk alone. Otherwise I would not speak to you like this. It occurs to me you do not, perhaps, believe we are only just down from the trees?"

Johnny smiled, relaxing. "No one who has seen a Benin bronze could ever believe that." He paused, regarding the trader attentively. "Your English is remarkably good. I find it unlikely that Kano Brass is your real name."

"You are right, it is not. But it serves me well as, shall we say, a trade name."

Johnny stood up. "I wonder if you were so interested in us before the date for independence was set."

The trader looked at him gravely. "There is certainly more interest now. We live in exciting times and knowledge is money."

"Then perhaps I can buy Benin bronze with information as well as money?"

Kano Brass thought for a while, "Later, perhaps. It is probably best to spend quite a lot of money first. I believe you have a saying about oiling wheels."

Johnny nodded, accepting the advice. Then he walked unhurriedly away, exploring the gardens and admiring the palm trees as he stood in their shade, deep in thought. When he decided to return to his room, the lawn where Kano Brass had been was empty.

THREE

By the end of that day he was becoming bored. The other subalterns, more interested in sport than soldiering, either went to the Polo Club to pick up pointers or practised in the cricket nets; but neither activity appealed to Johnny. As if he sensed this, Captain Scott was surprisingly brisk the next morning when Johnny stood before him.

"You and Chilfer will be off to Abeokuta in the next few days. Shortly afterwards one of you will probably be sent back here for a time. There's trouble over taxes, as usual, but this time it's looking serious. There may be protest marches and they often get out of hand and become riots. In a city as large as Lagos I'll need several platoons on standby in different areas, in case the civil authorities call us in, and I'm short of one platoon commander. Do you know anything about crowd control?"

"No, sir."

"It's perfectly simple. In the last resort, if you need to stop the mob getting close to an important government building, you can either order your men to fire over their heads, or fire into them. Since you'll be court-martialled if you fail to stop them and court-martialled if you kill any, just use your initiative and do what seems best at the time. Any questions?"

"No, sir."

"Good man. Meanwhile you need to get your uniform sorted out and understand the health regulations. On the last point, there's one regulation that's not included but is probably vital for randy subalterns, and I'll give it to you for free. When you go to the brothel and you've had your bit of *jig-jig*, pee on your hands and give your weapon a good rub down. It's an excellent antiseptic."

"Thank you, sir."

"As for uniform, the local tailor is waiting for you outside your *giddah* and he'll measure you up for your day uniform, your casual evening wear and your formal kit of white dinner jacket, black trousers and a white monkey jacket for mess nights. You get a uniform allowance of £40, but if you barter hard enough you may get it all made for a tenner. He'll also get you a felt bush hat that'll fit you properly and that'll button up on the left side in case you ever need to shoulder arms. Mostly you'll have a ceremonial sword on parade, and I assume you brought your Sam Browne with you?"

"I did, sir."

"Two things more. You're never allowed to drive yourself when you're on army business, so always order a car and native driver from the transport pool. It used to be quite a sport for the locals to drive their livestock in

33

front of an officer-driven car and then sue the army for damages in the local courts. Now they can only sue the driver and it's not worth it because he's got no money. Secondly, you need to be occupied while you're here or you'll sink into lethargy or be cheated by rogue traders. I've sent Chilfer to supervise a working party for a few days at HQ, and I noticed from your record that you've done a bit of boxing."

"I boxed for my school, yes, sir."

"This'll be right up your street, then. One of our corporals, Kalu, has been selected to represent the 3rd Battalion in the Regimental Boxing Competition. Apparently he's pretty good and his first match is tomorrow. He's been working out in a ring rigged up for him behind the transport sheds, but he's got no one to train him or act as sparring partner. There's some kit down there and I'm hoping you'll volunteer to take the job on."

Recognising that it was not a request but an order, Johnny stared straight ahead and said "Yes, Sir." with suitable enthusiasm and firmness.

Corporal Kalu was shadow-boxing in the ring when he arrived. It had been set up in a space where the bush had been cleared and so there was some shade from nearby trees. He looked lithe and fast, but as soon as he saw the officer he stopped and stood to attention, very soldierly even in vest and shorts, with gloves on his hands.

"Stand easy," Johnny said, raking around in an old tea chest and finding tracksuit bottoms, a pair of gym shoes that looked his size and a regimental vest.

"Do you think you can win the competition?"

"Just tomorrow, Suh, or all five fights?"

"Tomorrow."

"Yes, suh. Man from No. 5 Battalion no good."

"And all five?"

"Maybe. Man from No. 2 very strong."

"I'd better give you what help I can. Training first, then we might have a bout in the ring to see what you're made of. Get on with your practice while I change."

When he was ready, Johnny dug into another tea chest, found what he wanted and clambered into the ring.

"Have you used a pad before?"

Kalu looked at the felt covered metal frame which had a looped handle at each end. "No, suh."

"It's very simple. If I hold it out to right or left, you use a straight jab. If I hold it in front of my stomach, you come in close, left, right, left, right. Upside down in front of my face, give it an uppercut, as hard as you can; and if I tilt it either side hit it with a left or right hook."

He crouched, well-balanced as the school RSM had taught him, circling his opponent, keeping his distance then darting in close and out again, offering the pad,

35

demanding different responses. Although Kalu was slow at first, watchful, assessing what was required, he hit hard when he saw a real opportunity. But as soon as he felt more comfortable with the technique Johnny was overwhelmed by his speed, by the force of his punches and by his astonishing ability to predict what he was going to do with the pad, hooking, jabbing and uppercutting almost before he'd got the pad properly into position. When he could take no more, arms aching, stomach throbbing and legs weakening, he made Kalu skip, first on two legs, then on one, then on the other. He had him running round and round the area, alternately jogging and sprinting, and finally doing press-ups, on two hands and then one. But though he made him sweat profusely he never succeeded in exhausting him completely.

As he watched all this, assessing his strength and stamina, Johnny had been thinking; and now he came to a decision. If he was to get a lot of money for Kano Brass, he would have to bet on Kalu. But the only way to know how safe the bet would be was to fight him himself.

"Get in the ring," he said, pulling on a pair of gloves and using his teeth to lace them up as tightly and safely as he could. You're not afraid to hit an officer?"

"You my trainer now?"

Johnny nodded.

"Then it's OK, suh."

36

They touched gloves and circled, testing each other, searching for a weak spot. None of the punches was too hard, and most of them were blocked. But Johnny was manoeuvring his opponent into a dazzling beam of sunlight which pierced the tree branches. As soon as he saw Kalu was partially blinded he gave him two really hard punches and knocked him down.

He stepped back, giving Kalu time to get to his feet and recover, knowing what he must now expect. Kalu came at him swiftly, and this time he didn't pull his punches. Johnny tried to protect himself, went into a clinch, but he was no match for the other man. His nose was soon dripping blood and he was gasping for breath after a blow to the solar plexus, followed by one to the head which split his eyebrow. Vaguely he saw the right hook and clumsily blocked it; but it was a feint and his head seemed to explode as the left hook knocked him down.

He lay there, trying not to lose consciousness. But he must have done so, for when he came round Kalu was kneeling beside him, cradling him against his shoulder and pouring water over his face.

"Very sorry, suh," he said anxiously.

"That was a bloody good punch, Corporal, and I'm betting money on you to win tomorrow. If you lose, I'll put you on a charge for assaulting an officer. Do you understand that?"

"Yes, suh," answered Kalu, and his face broke into a huge grin. "You make plenty money."

Kalu was right. He won every fight up to the final and Johnny, putting all his available money on him, made a large sum. He then bet against him in the final, when he was fighting the man from No 2 Battalion and made even more. He had no doubt the trader would quickly hear about it, for he'd noticed how unwarily white officers talked in front of their boys, bar staff, mess waiters and visiting tailors and barbers. If all they overheard, together with everything the battalion clerks knew, was passed on in return for a small *dash*, those who were interested, like Kano Brass and doubtless his masters, would have already amassed a great deal of information about them all. So Johnny made sure his temporary houseboy knew why his face and body were so bruised and why a piece of sticking plaster held his eyebrow together; that the bar boy overheard his boasting when he ordered celebration drinks after Kalu's first victory; and that Captain Scott received a brief written report on his training of the boxer indirectly, through his office clerk.

Confident that by the time he met Kano Brass in Abeokuta his improved financial situation would have been noted, as well as his willingness to take personal risks to achieve his aims, he suffered only one setback. Captain Scott, assuming Kalu's success was the result of Johnny's excellence as a trainer rather than the boxer's natural ability, kept him at the detachment until the tournament was over. Only then was he allowed to follow Jack Chilfer to Abeokuta.

FOUR

Johnny liked his first glimpse of Abeokuta, a small town looking slightly bewildered as it rose from the surrounding bush, its size dwarfed by the spread-eagled area of the army base beyond it. He was saluted at the gates and then driven past the line of battalion offices and the shabbier hutted area for the platoon commanders. As they went up the hill he spotted the distant lines which were the living quarters for the native troops, the more impressive Sergeants Mess for the white NCOs, the sports ground with marked-out hockey and football pitches and the lengths of matting-covered concrete in the cricket nets.

At the top of the hill, with a fine view over the town and the promise of a fresher breeze, stood the senior officers' bungalows, the subalterns' hutted *giddahs* and the Officers Mess. They were scattered among the palm trees, lawns and flower beds of the battalion gardens which were lovingly tended by a team of gardeners who watered them in the dry season and drained them when the rains came. Johnny was dropped off at his quarters, a single room in a partitioned wooden building with a tin roof and a verandah overlooking the lawns. The driver, before moving off, handed him a written instruction, sealed in an envelope, to present himself at the CO's office at 07.30 the next morning. His boy, Owdu, a short energetic-looking man old enough to have been his father, introduced himself with a salute and a beaming smile. He carried Johnny's kit into his room, unpacked it and laid the clothes lovingly out on the bed and over the chair. Then he brought him a cup of tea, cleaned his shoes, seized the sweaty travel clothes Johnny had removed, and in an astonishingly short time returned them to him washed, ironed and starched where necessary.

Within a few days, Owdu became invaluable to him. He spoke little, though he answered intelligently if asked about local customs, religion and magic. He bought all the necessities of life: soap, toothpaste, shaving cream and shampoo, got Johnny's boots and shoes mended, made the bed and cleaned the room. Johnny taught him to wash his brush and comb, and whenever he was in a hurry in the morning he would return to find his razor had been cleaned as well. He never complained and he cheerfully coped with three changes of clothes a day. But what was more important, Johnny liked Owdu and he trusted him.

Nobody else was about on the day of his arrival, for it was the afternoon siesta. So once he'd placed a few personal items on his chest of drawers and on the small table beside his mosquito-netted bed, he put on shorts, shirt and hat and went outside, noticing Owdu's surprise. The sun was very hot, but he explored the area thoroughly, wanting to get his bearings, noting the boundaries and discovering places where he could be out of sight and in the shade. When he got back he found a green military bicycle leaning against the verandah which, Owdu explained, Transport had designated for his use so that he would not have to walk.

The next morning he stood facing his overweight, irascible Commanding Officer, Lieutenant-Colonel Charles Charrington, familiarly known, though never in his hearing, by his wife's nickname for him, Crocus.

"Very fiery man," Owdu had informed him with a grin. "When he rage and shout you go deaf. But good leader, everybody obey, everybody like him, good heart. But everybody fear him except Mrs Colonel, he never shout her, do what she say mighty quick."

"I want you to be Battalion Mortar Officer, Callin," the CO told him, fulfilling the trader's prophecy. "They're a good lot in the Mortar Mlatoon, all Hausas from the north, but they're Muslim, not Christian, so don't preach at them, they don't like it. They're bloody good soldiers, fighting's in their blood, and they hate the southern Igbos and Yorubas which can cause trouble in the Battalion. Before we English came to Nigeria they'd been slaughtering the southerners for hundreds of years, and they'll probably do it again as soon as independence is declared. That'll be their business by then, so we don't discuss it. If they respect you, they'll die for you. If they don't, they'll ignore you and do what's necessary anyway. Any questions?"

"Does the platoon have three inch mortars?

"Yes, of course they bloody do. You didn't think a battalion goes into battle with little hand-held two inch jobbies, did you?"

41

"I've only ever fired two inch jobbies, Sir. I know nothing at all about big jobbies."

The colonel's already high colour reddened alarmingly as he peered closely at Johnny to see if he was trying to be funny.

"Then you'll have to learn about big jobbies, won't you, Mr Callin, and that's why I'm sending you to the Gold Coast on a three week course. You'll leave for Lagos in seven days, staying with the detachment until arrangements are made to fly you to Accra. For the duration of the course you'll be seconded to the Gold Coast Regiment, so they'll look after you. I could have sent you on the twelve week course organised by the Sierra Leone Regiment but I can't spare you for so long. If you're as smart as you look you'll pick it up in a quarter of the time. And in case you think you're being short-changed, the only course in Nigeria is a week in Ibadan, and you'd be off playing polo most of the time and come back knowing fuck-all. Any other questions?"

"No, sir."

"Then go next door, present yourself to my adjutant and he'll sort out everything else."

Johnny saluted, about-turned, marched smartly out to the verandah, right-turned and went along to the office of the pleasant, bespectacled Major Williams who was sitting behind his desk there, his phone to his ear. The adjutant pointed to a chair, listened a moment longer, then reluctantly put the phone down.

"I don't think victory's going to be easy," he said with a sigh. "We're going to have to fight pretty hard to win this one."

Johnny, bewildered, wondered whether he was referring to the war in Korea. Uncertain how to reply, he simply nodded, but Williams realised he didn't understand.

"I'm listening to the Test Match, man. Just dial 14 from your office and you'll get the commentary on your phone. Signals kindly set it up for us, put a receiver by the radio in their HQ and Bob's your uncle. Whenever the Test's on it looks as though there's some military emergency, requiring all the battalion officers to be busy on the telephone. I was just listening to the experts' prediction, which was rather gloomy. You are a cricketer, I assume?"

"I haven't played for several years," Johnny answered cautiously. "I specialised in tennis at sixth form level."

"Splendid. I'll add you to the cricket team, then. Bowler or batsman?"

"Batsman."

Williams looked mournful. "We've got batsmen, old boy, but we really need a bowler. Still, you're young and keen, I'm certain you can bowl a bit. There's a match against Abeokuta Town this evening, all Europeans of course. I'll see you there."

The match proved useful in two ways. He met several Englishmen who worked in Abeokuta and he paid particular attention to the bank manager, Mike, who looked after the battalion pay rolls. Although it was attributable more to the poor quality of the batting than his own awkward, around the wicket spin bowling, he took 3 wickets for 11 runs. This earned him a reputation as a sportsman which seemed to matter a great deal more than military prowess.

He'd already passed another initiation trial in the mess at lunchtime. It had been African curry, with numerous saucers of different varieties of chopped vegetables, fruit and nuts to accompany the rice and curried meat. As he entered the mess, cautiously watchful as ever, he'd noticed a grinning subaltern rapidly remove a saucer with something red on it. He dutifully asked what the various saucers contained and was warned he should take as many chopped tomatoes and cucumbers as possible to counteract the strength of the curry. He did so without comment, took a large mouthful of rice, curry and tomato, preparing himself for what might happen. Immediately his mouth and throat were on fire, his eyes watered and he gasped for breath, desperately reaching for a glass of water as the others at the table fell about laughing.

"You took chilli instead of tomatoes, old boy," his neighbour explained, wiping tears of laughter from his eyes. He got up, brought the saucer of tomatoes which had reappeared, and ladled them onto Johnny's plate. Pretending to be even more incapable of speech than he really was, Johnny joined in the laughter and was slapped on the back and told he was a good fellow.

As a good fellow and a sportsman, his life quickly settled into a routine. He took over his Mortar Platoon

Commander's office and introduced himself to his men, smartly paraded outside. Most of them towered over him, and all were more Arab than African, with the proud military bearing of true warriors. He liked them at once, hardy men who would certainly never give him their loyalty unless he deserved it. He had already been told that few had passed the educational qualification in English required for promotion, and none had risen above the rank of corporal, though the senior one had the honorary rank of Platoon Sergeant. But it didn't seem to worry them, for they were men who were well aware of their fighting qualities, and despised the clever southerners who climbed to the highest non-commissioned ranks. He wondered how they would have reacted if one of the scattering of Nigerian subalterns, all southerners and none in his battalion, had been put in charge of them; but he assumed that would never happen until independence was achieved. Then it might well be one of the many tribal difficulties that would threaten the racial integration the English believed they had achieved.

To his relief, Johnny found they could understand his English perfectly even if their own was meagre. He explained he knew nothing about mortars, was soon going on a course, but meanwhile he wanted to learn as much as possible from them. So he watched carefully as they assembled a mortar, went through the firing technique, then took it down again and each carrying a part, ran with it into the bush, others following with boxes of bombs. None seemed to tire despite the heat, so he made them do it again and again until he was certain he'd learnt what was required. On the last time, he ran with them, insisting on carrying the long and heavy barrel even though it meant they only got a hundred

45

yards into the bush and his back ached for the rest of the day.

In the evenings, though not on that day, he played tennis on the concrete court, swam, restlessly explored the surrounding area, and read six-day-old English newspapers. He began to smoke small cigars which were on sale for four shillings and sevenpence for fifty; and he drank gin and tonic in preference to whisky, though he did so sparingly for he was always conscious of other financial requirements. Twice in that week before leaving for Accra, he watched films projected onto a screen erected on the lawn outside the mess. It was a thrilling experience to sit in the fresher evening air, so far from home, and watch recently released movies, though both were unfortunately black-and-white versions instead of the original Technicolor. The moths loved it as much as he did, fluttering in the projector beam and sometimes landing momentarily on the screen. Johnny decided that one unusually large moth could read his mind, going close to the screen whenever something caught his attention, but only settling on a scene that personally affected him. In 'Belles on their Toes' it hovered over every appearance of Jeanne Crain, one of the 'Picturegoer' pin-ups he'd placed on the wall of his room. But at the end of 'Ivanhoe' it alighted on the mouth of Elizabeth Taylor's Rebekah as she said her heart was breaking, moving to her father's lips as he responded with the words Johnny might have used about the years after the death of his parents: "My heart broke long ago, but it serves me still."

Since his arrival in Abeokuta, he'd been looking out for Kano Brass; and one day he returned to his *giddah* after lunch to find him sitting patiently on the verandah outside his room.

"I hear you have settled in well," the trader said quietly, after glancing round to be sure no one else was in the vicinity. "Your men respect you, and I must congratulate you on your unusual bowling technique. It seems it was as successful as your gambling on the boxer you trained. Your bets did not, of course, raise enough for a complete Benin bronze, but I have managed to acquire a fragment which I can offer to you for the bargain price of all you won. Even that is only possible because we wish to encourage your collecting."

"We?"

"I speak of the many traders who wish to serve you."

"Do you indeed?" commented Johnny with a smile, though his heart was beating faster as he stared at the small bundle of cloth that was being held out to him. He took it, fingered it, sensing what it might be from its shape. Then, with slow deliberation and mounting excitement, he unwrapped it.

He recognised it at once, proving to himself how valuable his years of work in his loathed uncle's antique shop had been. It was a seventeenth century leopard, typically and wonderfully Benin, not truly bronze but leaded brass, once part of a much larger piece made for a Queen Mother's altar, showing her flanked by attendants and protected by leopards. But it was perfect in itself, the leopard representing the power of the ruling Oba, an object so exquisite that he felt almost sick with pleasure.

"The workmanship is breathtaking," he said huskily. "It's almost as powerful as an Ife piece."

Kano Brass threw up his hands in mock horror. "Please, Mr Callin, do not ask me to get you a 13th century Ife crowned head."

Johnny shrugged, realising the comment was an indication their relationship had reached a new level, where his knowledge was taken for granted and so he could be gently teased about it. "I doubt if much is really beyond you," he replied, "but as only seventeen heads were found there, and all are carefully documented, I shall not mention them again"

The trader bowed his head slightly, acknowledging the politeness. "I am pleased what you hold in your hand affects you so powerfully. But you must study it more carefully in your room before you finally accept. It is costing you all the winnings you so painfully acquired."

"I'd certainly like to have a closer look at it, but I don't need to consider the price. I'm holding a miracle in my hand, and it's not something to haggle about. On the assumption that this may lead to more pieces, even more complete ones, I'll pay what you ask."

Kano Brass nodded solemnly, treating the matter with the same reverence as Johnny. "We both understand such pieces are beyond bargaining, and that is why I do not normally come to Abeokuta, a place frequented by the sort of traders who think barter is part of the game. I'm sure I do not need to remind you to keep it well-hidden, for a purchase of this nature is not usual and would provoke comment."

"But you have more?"

Kano Brass permitted himself a discreet smile, "I do not have them myself, being only a trader. But I am in contact with people who may be able to acquire them. Now give me back the fragment, shaking your head in refusal, and I will pass you a copper balancing toy, which, for the sake of anyone who may have seen us together or who may later enquire what you purchased, you can place openly in your room and show to people. When I pass it to you, and you take it into your room to consider, the fragment will be out of sight in the base. Once you have checked it and are content, hide it away, roll up the money very tightly so that it looks a small amount, then come out and hand it to me. I assume you did not put your winnings in the bank where there would be a record of it."

"I'm sure you've already ascertained, through the bank clerks in your pay, that my gambling was strictly cash," Johnny said. He took the balancing figure that was offered to him, curled his fingers securely around the underside of its domed stand and forced himself to walk unhurriedly to his room. There, with the door closed, he used a powerful jeweller's glass, revealing even more of the leopard's glory, and then went out with the money.

The trader rose to receive it, and, as he slipped it beneath his robe, he murmured, "When you are in the Gold Coast, it is possible you will be approached and a deal may be proposed."

That evening there was a Guest Night in the mess and everything was at its best. The mahogany tables

49

gleamed, the battalion silverware shone, the shaded candles flickered, the officers stood taller and slimmer, chin in, chest out, their starched white monkey jackets glittering with gilt pips, gold buttons and brass palm tree lapel badges, the black bow ties set off against the red cummerbunds and blue or black trousers. A full-dress band was playing on the lawn outside to welcome the guests, one of whom was Mike Dwyer, the Abeokuta bank manager. He introduced his wife, Maisie, who could not have been more than two years older than Johnny, though she seemed younger and a great deal sillier. But she was pretty in a giggly blonde way, and he made sure he listened to her chatter and appeared interested in everything she said.

After the food and wine, the serious drinking commenced, followed by the mess games. Mike was made an honorary member of the mess by being crammed into the open side of a large military drum, rolled at speed across the lawn and then down the long garden steps. As he lay gasping at the bottom, still stuck in the drum and his head spinning with the motion, a large amount of whisky was poured down his throat and he was carried back to the mess in triumph on the shoulders of the subalterns. He spent the rest of the evening bleary-eyed, slurred of speech and half-somnolent on a sofa, leaving Maisie to her own devices. Overwhelmed by the occasion, deafened by the raucous level of masculine hilarity during the increasingly wild antics of the officers, she timidly attached herself to Johnny and Jack.

After some lower level activities like arm-wrestling and horse and rider encounters, a roar went up demanding High Cockalorum. A number of eight-man teams were formed which scrummed down and braced themselves against the mess wall. The guests and senior officers then took it in turns to run across the mess, leap in the air and crash down on the rugby scrum in an attempt to crush them to the floor. This went on, with rising excitement, until only a single scrum survived. Jack was one of the props in the front row of this one, leaving Johnny to stay protectively with Maisie, and they had held up manfully. But then, as was traditional, they had to face their final and greatest challenge. Crocus himself, fifteen stone of gin-fuelled commanding officer, hurtling across the floor and farting so much as to seem jet-propelled and momentarily airborne, fell on them like an avenging fury. It was too much for the scrum which gave way, collapsing on the floor in a heap of tangled arms and legs. There were roars of approval for their indomitable colonel until it was realised that he had accelerated a fraction too much, misjudged his forward momentum and driven his head straight through the wall panel so that it was now bellowing in the empty dining room while the rest of his body remained in the mess, twisting impotently in the air. His initial shout of triumph changed to oaths of indignant anger as he realised his predicament, and his officers ran to hold him up. Despite the fact that his roars of rage were making the regimental trophies rattle in the dining area, his wife's pithy comment was perfectly audible above the din.

"You bloody idiot, Crocus," she said. "Now pull him out before he does himself an injury."

After several hours, few were still on their feet. Johnny, flat out behind a sofa, found that Maisie had crept in beside him and her unexpectedly soft and shapely body was wedged against his. His virgin response to such arousal was to get his arms around her and kiss her passionately; and it seemed to him that she responded eagerly. But his bliss was rudely shattered by a blast on the hunting horn that signalled the departure of the disinterred colonel and his lady, and so the official end of the Guest Night.

"Go and hide yourself on the verandah of the neighbouring building and you'll see something funny," whispered Johnny, and as soon as she'd slipped away he went outside to follow the colonel and his wife to their car. He nudged Jack Chilfer, with whom he'd planned this escapade, and they drifted over to the two brass cannons at the entrance to the Mess. Beside them, hidden in the shadows, they'd placed two thunder flashes used in battle-simulation exercises and a couple of grapefruit. As the colonel's car drove away in stately splendour they each lit a thunderflash by striking its end, slid them into the cannon barrels, rammed the grapefruit down on top of them, and hastily slipped away into the darkness. Both cannon exploded and the grapefruit were propelled through the air, one splattering onto the road in front of the car, the other, to general acclaim, scoring a direct hit on the rear side door.

Everybody felt it had been a splendid evening. Maisie gave Johnny another kiss and said she'd never seen anything like it, which probably concerned the flying grapefruit, but which he liked to think might refer to the swelling barely contained inside his trousers.

Johnny, in his turn, whispered that though he was being sent away on a course he desperately wanted to see her on his return.

Then the evening was hijacked by the serious late-night drinkers and the guests gradually went home. Johnny retired to his bed where, beneath the mosquito net, he stroked the Benin leopard, overawed by its beauty. An idea was already forming in his mind about how he might raise the money for another such piece; and as a delightful corollary to that thought, he wondered how it would feel to hold and stroke Maisie's naked flesh instead of the bronze.

FIVE

A West African Airways Corporation Bristol Freighter carried him to the Gold Coast. It was an enjoyable contrast to the Hermes which had brought him from England, when the travellers had all been army personnel. Now, as the two sides of the large nose of the freighter opened in a wide grin to receive its passengers, and there was a surge forward to get seats or floor space, he saw that on this flight his companions were largely native and not all human. Loud, colourfully-dressed *mammies* with huge bundles on their heads and children clutching their skirts herded sheep, goats and chickens in front of them into the body of the plane. Although there were a few other Europeans, he was the only army officer; and, as such, a seat was carefully left free for him. Then the nose closed, the engines thundered deafeningly, the frame creaked and juddered, and after a short run the Freighter lurched lugubriously into the air.

There were no stewardesses, and he could not have spoken to them if there had been, for the noise in the air was almost as ear-shattering as it had been on take-off. All around him the *mammies* grinned excitedly, munching yams and fruit. Goats and sheep sniffed at his knees, a hen briefly used him as a perch, and he revelled in his first colourful and truly African experience.

54

Several of the women were bare-breasted, and the others unconcernedly revealed almost as much, only bothering to twitch the cloth to cover their nipples if they happened to notice his glance fall upon them. By the time the plane began to drop down to Accra, he realised he'd been so absorbed in the abundant life around him he'd never once felt airsick.

There was nobody to meet him at the airport, but in the distance he spotted a smart young black officer in a similar uniform to his and he went across to him. Native officers from Nigeria, Sierra Leone and the Gold Coast were, he knew, all Sandhurst-trained; but they were quite a rare sight and he wanted to meet one.

He held out his hand, introducing himself and noting as he did so that this lieutenant wore the insignia of the Gold Coast Regiment.

"I'm Ralph Okoro," the subaltern replied. "Are you for the mortar course?" He spoke English beautifully, and Johnny could not help noticing the matching beauty of the man himself. It rattled him, and when he'd nodded, he spoke the first words that came into his mind, regretting them as soon as they left his mouth.

"Are you here to meet me?"

"I'm returning from a conference in Paris," Okoro explained, generously overlooking the suggestion that any officer, let alone one with a pip more than Johnny, would do anything as demeaning as meet course members as though he was a mere driver. "But I know about the course because I helped to arrange it months ago, so I'll give you a ride in my taxi. I'm going to B Mess. Is that where you're staying?"

Johnny, still overwhelmed by Okoro and embarrassed by the unfortunate impression he must be making, compounded it by haplessly appearing to criticise the organisation of the course. "I've been given no details, but I'd be grateful for the lift and then I can sort it out."

"Cockup as usual, and at our end," Okoro said with a deprecating smile. "Welcome to the Gold Coast, and call me Ralph."

Grateful for Okoro's diplomatic grace but still annoyed with himself, Johnny tried to relax beside him, and realised that it was in fact the presence of the man himself that was unnerving him. For the first time since his parents' death he was in the presence of someone he could acknowledge as superior to him; and instead of fighting it, struggling to regain the upper hand, he surprised himself by gladly ceding the leadership role to him. This was someone who could, for a brief period at least, relieve him of the pressure of always being on his guard, lest anybody should again dominate him as his uncle had. Somehow, with Ralph, taller, better looking, more elegant, naturally authoritative and so much more at ease with himself, he could allow himself the luxury of drifting behind somebody better and stronger. It was as though he'd suddenly found an older brother, though that was not how he thought of Ralph. But at this stage he didn't really care how he *did* think of him, or what part he might play in his life. It was the strangest feeling, almost akin to finding God, and he was filled with happiness, content to wait and see how it all developed.

The army camp was some distance from Accra, a city that seemed just as bustling and overcrowded as Lagos. But it was close to the sea, and that thrilled Johnny.

"Do you surf?" Ralph asked him.

"I tried it once in Lagos and it was an amazing experience, even though I was so useless. I ripped my trunks to pieces on the sand, swallowed a lot of sea, but there was something so special about it that I knew I had to master it if I ever got the chance."

"I'll take you out tomorrow morning and give you a few pointers. It's not so difficult, once you know the basic technique and the best places to practise."

"I'd love that," said Johnny instantly, his heart beating unusually rapidly, "but the course may start tomorrow."

"Don't bank on it. Usually nothing much happens for several days as people drift in, and somebody finally gets a grip."

At B Mess it became clear that nobody had been expecting him. But in a very short time Ralph had officially attached him to the Gold Coast Regiment, got him temporary membership of the mess, found him a pleasant room overlooking the gardens and produced a boy for him.

"There's an open-air film tonight on the lawn, 'Diplomatic Courier' I think, and I hope I'll see you there. As I suspected, the course doesn't start for three days and so we can fix up some surfing when we meet this evening."

Johnny enjoyed the film, feeling that in some ways its revelation of deception and trickery shone a mirror onto areas of his own life. Ralph said he'd pick him up at 08.30 and he was punctual to the minute. But instead of the car Johnny had expected, Ralph was on foot, wheeling two bicycles.

"You'll find it easier to find your way on your own if you cycle the length of it with me today," he explained, and so Johnny carefully noted landmarks as they pedalled along. Ralph did not talk as they cycled, and Johnny liked him for that as he did not want to be distracted from all there was to see, and he was never a great talker himself.

At the beach they got into their trunks, took a surfboard each from the military store there, and splashed out though the shallows until the sea was up to their waists and the largest rollers were pushing past their shoulders.

"Hold the board straight out in front of you, bend your knees, look over your shoulder until a big roller is rising up behind you, then push off just as it reaches you, throwing yourself onto the board and letting yourself be carried up the beach without the sand shredding your shorts."

Johnny was amazed how quickly he got the hang of it, though he lacked the elegance that marked Ralph's runs. The sensation of being carried effortlessly at what seemed to him to be such a tremendous speed was not only exhilarating, there was something mystical about it; he felt a surge of gratitude to Ralph for giving him such a fresh and unexpected experience.

After half an hour, when he felt really confident, Ralph showed him how to mount the board with one knee forward, the other leg straight out behind to balance himself. It was more difficult, but once he'd mastered it the satisfaction of truly seeming to ride the wave was immense.

When they'd had a break, drinking tea from the thermos Ralph had brought with him, he showed Johnny how to rise from the kneeling position to stand on the board and guide it with the downward pressure of his feet. Though he never fully mastered it that day, he achieved a few partial runs before falling off that left him with an insistent determination to persevere, longing to be able to stand with the same apparent nonchalance as Ralph and carve his way left and right along the roller.

"Did you enjoy the film?" Ralph asked idly as they lay side by side relaxing on the hot sand.

"Very much," Johnny replied.

"Do you remember a scene in it where Tyrone Power discovers somebody has slipped something into the top pocket of his jacket, a photo with the name of a *rendezvous* hotel on the back? I was reminded of that when I got back to my room last night and found someone there who wanted me to give you a slip of paper, also with a secret meeting place on it."

Johnny felt the hairs prickle on the back of his neck, and in an instant his casual airport meeting with Ralph took on a possibly different significance. He wondered whether a moth had landed on the screen at the very moment when the *rendezvous* photo was secreted, but he said nothing, only staring expectantly at Ralph.

"It's a bit difficult to slip the note anywhere when you're only wearing trunks," Ralph said with a slight smile. "But it's urgent, for this evening."

Johnny sat up, pretending to be surprised, remembering what Kano Brass had said, but still a little perturbed, for he knew no one in Accra. "Who was he, what did he want?"

"I can't tell you the answer to the first question, and he's not the sort of man to whom you would ask the second question. He has power and influence, and I'm just the messenger boy."

"But you knew him, you'd met him before?"

"A group of us have had dealings with him, yes, though I can give you no details. With independence for the Gold Coast only four years away, and for Nigeria and Sierra Leone shortly afterwards, there are many groups who exchange information."

"He's a politician, then?"

Ralph laughed. "I suppose all of us are who take an interest in the future of our countries. But I rather think he wants to talk to you about antiquities. Do you have an interest in such things?"

60

Johnny's heart thumped with elation. "West African antiques, yes."

"An interest you inherited from your parents, I suppose?"

The question convinced Johnny that his meeting with Ralph had not been the chance encounter it had seemed. But he'd always realised that sooner or later there would be some form of interrogation, and he decided he'd rather have it here, with Ralph, in the open, than in less pleasant circumstances. He lay down beside him again to avoid his gaze.

"Both my parents are dead," he answered. "They were killed in the war, my father in North Africa at El Alamein when I was eight, my mother two years later when a flying bomb destroyed our house while I was out cycling."

He heard Ralph shift in the sand, and then he felt his firm hand grip his shoulder.

"I'm sorry. It was a casual question and I should not have asked it."

Johnny put his hand on top of Ralph's for a moment. "It's all right, I have no problem talking about it, not now. But neither of them was at all interested in antiques. That came from Uncle Alan, the only relative I had left. He was a dealer with a shop in Croydon and, unusually at that time, he specialised in West African antiquities. He saw the Benin bronzes when they came to England in 1948, and he took me to see them during the Festival of Britain three years later. He had what he claimed to be a Benin plaque hanging on the wall of his living room, depicting the Oba Ozolu on horseback with his companion Laisolobi beside him, both gripping the same *eben* sword."

"I seem to remember that's the symbol of leadership, and that Laisolobi turned against his king when he became dictatorial and put his troops at risk."

Johnny looked at him, delighted. "You know the story, then?"

"All officers placed in the tricky position I am in are always reminded of the story. It's a powerful warning against going your own way without consulting others who have hitherto been faithful to you. But I'm astonished your uncle had that bronze, it's almost priceless."

"As soon as I'd studied enough, I realised it was a twentieth century copy, still powerful in its own way but roughly cast, and lacking the exquisite detail and the extraordinary facial features, especially the eyes. As a boy I desperately wanted to be like the smallest figure in it: helmeted, armoured and ready to blow his horn, though of course I learnt later he wasn't small because he was a child, but because he was only an unimportant attendant."

"You sound as though you were lonely."

"I was. So I filled my life with the study of genuine Benin bronzes. They became my passion, and I learnt everything I could about them, becoming even more knowledgeable than my uncle."

"And you wish to acquire something genuine to give your uncle, to replace his copy and to thank him for taking your parents' place?"

"He never took my parents' place. He was a vile man and I hated him. Until I learnt to box and became physically strong enough to look after myself, I pretended I was that little figure in the bronze, because the horn might raise the alarm whenever I heard my uncle approaching my bedroom, and the helmet and armour might protect me from his unwanted attentions. So all I need now is the enormous satisfaction of getting a collection of bronzes finer than anything he could ever have dreamed of owning."

They were both silent for a time, the distant, almost threatening, thunder of the surf contrasting with the safe warm embrace of the sand. Then Ralph spoke.

"It's ironic that we are lying at the edge of what used to be called The Slave Coast and each of us is, in some way, enslaved: you to the past, I to the future. Your people drew a line on the map and said it was one country, Nigeria. But it was three countries: the land of the Muslim Hausa in the north; the Christian Yoruba in the south-east; and, in the west, the Igbo whose beliefs are a mixture of Christianity and Animism. Though I work here as it gives me freedom of movement and because independence comes three years earlier, I am an Igbo from Nigeria."

Ralph's voice had altered when he spoke so personally, just as Johnny's had become tight with distaste when he'd mentioned his uncle. But what throbbed in Ralph's voice when he said he was an Igbo was a passionate pride.

"When we finally get our independence in 1960," Ralph continued, "I believe, and so do many others, that the country will gradually split apart. The Hausa and the Yoruba will probably make common cause against us because their tradition is rule from the top, whereas we are used to a more democratic way. I do not doubt for a moment that eventually there will be civil war. In preparation for that, we, the Igbo, have to be rich enough and sufficiently well-armed to break away. That is why I leave tomorrow for your country, to attend a weapons training course at a place called Hythe. Do you know it?"

"Yes, I've shot there: rifle, Sten gun, Bren gun, even revolver though I didn't hit much with that. I also threw grenades there, fired two inch mortars and learnt to blow up the shells and grenades that didn't explode. So the instructors have a lot of expertise, and it's lucky you're going now, in our summer, because it's pretty bleak at all other times. I imagine you may be looking at heavier weapons, too?"

"Yes. And I've been led to believe I shall meet with people who, at a price, will be able to supply arms."

"It must be dangerous work."

"I have a cause to serve. Can you call revenge on your uncle a cause? Because what you are doing is dangerous too. You, like me, are getting involved with people who are not at all nice and I worry about what may happen to you."

Johnny turned, propping himself up on one elbow to look down at Ralph.

"I'm not an idealist like you, Ralph. I wish I was, but my life after my parents died didn't allow idealism. I not only lost them, which hardened me, but I was also deprived of the few personal items that might have helped me to cope. They were silly things like a tent and a bicycle, but they were all I had to dream about. I resented their loss; and deep down I grew greedy to replace them with possessions that would once again be special to me. I learnt to look after myself at quite an early age; I have no illusions about people, I expect to survive and, by whatever means available to me, I'm determined to get those particular objects which might restore my pride. Maybe, when I've done that, I'll become a better person. Then, perhaps, I'll return here to fight at your side."

They lay beside each other for a few moments more, and then Ralph sat up.

"Time to go our separate ways," he said sadly. "I am so glad I met you, because it has altered a little the feeling of hatred I've always nursed against our white oppressors. I don't want you carrying incriminating evidence, even in your top jacket pocket, so I'll send my driver to you an hour after we get back. He will take you to your meeting, then bring you safely back afterwards. Do not, of course, wear uniform."

He paused, then took his hand and said gently, "I won't forget you, Johnny. Perhaps, as you say, you'll come back one day to join me as we try to break away and set up our own country. Almost everybody will be against us, including Britain who will of course support the *status quo,* by force if need be. In that case, you should certainly consider that helping me might be seen as treachery."

SIX

He was driven into Accra, but the car did not stop at one of the hotels or large restaurants he'd expected would be his destination. Instead, the driver took him into crowded backstreets where the air coming in through the open car window was heavy with the smell of West Africa, a mixture of rice and *garri*, wood smoke and refuse. Groups of men in striped suits and vivid ties padded softly along the line of small shops and tiny bars, while *matas* with trays of cigarettes and sweets on their heads stood around glowing braziers, as if the damp evening heat and their colourful robe-like dresses were not sufficient to warm them.

The driver pulled up by a neon sign which blazed 'The Afrikander' at them. Inside he could see garish lighting, and hear the beat of tinny amplified radio music.

"This the place for you," the driver said. "If he no there, you wait inside, they know you come. Massah say not fear, all be well. I take him car for tree, wait there for you." He pointed to a tiny square with an old stone well shaded by a squat African tree with thick dusty leaves.

Johnny got out, understanding why he should not be wearing uniform which would have been crazily conspicuous. He nodded to the driver and deliberately ambled towards the swing doors as though he had no pressing engagement, and then went through them as if it was a familiar haunt of his.

He was confronted by dirty tables, some with half-drunk men sprawled over them, root beer or palm wine beside them. Behind the bar an overweight man in a smart spotted shirt, which contrasted with his unshaven face, looked at him without apparent interest and jerked his thumb at a tapestry curtain in the far wall. It had a white card beside it and when he got close enough to read it, the faded gold lettering proclaimed 'First Class Guests Only. Must spend two shillings or more.'

He gave the barman the two coins, ordered cola and pushed his way past the heavy curtain. It was a small room, neatly furnished in oriental style. Dim lighting played on highly-coloured paintings of harem life and cast shadows around the rather tawdry silken couches. For a brief excited moment he wondered whether his meeting would be with a girl, but the mustiness of the room suggested it was not often used. He looked up when the curtain was pushed aside, but it was only the barman with a glass of the West African version of Coca-Cola, a saucer of groundnuts and a smaller glass of a clear, slightly oily liquid which he guessed was home-brewed gin reserved for two shilling customers.

He swallowed half the cola, for it was hot in the room. It was less sweet and far more refreshing than the real thing. He chewed some nuts, washing them down with a cautious sip of the other drink. It had a power that almost made up for its vaguely disgusting flavour.

Two men came in together, casually dressed, sharp-eyed and with expensive shoes. One stayed by the curtain, the other shook hands formally with Johnny.

"I am Suli," he said, his English clear and confident. "I am sorry you were kept waiting, but I wished to be sure you'd not been followed. In this business one cannot be too careful."

"Which business is that?" Johnny asked him.

"That is for you to tell us," Suli replied, smiling as the waiter was allowed through with a glass of beer and a saucer of nuts. As these were put down, Johnny studied Suli. He was youngish, he had a nice smile, he was sure of himself, he'd undoubtedly attended an English university and he was probably a middleman, important but not that important.

"You know I'm interested in antiques?" Johnny asked when the waiter had gone.

Suli nodded. "Very rare antiques, very expensive antiques, antiques from Benin that are not normally traded."

"Yes, I know all that. Can you get them for me?"

Suli seemed startled, but not displeased, by his insistence on getting instantly to the crux of the matter.

"At this stage it is perhaps a different question that should be asked. Can you pay for them?"

"I won't waste your time by pretending I can pay cash, as I did the first time. But I do have a proposal."

Suli nodded. "Then I will listen to it and judge whether we can proceed further."

There was something in the way he said it that made Johnny revise his first estimate of him. He wasn't a middleman and he wasn't unimportant. This was a man who could make decisions and, as Ralph had indicated, a man with power who could be nice, or very nasty. Much might depend on Suli's personal reaction to him.

"I might be able to arrange for you to get into a bank at night so that you could remove money from it. Obviously I would leave it to you how much you chose to take."

"Obviously," said Suli. Then he began to laugh, joyfully and unrestrainedly, and it occurred to Johnny he was probably somebody's son, somebody near the top or even at the top, somebody indulged and given a certain freedom in his decisions.

When Suli finished laughing, he clapped Johnny on the arm. "You have managed to amaze me, Mr Callin, and that delights me because it does not happen often. Where is this bank?"

"Abeokuta."

"And you are suggesting we do not take all the money, but just some?"

"It's really none of my business, but I felt it might be safer that way. Banks need to retain public confidence, and if the sum is not too crushing, it might be settled internally, without publicity, by private arrangement with the insurance company. That keeps the police out of it, which might be good for me and whoever you tell to do the job. But none of that is for me to decide."

"Could you set it all up without help?"

"No. I've never actually robbed a bank and know nothing of the techniques; so to fulfil my side of the bargain I would need three things. First, pads of some special material in which I could make pressings of the keys to the entrance doors and the safe."

Suli raised his eyebrows. "For someone who knows nothing, you have excellent imagination. What are the other two things?"

"I would need to see a photo of what I would obtain from the deal."

"And the third?"

"I find the third quite embarrassing and I'm not prepared to talk about it in squalid surroundings like these. If you are interested so far, I suggest the two of us go somewhere smarter, where we can get decent drinks and some food. A place with girls, clean girls, would be better still."

Suli stood up. "I have a white sports car outside. Join your driver, tell him to follow it and drop you off where I get out. He must then drive back to the barracks. I'll return you to your quarters when we've settled everything."

71

Johnny wanted to keep Ralph's driver close at hand, but knew it would be the wrong moment to seem distrustful. "I'll see you there," he said, and Suli's amused smile showed that his momentary hesitation had not gone unnoticed.

The Golden Palm was in the richest area of Accra, and a slit-skirted girl of great beauty led him to Suli's table. It was just for two and it was in an alcove which gave them privacy. A gin & tonic and a whisky appeared, and food was put before them. There was music playing quietly and the atmosphere was orderly and relaxed.

"I am intrigued that you are embarrassed by your third requirement," Suli said. "I hope you can trust me enough to tell me."

Johnny drained his glass. "The bank manager's wife seems to have taken a fancy to me. She's young, attractive enough, and I'm sure that if we became close I could trick her into loaning me her husband's keys for the brief time necessary to get impressions, but without raising her suspicions. It would probably work best as part of some lovers' game."

"You'd seduce her?"

"Yes. If I knew how to do that."

Suli looked at him with interest. "You've never been with a woman?"

"No. My uncle, who brought me up, was an unsociable man who hated women even more than he

72

seemed to hate me. So I went straight from school to the army without any experience of girls."

"I can arrange for you to get laid here, tonight."

"It might be a start, but I want more than that. If I'm to get really close to the bank manager's wife, emotionally close, I need to learn how to treat women, what they like and what they don't like, how they react, the most effective ways of loving them. This robbery is a big deal, especially for me, but maybe for your people too. It should get me what may prove to be one of the central pieces of my future collection, and it'll get you funds; so I won't risk messing up because of my incompetence with a woman. I'm not looking for pleasure, more a university course in anatomy and female psychology. Of course, I shan't object if there should be some pleasure in it as well."

"And you want that here, not in Nigeria?"

"My course here lasts a month, I'm not known here, I'm out of sight of all who might recognise me in Nigeria, so it seems the perfect opportunity. And if you can arrange such a parallel course to my one on mortars, I think it's best if I start my instruction uninitiated, as I am now. So I'll decline your kind offer of a girl for tonight."

Suli leant back and studied him thoughtfully.

"I've never heard anything so crazy. It's all in your head, you've got everything worked out there, but real life, real people, essentially one real woman and one real man, may not combine in quite the same way as in your thoughts. You have the drive and ambition of an experienced man, but I have to remind myself you're really very young. That worries me."

"I've lived a hard life and I've done bad things. It's aged me."

Suli, never taking his eyes off him, nodded slowly. "If I were to take advice, as I ought to do, I would be told to have nothing to do with such a ridiculous scheme. But I'm hooked, I just have to know how it'll all work out, so I'll back you up to the robbery itself. If you can convince me at that stage that no one suspects anything about it, not even the woman, and that we can walk into the bank without any possibility of a trap, then the game's on."

"Thank you," Johnny said, the relief clear in his voice. Then he settled to the eating and drinking, a sense of triumph growing inside him as he relaxed and enjoyed Suli's company.

Suli drove him back in his sports car, and its speed, and the luxury of the interior, seemed to Johnny to be the perfect ending for the evening. But just before they reached the camp gates Suli pulled in to the edge of the bush, reached over and gripped his arm. "I want you to enjoy your dreams, Johnny, but you have to face one reality. However intrigued I am, however much I like you, I won't allow anything to endanger the activities of our group. If, at any moment during your preparations, I have reason to believe you or the woman is putting us at risk, I shall act. You will not dream again, there will be no collection of Benin bronzes and the woman's enjoyable experience of a great lover will come to an abrupt and final end. Do I make myself clear?"

"Perfectly," said Johnny.

So he reached his bed in exactly the same state of sexual innocence he had been in when he'd left it that morning. But twice a week after that he had an appointment with Candy at the very selective brothel next door to The Golden Palm; and, although she held no official degree, Suli assured him she was particularly well-qualified in the University of Life.

SEVEN

He returned to Nigeria, an expert on all aspects of loading and firing 3 inch mortars. Whether the target was in sight or completely hidden from him on the other side of a hill, he could hit it with remarkable accuracy. He could destroy with high explosive bombs, lay smoke to cover an infantry attack and move his platoon and their mortars at high speed across difficult terrain, thanks to the new model Land Rovers.

Shortly after his arrival back at Abeokuta the CO and the adjutant watched a display Johnny put on for them in a battle camp area well beyond the battalion housing area. His platoon, after only a few days' practice, reacted well, showing as much confidence in him as he had in them. Crocus grinned with satisfaction and ordered him to prepare a similar show for the forthcoming visit of General Sir Lashmer Whistler. Unsurprisingly, neither the CO nor the adjutant expressed any satisfaction about the sexual expertise he had acquired alongside the mortar course, since they were blissfully unaware of it. But Johnny had taken the opportunity to put it to the test two days earlier, and was content that Maisie had been equally satisfied with that side of the course.

They had met in The Residency in Abeokuta, at a welcoming party thrown by Schofield, the new incumbent. Mike arrived with Maisie shortly after the 3rd Battalion subalterns, who had come as a group. Johnny was well aware that the general opinion of her, passed down in mess gossip from the senior ranks, was that she was rather common, mutton dressed as lamb, and possibly no better than she ought to be. Most subalterns followed the line, privately referring to her as The Shop Girl, many probably using the contempt as armour to disguise their lust for her. Johnny, who never talked much about girls or sex, was laughed at for being nice to her, but it went no further than that, for he was known to be friendly with Mike, playing cricket and tennis with him and keeping fit with him by swimming lengths in the battalion pool near Abeokuta railway station.

So it was no surprise when he strolled across to greet them, made sure they'd got drinks and urged Mike to go and make himself known to Schofield.

"I missed you so much," Maisie blurted out as soon as Mike left them.

"Not as much as I missed you," he assured her. "I was really desperate in Accra."

He looked casually round the room as he talked, smiling as though they were involved in idle chitchat.

"Now it's the hot season, Mike's had our pool filled. Can you come to try it out tomorrow as soon as you're off duty? Mike's going to be busy at the bank as usual."

Johnny began to steer her towards another group that was forming nearby. "I'll go to the battalion pool first, then come on to you."

He introduced her into the group and then left her with a languid wave.

"How was the Shop Girl?" Jack asked him with a grin.

"She's a nice little thing," protested Johnny. "I don't know why you chaps have such a down on her. Mike likes her, after all."

"But what can you talk to her *about*?" Jeff Holmes asked perplexedly. "She's not interested in sport, knows nothing about cricket, doesn't seem to read books and appears to go deaf if you talk about army life."

"Talk to her about Mike," Johnny suggested.

"Oho, now the secret's out," crowed Nicholas Birch. "You talk to her about Mike because you're hoping she'll persuade him to give you a decent loan from the bank." There was laughter, and for the rest of the evening he had to put up with teasing questions about the state of his finances and how the negotiations were going for the desperately needed advance.

The next afternoon he reached the battalion pool early, swam five lengths, made sure he was seen by the few others there as he walked about drying in the sun, then slipped out unobtrusively into one of the waiting taxis and was driven to Mike and Maisie's house.

Knowing the eyes of the houseboys would be on them even if he couldn't see them and that their ears would be sharp, he greeted Maisie, who was already in the pool, in his usual casual way. He ascertained that Mike was not there yet, followed Maisie's called directions to the bathroom, changed back into his trunks, strolled out into the burning sun and plunged swiftly into the pool. Though he carefully avoided contact with Maisie, and splashed often to make their words inaudible to any garden boy, they were at least able to converse.

"How have you been?" he asked, remembering Candy's maxim that a man should always let the girl talk, listen to her with great interest and never interrupt to talk about himself. So he heard about her boredom, her headaches, the inadequacies of the house servants and, rather more by implication, of Mike who seemed more interested in his work than in her.

"Did you really miss me?" she asked finally.

He averted his eyes, trusting Candy's insistence that girls liked a remorseful sinner and always eventually forgave him.

"I missed you so much I got desperate," he blurted out, gulping and refusing to look at her.

"What is it, Johnny?" she asked curiously but softly. "Did you do something bad?"

He nodded miserably.

"Because you missed me so much?"

He nodded again, unable to speak but mentally acknowledging Candy's shrewdness.

"What did you do?"

He stared at her now, despondently resolute and noting her shining eyes. "I can't tell you, Maisie. It was just too awful. I thought of you all the time, and it was worst at night when you were before my eyes but I couldn't touch you however much I longed to."

"You must tell me, Johnny, and then I might be able to help you."

"But I can't tell you here, in your own home, your home and Mike's, and your houseboys all around. Isn't there anywhere safe we can go, where we'll be completely alone, just the two of us? I'm so ashamed, you see."

Maisie seemed to ponder, though he was sure she already had a plan.

"I'm looking after a friend's house in another part of the town, more isolated than here. She's abroad for two months and I go there most days to check nothing's wrong. I could pretend to be taking you back to camp after your swim and go the long way round."

He stared at her, looking stunned. "That's perfect, Maisie. It's a wonderful idea and it's so clever of you to think of it."

Flatter her, Candy had told him. Tell her how intelligent she is, how remarkable. It's not something most women hear.

He clambered out of the pool, dried, went in and changed. As he came out, Maisie passed him, going in. She spoke clearly, for the sake of any listeners.

"I'm sorry you've had a wasted journey, but at least you've tried out our pool. I can't think what's happened to Mike, but it's silly to take a taxi when I've got to go out anyway. Give me a moment to change and then I'll drive you."

As he waited in the shade of the garden he rehearsed in his mind some of Candy's other lessons. A girl likes to be surprised. Often she'll act on impulse. Never force the pace, never seem to demand, let her give and then feel the better for her generosity. At first be slow in loving, almost reluctant at the same time as showing how much you are on fire for her but holding back out of respect. But once she's allowed you in, let yourself go, never give her time to reflect, to change her mind, overwhelm her with pleasure, using your imagination as much as you use your something else.

They drove out openly together, but when they were about to move away from the direction of the camp she told him to crouch down on the floor so that it looked as though she was alone in the car. He wondered whether she'd done this sort of thing before, and hoped she had because she would be more used to hiding it. But, oddly, he was conscious of a hope she hadn't.

She drove up close to the side door of her friend's house, unlocked it and left it ajar. Then she opened the passenger door wide, and he scurried out into the house. She followed him, locking the door, and they were in each other's arms, kissing, pressing close together,

81

gently moving their bodies, one against the other. Then she took his hand and led him upstairs into a bedroom. They lay down on the bed, facing each other, staring at each other in wonder.

"Now you must tell me," Maisie said earnestly.

"I went somewhere in Accra," Johnny finally admitted hesitantly. "It was a place one of the other officers told me about. They had girls there who would, well, would do things."

"Native girls?" asked Maisie, horrified and thrilled.

"Yes. You see, I couldn't bear it any longer. I could only think of you, imagining you holding me, kissing me. So I pretended she was you and I let her, sort of do things."

"You didn't...?" Maisie gasped, pulling back, appalled.

Let the girl guide you, Candy had advised. Listen to her tone of voice, watch her physical reactions, they'll show you the path ahead.

"No, of course not," Johnny said indignantly. "I'd never ever do that with a native girl. But I closed my eyes, let her undress me, touch me, hold me, and all the time I pretended it was you doing it. My darling, can you ever forgive me?"

And Candy had been right in that as well. For Maisie did forgive him, unbuttoning his shirt and trousers and insisting that it would now be her touching him, not some West African substitute, but he must show her what to do. So he kissed her in abject gratitude, took her dress off and, shyly and apologetically, instructed her so well and caressed her so effectively that soon his apologies faded and, though technically not conjoined, they both became speechless beneath waves of individual pleasure.

The next time they went a stage further, removing all clothes and minutely exploring each other's bodies. Following Candy's insistence that the girl must be constantly reassured that she is beautiful, not too fat, not too thin, and with wonderful hair, he must have quite literally hit the spot, because on the third occasion, properly protected, they became lovers in the fullest and most exquisite sense.

Thereafter Maisie refused him nothing; and Johnny, carefully keeping his eye on the ball, or at least his future Benin bronze, introduced some playful challenges which Maisie took to with pleasing enthusiasm.

This involved each of them bringing something difficult to their weekly assignation. For the first one he challenged her to come wearing a pair of knickers to which she'd attached a note saying how she most wanted him to love her. To his horror she, in her turn, told him she'd had an erotic dream in which he made love to her wearing his military sword and so he must bring that and his Sam Browne belt, complete with sword-frog.

Hoist with his own petard, he realised he would have to wrap the Orderly Officer's sword in cloth, with a cricket bat and tennis racquet disguising the shape, wear his Sam Browne under his shirt and travel by taxi.

Fortunately only Jack caught a glimpse of him hurrying across the lawn from his *giddah*.

"What the hell's that?" he asked. "A military banner?"

"Sports gear," Johnny answered blithely. "Cricket bat, tennis racket and some gear."

"Bloody big cricket bat," Jack commented.

Johnny leered at him. "You know what they say, Jack. Big cricket bat, big something else," and he pushed his loins forward suggestively and did a few thrusts.

He left Jack doubled over with laughter and reached his taxi sighing with relief that it had been simple Jack Chilfer who'd seen him and not anybody else. He was relieved also, in another way entirely, after the completion of the lengthy, passionate session with Maisie which was as hilarious as it was sensational. She had sewn a handwritten instruction note into her knickers that was explicit about the way he should behave with her when he had his sword on; and in a surprisingly short time he found himself at attention behind her, stark naked but for the glittering brass and leather Sam Browne across his shoulder and around his waist, the scabbard suspended from it, the sword upright in his hand, gazing fondly at the glorious curve of Maisie's back as she, propped on her arms by the bed, peered at him over her shoulder, her eyes wide with excitement as they fastened on the bared blade. His own weapon immediately stood to attention as well, saluting her beauty just as the sword was; so he took a smart pace forward to reach the target and served her loyally. In no time at all they were both fired up and it took all Johnny's military discipline to stay at attention, maintain the ninety degree angle of the sword point and hold the scabbard down the imaginary seam of his non-existent trouser leg. But it was amply worthwhile, for by the time Maisie uttered a final triumphal war cry and he had dutifully exhausted himself, he dared to hope she would never now refuse him anything.

That tempted him to move immediately to the final challenge, for the meeting with Jack had scared him and he knew it would not be long before their secret assignations became known and they would have to end. But the prize was so precious he dared not hurry anything. One more innocent request was probably necessary before he could be sure the game was so established that her third response would be an automatic yes. So he challenged her to drive to pick him up near the battalion pool wearing no underclothes beneath her dress. Maisie giggled and shrieked, saying she couldn't possibly do such a thing; but he knew she would.

To his relief, her challenge to him was comparatively easy this time, and he felt she might have been more concerned about the difficulties he'd experienced with the sword than he'd suspected. He was beginning to realise that she wasn't nearly as silly as she seemed, that it was an act she put on in public where it seemed to be expected of her. But with him, and possibly with Mike as well, she was quick to understand, alert to his feelings and full of an affection that increasingly seemed like love. So this time she asked him to write, on whatever part of him he thought suitable, a love poem to her.

Unexpectedly, the combination of the flouted underwear convention which, she claimed, allowed her fresh cotton dress to flutter caressingly against parts of her in the most delicious way, and his poem, written with more seriousness than he'd intended on the top of his thigh, altered their relationship.

When they were both naked on the bed, she leant close and read the poem, turning after a pause to look at him with a startled earnestness he'd never seen in her before.

"Is that really how you feel about me?"

Remembering how he'd felt when he wrote the words and how he still felt now, so close to her, he nodded, quite unable to speak.

She put her face to the poem again reading it over and over, her body utterly relaxed, her hair tickling his most sensitive place. Eventually she kissed him, a timid, wondering kiss, almost as though she understood that though today's truth might become tomorrow's lie, it was still a truth worth having. Then they turned to each other, hugging, holding on tightly to what was there in that particular moment. Dreamily, banishing reality, he made love to her and they achieved an ecstasy together that was different and deeper, reducing them to silence and unexpected thoughts.

After a time, as they lay entwined recovering from their strange bliss, Johnny overcame an unexpected reluctance and whispered to her that the next challenge should be so difficult as to be almost impossible to achieve, though he was confident that their love for each other would enable them to surmount it. He asked her to go first this time, expecting he would have to lead her a little. But she'd obviously been dreaming up future challenges and she turned towards him, nestling her breasts on his chest, her astonishingly blue eyes fixed on his.

"You know you have all that silver out on the table on guest nights in the mess? Well, I noticed a small silver soldier there, holding the menu. I imagine all the silver is usually locked away, but I challenge you to bring that piece to me and we'll have it in bed with us. Then, whenever I'm at a guest night after you've left the army, I'll be able to look at it and remember all we did together and how we felt about each other."

Johnny deliberately pushed her off him and sat up in consternation. "I'll never be able to get it. It *is* locked away, and think if somebody should find it missing."

Maisie smiled up at him, delighted at his appalled reaction. "Well, that's my challenge," she said smugly. "And may I point out that it was you who said our love for each other would enable us to overcome any difficulties."

She giggled, stuck her tongue out at him and turned her back, very pleased with herself.

"You're not as clever as you think you are," he said, rallying quickly. "Because if you admit you can't face up to the challenge I'm going to give you, then I don't have to do mine. And as yours really is almost impossible, and you'll never be able to do it however much you want to, I'm in the clear."

She turned to him in one of those lithe fluid movements he'd come to adore. "Tell me your challenge then, and I bet I won't shirk it like you're trying to do."

"Just for once I long to feel as though I'm a banker and you're my wife. And to achieve that I need to make love to you holding in my hand, not a sword this time, but the keys to the bank."

Maisie frowned, thinking this through, and Johnny felt his hopes fade. Then she tilted her little chin and looked up at him. "I love it that you want to feel as though I'm your wife, and I'm not going to give up as easily as you did. I'm so confident I'm prepared to swear I will answer your challenge."

"What will you swear on?"

"On my favourite part of you, of course," and she proceeded to do just that. He then admitted he'd been craven, swearing on his favourite part of her that he would, after all, do her bidding. Then, to ratify the pact, they decided to unite the two parts.

"You are remarkable," he gasped as they lay panting with exhausted joy. "But I bet Mike keeps the keys with him all the time, so I just don't understand how you're going to pull it off."

Maisie gave a self-satisfied grin. "Because he doesn't carry them with him when it's a Bank Holiday. And, in case you've forgotten, you silly little soldier, it's Bank Holiday Monday next week and, as usual, he's going off with his friends to play golf in Ibadan."

"Where does he put the keys then?"

Maisie gave a scandalised little screech, slapped him on the wrist, and said she couldn't possibly say. "It's a deadly secret," she insisted, "even from me."

But Johnny, though his heart seemed to have missed a beat, quickly discerned the twinkle in her eye. "You little minx," he said admiringly. "You know, even though you shouldn't, and what's more you can get at them."

"I'm not just a pretty face," replied Maisie, pouting in delighted triumph. "I have to keep an eye on things, and it just happens that, with a little manipulation, the key to the drawer in my bedside table, though different, can be made to open the drawer on his side, if that should prove to be the hiding place. And it's no good crowing like that as if I'd done what I shouldn't, because you've got to understand that if something happened to him and he ended up unconscious in hospital, people would expect me to know where the keys were. I certainly wouldn't want them to think he keeps secrets from me, as though he doesn't trust me."

A sudden bitterness in her tone made Johnny think that this was a wound that had cut deep, and he wondered whether his path had been made smoother because in a way he was the instrument of her revenge.

He lay with her a long time after that, holding her close and failing to keep at bay the thought that their next meeting would have to be their last.

EIGHT

Johnny decided a frontal assault was the only way to get the silver soldier. So, a few days before the Bank Holiday, he approached the adjutant.

"I'm worried about the overall security of the mess silver, sir. I was brought up among antiques and my uncle taught me a great deal about the care and protection of such valuable items, constantly stressing the importance of a full photographic record. If you could use your authority to have all the pieces laid out in the dining room after lunch, tomorrow perhaps, I'd be happy to take the pictures and pass the prints and negatives into your safekeeping as soon as I get them developed. For obvious reasons, I'd like to have one of the military police on guard in the room while I do it."

"That's a very kind offer, old boy, and you're absolutely right. We ought to have some sort of pictorial record, for the insurance as much as anything else. I'll pass it in front of the CO when I see him shortly, and then I'll get the mess boys to lay everything out for you tomorrow. I'll get you your military policeman, too, and you'll have to sign for the key to the large filing cabinet where the silver's kept, take responsibility for having everything locked away afterwards and then returning the key to me."

As soon as the photographs were ready he handed them over, deliberately choosing a moment when he could see Major Williams was bogged down with paperwork.

"Good man," the adjutant murmured absently, pushing the bulging envelope into a drawer and returning to his papers.

"I won't hold you up, sir, I can see how busy you are, but there's a slight problem with this little fellow." From the pocket of his bush jacket he produced the little silver soldier, standing at ease in his Nigeria regiment uniform with his rifle and fixed bayonet in the correct position in his right hand. "The bayonet's slightly bent and there are one or two areas of discolouration. My uncle trained me to do silver repairs and I'd like to sort it out before the next mess night. If you give me permission, I'll have time on the Bank Holiday Monday."

"Fine, fine, the key's still signed out to you," Williams mumbled. "Very good of you, I'm sure."

He returned to his work, Johnny saluted and retired, carrying off in his hand the means to another Benin bronze.

That evening he found Kano Brass waiting patiently outside his *giddah,* his wares laid out in front of him. Johnny pretended to look at them with interest.

"This silk is very fine," the trader said in a wheedling voice, handing him a rather garishly tasselled tablecloth, carefully folded and not made of real silk. "Please take it inside, see if it will look well in your room, then buy it from me with a few coins."

As soon as he was indoors, with the door half-closed, he extracted the photograph hidden in the folds. Feeling weak with excitement, he seized the large magnifying glass from his desk and sat down to study it while pretending to assess the tablecloth. This was a much larger copper alloy plaque from the late 16th or early 17th century, missing its right-hand side but showing the central and left hand figures of the customary trinity. Both wore a particular style of helmet and the taller central figure had a staff in his hand surmounted by the head of a crocodile biting a fish. Despite the loss of one flanking figure, it was a strikingly powerful image and after minutely checking every detail of the clothing, ornaments, facial features and the vestiges of *ebe-ame* river leaf depicted in the background decoration, there was no doubt it was genuine.

Controlling any outward show of excitement at the wonder of what he'd seen, he went back to Kano Brass, nodding and passing over the coins. Then he sat down to look casually at other items.

"What did you feel?" the trader asked quietly.

"I'm still shaking," Johnny replied. "The features are so strong and it's a masterpiece of casting."

"Do you know what it portrays?"

Johnny smiled at him. "It's a portrait of a trader with one of his companions. They wore helmets like that because they were important people, and he's carrying a trader's staff."

Kano Brass nodded, a professor encouraging his pupil. "You are right, of course, though there is more to it than that. These are the emblems of the royal guild of traders. We were greatly respected in Benin."

"And when we Europeans first saw examples like this, we refused to believe such work could have been done by Africans and decided instead that descendants of the classical Greeks must have settled in Nigeria. It was hard for us then to believe that non-European races could equal or even surpass us, and although we accept it now, we mostly forget it."

Kano Brass bowed. "I was too tactful to mention the Greek tribe in Nigeria, but I am happy you know that story. If I may presume to say so, you are a strange man and I am glad to have met you. One day perhaps I shall understand you."

"I'm not entirely sure I understand myself," Johnny said, standing up and preparing to leave. "Come back in a week. I shall have something for you then."

When he met Maisie on the Bank Holiday he sensed at once that something had deepened in their relationship. She was quieter, no longer the giddy youngster revelling in the excitement of her affair. There was no shrieking of delight when she saw the silver soldier, just a great contentment that he had done something so very difficult for her. Nor did she wave the bank keys gleefully in his face, but simply put them in his hand as if she was offering him a gift. As they clung to each other instead of rushing to remove their clothes, he wondered whether she, too, sensed that it was over, that the danger of discovery was forcing them towards a necessary sacrifice and, like him, she was trying not to think of the pain to come.

Gradually a desperate need to assuage that future misery overwhelmed them and they began to shed their clothes, each holding on to the object they'd received as though it was a talisman that might yet protect them.

"I don't know what's wrong with me, but I'm suddenly nervous and I have to go to the bathroom," he said distractedly when he'd only removed his trousers, and once there he carefully made the pressings in the two cigarette cases filled with a waxy substance. Then he buttoned them into the inside pocket of his cotton jacket, wiped the keys, and hurried back to Maisie who was naked on the bed, holding the soldier against her breast as though he was a love child. Then she placed him carefully under the pillow as they began to make love. He put the keys there too, as if they were both making the point that the phase of challenges and erotic objects was over, and now they would concentrate entirely on each other. All that should matter, as time ran out, was their mutual love.

At first he felt shame sweeping through him, which was not a sentiment he'd often experienced. But gradually it was obliterated by the unexpected truthfulness of their emotions. He knew he had received, was now receiving, something genuine and wonderful from Maisie, something that would stay with him. And he was equally certain that he was now giving her something that was not a deceitful lie, not a betrayal, but his heartfelt appreciation of the real Maisie she had allowed him to discover. By the time they climaxed she was crying helplessly, and his eyes were full of tears.

"There's something I've been keeping from you," he said when they were both dressed and getting ready to leave. She seemed to freeze, as if she already knew what he would say.

"Somebody must have seen us. There are rumours around the camp and I've been getting strange looks and snide remarks. I took no notice because I love you and so I just couldn't stop seeing you."

Maisie put her arms round him and it was as though she was clinging to a tree in a desperate attempt to prevent the flood from carrying her away.

"What rumours?" she asked, and her voice was scarcely audible. "What remarks?"

"It's gone beyond rumour," he replied. "This morning, off duty as we all were, the adjutant came to my *giddah* and we took a walk among the palm trees. He's a decent old stick, more like a country squire than a soldier, and I could see at once he was acting under orders from the CO. He told me the colonel had heard that I was making a fool of myself with the bank manager's wife and that I'd better put a stop to it immediately before I was marched in front of him and the whole matter of improper conduct became official."

"What did you say?"

"The only thing I could say, the most difficult thing I've ever had to say. I stood to attention, said I would end it and that after today the colonel would have no more cause for concern. I wasn't going to give up my last chance to be with you and I don't know whether the adjutant guessed that's what I would be doing today. But he's a kindly man at heart and, even if he did, I think he'll simply report to the CO that it's over."

He felt Maisie shiver against him. "I've been getting looks, too. Do you think Mike knows?"

"I very much doubt it. Not because it's always said the husband is the last to hear, but because it sounded as though it was an army rumour about a lovesick subaltern, not a civilian one about an unfaithful wife. I don't think anybody believes you took me seriously, and certainly not that we were lovers. I would guess that I was seen as a fool with a crush on the nearest attractive woman, and your only fault, if any is attributed to you, was indulging me instead of slapping me down immediately."

"Will we never see each other again?"

"That might be the best way for us both, because I'm being sent on manoeuvres in the north fairly soon, and it's not all that long before my time's up and I'll be flown home. But we won't be allowed such an easy way out, because in the meantime we're bound to meet at social functions and people's eyes will be on us."

"I don't care if they are, I'd still rather see you across a room than not see you at all."

"We can meet as good friends, me rather chastened and feeling silly, you forgiving and a little amused. But it must always be in company, we must never be alone together. You must stay close to Mike, and I'll talk to him a lot more than I do to you."

"I don't think I can do it."

"Anything else will raise suspicions. I'm certain Mike knows nothing, but if you suddenly start to be reluctant to go out to events you used to be so keen on, it might raise questions in his mind. And as others would be expecting you to avoid me, it would confirm whatever they think now. And there's another thing. You mustn't ever undervalue yourself by saying you can't do something. I've seen what you've been able to do for me, so I know just how strong and brave you are. For both of us it'll just be a different way of loving each other."

"Very, very different," said Maisie sadly, pressing herself against him. "But you're right, I can do it, and I will, but only because I've known what love can be like, and that's made me very strong."

They met sooner than they expected, though they did not speak and only acknowledged each other with a friendly wave. It was when General Sir Lashmer Whistler KBE, CB, DSO paid a visit to the 3rd Battalion as part of his West African farewell tour. He was Royal Sussex Regiment, and so Johnny and Jack were to be presented to him. But before that there was a full parade in which Johnny stood before his Mortar Company, sword in hand and wistfully recalling the last time he had carried it and what had been before his eyes on that occasion. This was followed by an official lunch when Johnny was seated close to the general who eyed him keenly as though he might know a lot more about him than Johnny would have wished. And afterwards, while they had coffee standing in the mess, Sir Lashmer drew him aside.

"Weren't you one of the very few cadets at Eaton Hall who was appointed under officer?"

Johnny nodded.

"And didn't I hear that while you were training the battalion boxing hopeful in Lagos, you actually went into the ring with him?"

Johnny nodded again. "I needed to discover whether he was really any good, and it seemed to be the obvious way."

"You knocked him down, then he knocked you down?"

"That's a polite way of describing it, sir. I caught him with a lucky punch when the sun was in his eyes, and then he demolished me."

The general smoothed down his thinning hair, stroked his greying moustache, and then said quietly, "You've proved yourself a capable officer here, especially in the way you've made the Mortar Platoon so effective. You're a credit to the regiment we both represent, and if there's anything I can do for you before I leave Nigeria, you must let me know."

He was about to turn away, but Johnny took him up on it straight away. "I'm adventurous, sir, and when my time's up in April I'd like to drive back through part of the Sahara. I'd keep my eyes open, of course, because with Independence not so far away it might be useful to discover whether there's anything afoot over the northern border. I'd submit a report to the CO at Chichester when I report to the Regimental Depot to sign my discharge papers."

Sir Lashmer's gaze had suddenly hardened, and Johnny was uncomfortably aware he was being sized up by a pair of eyes that were disconcertingly shrewd.

"Why would you think that necessary?" the General asked.

"I kept my ears open when I was in Accra," Johnny answered, his voice low. "I heard rumours of a possible breakaway Igbo state, and a counter move by the Hausas to seize overall military control of Nigeria to prevent it. You know far better than I do that it's just talk at this stage, probably a lot of hot air. But I'll be up in the north shortly on manoeuvres, and if subsequently I could get over the border on my way home, I might pick up a bit more information."

The general's eyes had never left his face, but Johnny felt that he might have surprised him and that at least he was being taken seriously.

"Driving back across the desert has been permitted on a few occasions," Sir Lashmer conceded, "but always for short-service officers, not national service chaps like you. But in the rather special circumstances you

99

mention, I'll talk to my security adviser and do what I can for you."

He found himself alone then as the general went to speak to Jack Chilfer, and Johnny took the opportunity to walk out into the gardens to ensure he kept away from Maisie. Although, when he'd described it to her, he had dramatised the adjutant's warning somewhat beyond the truth, he had been given a nonspecific warning about overfamiliarity with civilian wives. It had rung so many alarm bells that he'd taken it very seriously indeed, and so acted swiftly to end the affair before it became known and ruined both of them. And in the days that followed it became apparent that he had done so only just in time. Although nothing was said, he suddenly found that extra posts were found for him so that he had virtually no free time. He was appointed Education Officer, supervising the school for the native troops' children, and Chop Master, responsible for the Officers Mess menus and the oversight of the budget which was frequently overspent, because so much food slipped out through the back door. Then, following the decision of the London Conference on Independence to make the capital, Lagos, independent of both the Yoruba southwest and the Igbo southeast, there was such political unrest that a State of Emergency was declared, all battalions were put on high alert and he was ordered to appear before the commanding officer.

NINE

"I need somebody reliable to take over as cipher officer," the CO told him. "Major Williams retires from the army in a week, and he's so frantically busy preparing the handover he's got no time to decode and encode the number of messages necessary because of this sudden State of Emergency. Within these four walls I can tell you he's never been that quick at it, and he's prone to make mistakes, but it hasn't mattered because nothing was ever particularly important. But now we're going to get urgent confidential messages to be decoded, and the reply from me will have to be sent faster than a whore can get her knickers off. So I'm appointing you Cipher Officer and you'll dance attendance on me whenever something comes in or has to go out, middle of the night or just when you thought you'd have siesta. Have you got that?"

"Yes, sir."

Crocus stared at him suspiciously, as if his answer sounded glib.

"You do know the decoding and encoding drill?"

"Yes, sir," Johnny lied.

The tips of the Colonel's ears turned pink. "No you bloody don't. I checked your record and you haven't done the course."

"I'm a fast learner, sir, and if I can look at the code books from the safe I'll be up to speed by tomorrow."

"I'm worried that you even know the code books are in the safe. You seem to have big ears, so you probably also know that they're never allowed to leave the adjutant's office. You'll report there tomorrow, do your homework, and if you're not up to scratch by lunchtime you won't be eating. If you grasp things as easily as you lie to your commanding officer, you should manage it easily."

"I'm sorry about that, sir. I was overeager."

"Apology accepted," Crocus growled, but he still looked askance at Johnny as though he'd banked up his anger, but it was still glowing hotly. "I've never had a national service officer quite like you, and you worry me. You're efficient, I'll say that for you, but sometimes you seem like a smart Alec, and you'd better get it through your head that I do *not* like smart Alecs. And, in case you're trying to look all sweet and innocent, I've heard about your Eaton Hall passing out parade when, right in front of the guests who included generals and a cabinet minister, the bronze statue of the Duke of Westminster suddenly seemed to come to life when the stallion he was mounted on pissed into the pool, loudly and at great length. Apparently some clever Dick had made a hole in the horse's pizzle, plugged it with wax, filled the statue with water and then left the rest to the predicted hot sunshine. And if that's a self-righteous shake of the head, you can forget it because I've discovered you know all about working with silver, and doubtless bronze too, so I wouldn't be at all surprised if you were the culprit. And that's just what I mean about being too smart for your own good, and I can't have behaviour like that from my adjutant."

Johnny stared at him, bewildered. "But I'm not your adjutant, sir."

Crocus snorted irritably. "If you'd shut up and listen to what I say, you might understand. I've heard a lot of good things about you, and I'm reluctantly persuaded you're the only available officer here who could handle the post which dovetails well with being Cipher Officer, so heaven help you if you let me down."

"I still don't entirely understand, sir."

"Well, I'm relieved to hear you're humble enough to admit there's something you don't understand," Crocus suddenly bawled, as though he needed the explosion to bring him to a decision he was still uncertain about. "I'm in a hole, the replacement for Major Williams is delayed, and I want you to take on the post of adjutant until he arrives or someone else is found. You'll start working with Williams for two hours every afternoon until he leaves, and then I'll expect you to do every morning as adjutant and run your platoon after that. Any questions?"

Johnny was astonished, but he felt he ought to protest. "I'm only a subaltern, sir, and the present adjutant is a major. I'm just not senior enough and my authority won't be accepted."

He saw the ominous reddening of the cheeks as Crocus got into his stride.

"Then you'll bloody well have to impose your authority and make it stick," he barked. "I talked to General Whistler while he was here and he seemed to have been very impressed with you, said you'd be ideal in a security situation, claimed you'd got your ear to the ground and knew more about what was going on than any junior officer he'd come across in Nigeria. Even persuaded me to give you special permission to travel home by car across the Sahara, which I thought insane, but it seemed to make sense to him. Are you going to throw all that away, and spit in the General's face just because you're wetting your pants at the responsibility?"

"No, sir," replied Johnny, rigidly at attention. "I'm not afraid of responsibility, I want to take on the role of temporary adjutant, but I felt I should point out a possible difficulty."

"Did you indeed? Well, I'm paid to foresee possible difficulties and I don't envisage any. Some adjutants are only captains anyway, and I suppose I might consider promotion to that temporary rank if it seems necessary. Now are you going to continue prancing about like a filly in season, or are you going to give me an answer a plain-speaking man like me can understand?"

"Yes, sir, I'll do it."

"Damned right you will," Crocus bellowed, seemingly unable to halt the momentum of his fury and taking off in another direction, uncertain of the detail but going for the overall target "You've had too much time on your hands anyway, and you've been sniffing around, grunting like a randy goat. I've got eyes and ears, you know, I'm not in my dotage yet, and I won't have that sort of behaviour either."

He was crimson in the face now, and didn't hold back a final salvo.

"This is just between the two of us," he roared, his words echoing round the camp as though a public address system had been switched on. "But from now on you'll bloody well keep your brandy snap inside your trousers and concentrate on being my right-hand man."

There was a deathly silence around the area, and slowly the flush in his cheeks receded.

"Glad to have you with me, Callin," he finally muttered gruffly. "I'm sure we'll rub along together pretty well. Now go and fix everything with Cliff."

As Johnny stepped out from the CO's office and paused to recover from the shock, he was only too aware of the amused glances through the open doors of the nearby company and platoon offices, the ironic thumbs up signals and several rather more obscene gestures which made it clear that everyone had heard the Colonel's comments. Attempting to ignore them, he gladly took shelter in the adjutant's office and settled down to learn everything he could about his new duties. For all his professorial fussiness and innate diffidence Major Williams was as effective a teacher as Johnny was eager pupil, and after several hours of intense concentration he felt confident about the codes and more aware of the range of an adjutant's duties.

He walked up the hill towards the mess not thinking of the lunch awaiting him, nor noticing the heat, but trying to balance the loss of Maisie, which still preyed on his mind, against the antique-collecting possibilities ahead. He'd handed the key pressings to Kano Brass the next day but had heard nothing since; and so, with no new acquisition as a counterweight, his regret for what he'd lost was especially keen. What he'd had with Maisie might not have been true love, but it was his first love and that made it special. Yet he'd still betrayed her in order to obtain something he desired with even greater passion. One day, perhaps, he might meet somebody more important to him than anything else, whose love would be preferable to any Benin bronze. But that hadn't happened yet; or if it had, and on consideration he felt it might have done, it had not developed into love and probably never would.

It was only as he drew nearer to the mess that he became aware that the heat was more intense than anything he'd ever experienced, hotter even than the day before which had led to talk of frying eggs on the surface of the road. Then, as though the sparks of the CO's impressive anger had kindled the crackle-dry grass and it was slowly spreading, they woke the next morning to bush fires threatening Abeokuta and their own battalion encampment.

Like the other officers, Johnny took his platoon into the surrounding bush to fight the flames. His men were armed with fire-beaters, a flap of rubber attached to a long wooden handle, and it was their job to hold the line, stopping the flames advancing any further while behind them other platoons cut a wide firebreak, using machetes to slash the bush and hack down the clumps of bamboo. Within each of these platoons, one section was furnished with axes to fell young trees.

The last line of defence stood behind them, close to the camp boundary. Grim-faced, they grasped in their hands hoses attached to taps within the living quarters. With these they painstakingly watered the ground, soaking it so that even if the grass suddenly flared it could not creep forward.

It was a memorable scene. The roar of the fire drowned all other noise, the sky was lost in the spiralling smoke studded with glowing sparks, the air was full of birds of prey, plummeting down through the inferno to seize the small rodents, lizards, snakes and insects running, slithering and hopping before the encroaching flames. But it was not only a feast day for the avian hunters. Every so often Johnny noticed one or other of his own men drop his beater, stoop, snatch and smash, then pocket the tasty bush-tucker provided by the inferno. The wind was a deadly fan, blowing destruction towards the camp; and each time a bamboo clump caught alight it acted like a flame-thrower, the fire crackling up to the tips at terrifying speed, arcing over the firebreak and torching branches as yet uncut. The heat was so intense it seemed to Johnny that his flesh was melting; and the sparks showering down on him were like a new and deadlier form of mosquito, biting his skin wherever it was exposed.

They worked for hours, often seeming to lose the battle as the fire got beyond them but always, somehow, driving it back. Eventually the fire was contained in areas already burnt, blackened and glowing, pulsing with malignant eagerness to hurry forward but defied. As evening drew on, and exhaustion threatened to overcome them, the wind dropped and they knew the camp was saved.

Slowly they began to move back, faces grimy with soot, legs, arms and hands scorched, eyes smarting, hair singed beneath the rims of their hats. Johnny wondered whether Abeokuta had survived and, more particularly, if Maisie was unharmed. After showers and fresh clothes they gathered in the mess, drinking as though they'd never stop, hearing the news that Abeokuta, too, was safe though many of the wooden shacks in the shanty areas had been devoured. Proud of themselves, relieved to be alive, leaving unspoken the fear they'd all felt, they drank themselves into oblivion and their boys carried them to bed.

Kano Brass reappeared the next afternoon.

"It seems wicked robbers took advantage of the fire," he mentioned quietly when Johnny was alone with him, in front of the items which he had brought to sell. "They broke into the bank when everybody was busy fighting the fire. It is believed that in the smoke and panic the safe may not have been properly secured."

"When was the theft discovered?" Johnny asked him.

"This morning, when the Manager went to unlock the doors. There were clear indications they had been forced open, so there is no concern about keys. The police, of course, are looking into it, but with the fire diverting everybody's attention it seems unlikely that much blame will be attached." He shrugged his shoulders, dismissing the episode from his mind. Then he added softly, "I've heard the fine depiction of two traders will soon become available to you."

Johnny did not reply, though the anticipatory thrill considerably reduced the pangs of loss that were still within him.

Kano Brass looked at him keenly, as though he was reading his thoughts. "In case it should be of any future interest, there is a rumour about a recent find, in good condition, a complete piece, not just a fragment."

Johnny felt the quickening in his blood and pondered the possibilities as he pretended to study the only passable piece before him, a life-size ebony head with inlaid eyes. If he were to succumb to this fresh Benin temptation he would be forced to betray the army itself, and to his surprise he was rather reluctant to do that. So he played for time, even though he knew that if the object was very special his present hesitation would rapidly disintegrate.

"I met a man called Suli in Accra who seemed to know about such antiquities. If I were to come across him again I might learn more about this discovery and possibly come to a decision."

"I'll ask around when I'm on my travels," replied the trader thoughtfully. "Perhaps I may find someone who knows of him and, if Allah wills, your message will be passed on."

By Christmas, Johnny was exhausted. He hadn't cracked in the heat as some had done, going down with

109

malaria and dysentery. But, worn out by the strain of being adjutant on top of his other duties, he did not have the energy to care about anything except the burden of responsibility. He hoped he was managing his temporary post quite cleverly, avoiding the temptation to throw his weight around, preparing his work meticulously, explaining rather than telling, and using his efficiency to save time for the other officers instead of adding to their burdens. He paid particular attention to the captains and the majors who were most likely to resent a junior officer in such a position of authority, and it did seem they were generally happy to leave the work to him.

The complicated jigsaw of his jobs allowed him constant access to the safe in the Adjutant's Office. It was where the code manuals were kept, and, day and night, he wore the key to it on a cord round his neck. But, frequently decoding or encoding messages during the blessedly brief State of Emergency, he became aware of much else of interest in the safe. As well as the West African Area Security Plan and a range of Action Plans covering civil unrest, localised mutiny and even a national uprising against British rule, there was the location of ammunition dumps, heavy artillery, the nearest air and naval support, and district evacuation plans, all of which might have a high value to Suli and his friends.

The new permanent adjutant was now due to arrive in mid-January, just before Johnny took his mortar platoon up to the northern region for a couple of months of battle camp and brigade manoeuvres. The preparations for an orderly handover kept him busy hours after every other officer had finished work, and everybody at the camp became used to seeing the lights on in the Adjutant's Office late into the night as Johnny sorted the files. Then, on Christmas Eve the water supply failed and a drought was declared. The usual round of parties, in Abeokuta and the army camp, continued just the same, the consumption of alcohol increasing in proportion to the rising sense of desperation. Trucks delivered water from the River Ogun, but it was so dirty it had to be mixed with chlorine before it could be used for the two washes of the body permitted each day. Teeth were cleaned in soda water and the drought was predicted to last for three weeks.

On Christmas Day the subalterns were invited to drinks by Morris, the District Officer. His men had seized and confiscated an entire shipment of rum being smuggled over the border from French Dahomey and as anything left would have to be poured out into the bush in accordance with the regulations, they set to with a will and after an hour most were unable to rise from the carpet of the living room onto which they had gradually subsided. Johnny, who was there because he was a subaltern but more restrained because he was Adjutant, doled out black coffee and helped them back to the Officers Mess in time for the Christmas Lunch. That was followed by the church service in the open-sided tin-roofed chapel behind the Company Offices. In the absence of the sick chaplain, it was taken by Nicholas Birch, who had once incautiously mentioned that he felt called to the priesthood; but his nervousness, which restricted the sermon to three minutes, was appreciated by all, especially those whose heads were still sore.

Early in the evening, after a brief rest, the open-air *Wasa*, the African celebration, took place. All the mammies wore their most flamboyant dresses and extravagant headdresses, while the younger men dressed in cowboy gear, indulging in fast-draw competitions with their toy pistols, and dancing athletically so that gun belt and chaps leaped and fluttered around them and stetsons were hurled exuberantly into the air. The musicians played energetically on their percussion instruments of hollowed-out wood, stretched hide or cast metal chime-bars; and, as all the participants warmed up, the dancing became a triumph of fluid movement, blurring cloth and exaggerated movement of female protuberances.

Kano Brass was there, and as he put his hands together and bowed a respectful greeting to Johnny, he asked if he was attending the fancy-dress party at the Abeokuta Club later that night. Exhaustedly, Johnny shook his head; but the trader mentioned that somebody was very much hoping to meet him there, and then moved on to greet other clients.

Unprepared for dressing up, Johnny hastily borrowed some clothes from Owdu, including his red Mess Night *fez*. Then he put together a tray of loose cigarettes, some chocolate bars and a few *cigarillos* and went to the party as a street vendor. The Club was not popular with the officers because its members were drawn from the lower class of whites, merchants, building superintendants, managers of the larger stores, as well as members of the Battalion Sergeants Mess. But Johnny, relieved to be away from the eyes of those who knew him well, felt perfectly at ease there and enjoyed himself. After a while

112

a bearded sheikh approached him, took him out onto the verandah and said, "Candy must have taught you well. We got everything we wanted and I'm sure you did, too."

Johnny stared at him, but the disguise was so good he could still scarcely believe it was Suli until he grinned at him. "We had no trouble at the bank, and we did everything we could to avoid suspicion falling on anyone. We even left some money behind so we seemed to be amateurs, though that went against the grain. And now I hear you may be interested in another piece that has become available." His eyes were very alert as he made sure two other Arab-like figures were keeping them wedged securely at the end of the verandah, ensuring that nobody could approach them or overhear them.

"It depends what it is," Johnny replied cautiously.

Suli passed him a photo. "There will be more detailed ones later, but you should be able to make a general decision from that."

Johnny peered at it and knew immediately he would sell his soul to get it.

"Yes," he said, forcing himself to speak calmly. "I might want to do a deal on this."

"I will not insult your expert knowledge by doubting that you understand a piece like this will require a very special offer."

"I'll make it as special as I can," Johnny answered, still straining after a remnant of noble forbearance.

"It's a little late for scruples," Suli said, and there was an edge to his voice even though he continued to smile. "We were only interested in you because you were an army officer who might gain access to military secrets, and now, as Cipher Officer, Intelligence Officer and Adjutant, you have the key to the battalion safe. That's what we've been building up to, that's the price for the bronze, and with the dangerous knowledge you have gained of me, I'm afraid you no longer have the option of declining the offer."

"I'm not declining it," Johnny replied stiffly, made obstinate by the implied threat. "I want the bronze and I can give you what you need, but there is a condition. I want an assurance that none of the information will be used until after Independence, when the army, to which I'm loyal in my own way, will have returned home."

Suli relaxed. "I can give you that assurance. We do not have the capability to fight the British, or we would have acted sooner. But there are papers there that may help us as we take control, especially the location of ammunition dumps and other secret locations from which valuable items could be diverted into our hands. You can open the safe?"

"Yes."

"When and how?"

"I work late in the Adjutant's Office every night, but it must be soon. A permanent adjutant is taking over on the first of January."

"Tonight then, at 2100 hours when everybody will still be at parties. I'll bring the camera and I can get into the camp without being seen. At 2105 come out of your office, leaving the door open, and walk slowly down the verandah to the CO's office as if you're stretching your legs and having a breath of fresh air. Then walk back. I'll be awaiting you in your office."

Johnny nodded, pushed his way through the revellers and took a taxi back to his quarters. There he put on his uniform, placed the photo of the Benin bronze in his pocket and cycled down to the Adjutant's Office.

He could see at once that the guards on the entrance gate fifty yards beyond his office were in festive relaxation mode, for no one else was about. They snapped to attention when Johnny looked in their direction, then grinned and waved shyly. He gave them a brief acknowledging smile, went in to his desk and tried to settle to work. At 21.05, when he strolled out onto the verandah, he was conscious of the silence, the darkness of the camp, the distant sounds of revelry. He walked down to the CO's office next door, breathing deeply, flexing the fingers of his right hand as though they were stiff, and easing his shoulders. He listened for the slightest sound, waited a little longer when he heard nothing, then walked back, feeling disappointed and a little worried.

At first, when he went in and closed the door, he saw nothing new in his office even when he put his desk light on again. Then he noticed a darker patch of shadow low down by the safe. It was Suli, shrouded in a dark robe, immobile.

115

"Make sure the blind completely covers the window, then lock the door so that we can't be taken by surprise," Suli said quietly. "If anybody does come, unlock it and go out onto the verandah to talk to whoever it is. If anybody has to come in, you may be sure that I shall be hidden."

He spoke with such authority that Johnny realised he was used to being in command, and it occurred to him that he might even be a former army officer from outside Nigeria. He did as he was bid and then looked questioningly at Suli.

"Please unlock the safe, then get on with your work, ignoring me. I have my own light as well as the camera. From now on we should remain silent except in an emergency."

Johnny took the key from around his neck, opened the safe, put the key back and returned to the files on his desk. Glancing up occasionally, he was impressed with Suli's speed and skill, taking one document at a time in his cotton-gloved hands, assessing it and either photographing it or stacking it neatly to one side. He worked so silently that if Johnny closed his eyes he could hear nothing except the click-beetle sound of the shutter.

But Johnny couldn't concentrate on his files, for every one of them reminded him that he was betraying his trust as adjutant and presumably committing treason, whatever assurance he had been offered by Suli. So he spent his time studying the photo of the Benin bronze, letting its beauty and its rarity soothe him. Of all the many ways in which the divine ruler of the Benin

116

kingdom could be depicted, Johnny had always been attracted to the fish-legged form; and this was what he was now offered. It was a large U-shaped plaque in which the *oba* wore coral regalia, the *ivie egbo* stone bead on his chest, and he stood upright on his electric mudfish legs. He concentrated on the exquisite detail, reminding himself that the bronzes were the compensation for what had been done to him, finally enabling him to face the world with memories obliterated and head held high. But some lingering guilt about his actions remained in him, mingled with the knowledge that though he might not be shot at dawn here and now, there might very well be, on some occasion, a price he would have to pay.

He'd lost track of time and jerked in surprise when Suli touched his shoulder, indicating that everything was back in the safe exactly as it had been and that he should lock it. Then Suli was gone and Johnny, weary in body and soul, put out the lights, locked up and cycled slowly back to his *giddah.*

When the drought, and its consequent lack of washing water, stretched into a third week, the ominous prediction of some epidemic proved true, though nobody had imagined it would be polio. The outbreak began in Abeokuta and then spread to the battalion barracks. Three soldiers went down with it, the camp was put out of bounds to any visitors, and all those inside were quarantined within the perimeter fence. Twice a day gargling parades were held, and no strenuous exercise was permitted. But finally it was over, the new adjutant arrived, the transfer papers were duly signed by both parties; and on that evening two figures were spotted by

117

the guards skulking near the Adjutant's Office. A window catch had been forced open, a few shots were exchanged, though no one was apprehended. But Johnny, with his greater knowledge, forgave Suli his threat and was thankful for his thoughtfulness; for now any eventual suspicion that military secrets had been compromised would be traced back to intruders on the evening after he had handed over to his successor.

Then, at last, Johnny was able to assemble his platoon and its equipment and leave on the long drive through Ibadan to Kaduna, and then a hundred miles further north to the arid plains between Zaria and Kano.

TEN

Johnny's guilt and exhaustion fell away among the open rolling flatlands of the north. The dry heat restored his energy and the stark thrill of distant rocky escarpments put into proportion his memories of Maisie and turned to dust the mildew of his treason. That was the past now. He had done what was necessary and so far he had got away with it. The possibility of a new life was almost within his grasp, one which would allow him to start afresh as a collector whose rare bronzes might open doors for him somewhere in another country.

On the command of his Platoon Sergeant, Kwa Katsina, a working party under Lance Corporal Musa Gasoul built him a *basha* that would be his home for the next two months. It was completed in four hours, a rectangular bamboo framed grass hut, twelve feet long, nine feet wide and six feet high, with a flat roof and two open-hole windows latticed with bamboo so that nothing larger than a lizard or a praying mantis could enter. Round the entrance end they erected a three-sided compound, placing his canvas bath against the far wall and building a rustic bench where he could sit and talk to visitors. Inside the single room two racks were constructed for clothes and equipment, and then his furniture was put in, consisting of a mosquito-netted camp bed and a canvas stool.

Johnny felt instantly at home in it and thanked each builder individually. Shortly afterwards, as he was relaxing in the sun on his bench, Private Ator Manu approached him with a diffident smile and volunteered to be his boy. Tall and strong, with tribal scars on his cheeks, he was the quietest member of the platoon. But Johnny had noticed that he was a hard worker, athletic and quick to anticipate orders when something needed doing, so he gladly accepted the offer. In no time at all Ator had set off, a kettle on his head, and he returned with a welcome tin mug of tea. Then, spotting Johnny's carelessly thrown-down mosquito boots lying on their sides on the ground, he swiftly but gently lifted them, upended them and shook out a scorpion. It began to scuttle away, its poisonous sting arched over its shiny black armoured back. But Ator was too quick for it. One hand seized the tail below the sting, the other gripped it behind its pincers, and he lifted it up, showing it to Johnny and warning him the venom was dangerous. Then he snapped off the thorn-like tip of the sting against a bamboo upright, placed the scorpion carefully on the ground again and let it scamper harmlessly away.

Johnny knew these men had the blood of Hausa warriors in their veins, had seen how rapidly they became efficient soldiers, ready and able to kill. All were stronger than he was; yet they were quietly amenable, to him at least and to each other. While they trusted him, as they seemed to do so far, they were constantly cheerful, never complained, nor did they sow discord in the ranks as was so frequent with the other tribal groups, Yorubas

120

complaining to their white officers about Igbos, and the latter returning the compliment. But he sensed, and never allowed himself to forget, that they would just as quietly go their own way if he misunderstood a situation or gave the wrong order. Meanwhile he felt at ease with them, utterly safe, convinced he had the best platoon in the battalion; and if there was war, he did not doubt they would die for him.

That first day they dug latrines, set up the cookhouse, built their quarters around the equipment stores and marked out the vehicle area for the service truck and the Land Rovers that made the platoon so mobile. And that evening, after some careful reading of his book on Nigerian tribes, Johnny called them all together.

"The first weeks we'll be firing the mortars, practising manoeuvres in the Land Rovers, and training to carry the mortars and the ammunition ourselves in case we're suddenly told the mechanised transport has been knocked out by enemy shells. That's all in preparation for the big and important Brigade Exercise, at the end of which one of the five battalions will be presented with the award for the Best Mortar Platoon. We're going to win that."

All nodded, their excited eyes fixed on him; and he paused to let the tension grow.

"We'll have to be faster into action and more accurate than all the others, and we can do that if we train really hard, starting early each day and working on into the evening. Will you accept that?"

Again they all nodded, wide smiles showing their approval.

"But we'll win, not just because of that, but because we're all Hausas. Others will have mixed platoons, some may be all southerners. But Hausas have a proud and ancient history. Your kingdom was founded by Magajiya Daurama as far back as the ninth century, you became Muslims in the eleventh century, you've been warriors ever since and these manoeuvres are taking place on your land. That will make the difference. As a Hausa platoon, in the Hausa kingdom, we have to win."

There was animated chatter and some enthusiastic shouts. Then Corporal Momon Sokoto, always the joker, called out with a grin, "You no Hausa, sah. You *oyinbo,* wrong skin!"

There was a roar of laughter and Johnny laughed too. Then he held up his hand for silence. "Corporal Sokoto is right, but I've thought about this and I know what we should do. I can't change my skin, but I can have Hausa blood." He pulled out his pocket knife, opened the blade and made a cut in his wrist. "Will you mix your blood with mine?"

There was a huge roar from the platoon, the knife went from wrist to wrist, and Johnny walked among his men mingling his blood with theirs.

"You Hausa, sah," proclaimed Sergeant Katsina. "We go win now; we no agree with lose at all."

Johnny, feeling he'd won an important initial victory, and touched by their devotion, looked at them all hard, staring each man in the eyes. "Thank you," he said. "Now we start each day at five instead of six, we work longer into the day and we work harder than any other Mortar Platoon here."

At 5.15 the next morning, after their ablutions and pre-dawn prayers, but before they, or he, had broken their fast, he started a daily regime of exercises. They ran relay races carrying the heaviest parts of the mortar, the 34-pound barrel, the 37-pound base plate, the 44-pound tripod and finally a wooden ammunition box filled with 10-pound bombs. Then, with two on each box of bombs, and everybody else carrying a part of the mortar, they undertook a cross-country run. The first day they covered a quarter of a mile, and each day thereafter they gradually increased it until they could manage a mile. Finally he made them do a 440-yard sprint and took careful note of who was fastest.

After breakfast they went out onto the range and fired their mortars. Again Johnny made notes on who was quickest at adjusting the elevating gear and the side to side handwheel, who was most accurate with the initial sighting, who unpacked and offered the bombs with the safest hands and who slid them most smoothly down the barrel, ducking his head appropriately as it reached the firing pin at the bottom and was automatically hurled into the air.

By the time they got back from the range, all of them were utterly exhausted. Nevertheless, Johnny insisted on rigging up a field telephone and testing all their voices for clarity and precision; and once again he noted his conclusions. That night, while the platoon slept, he worked by oil lamp at his improvised desk, seated on his canvas stool behind a plank stretching from one clothes rack to the other, poring over the mass of information he had acquired and assessing it. Then he took the necessary decisions.

When they were on the range the next day, he announced the new groupings, the bomb handler, the aimer, the firer and the observer who, when the target was out of sight behind some obstacle, would climb a suitably placed tree, run up the nearest hillock or scramble to the top of the intervening escarpment, watch the bombs explode and then use the field telephone to tell them the number of degrees to adjust the barrel, right or left, up or down. Johnny would receive the message, issue the necessary orders, tell them to fire single rounds or at will and generally watch the situation and apply spurs whenever greater speed was required.

On the third day, after a few adjustments, he felt the crews were as perfect as possible. So they began to practise driving the Land Rovers from area to area, halting, unloading and carrying the equipment to a suitable firing area, assembling the mortars and firing as soon as ready. That gave him the final information he required, the names of the best drivers and the fastest and most accurate team.

From then on it was daily practice and familiarisation with the terrain so that no choice of testing ground would catch them unprepared. As well as firing high explosive bombs, they learnt to lay smoke screens using white phosphorous, moving the barrel horizontally a few degrees between each bomb so that the line of smoke would obscure the advance of troops or tanks.

But for Johnny there was so much more to it than military preparation. He became fascinated with the area itself, the rock formations, the changing colour of the vast sky at dawn and dusk, the wildlife he now saw with more knowledgeable eyes. The vultures fascinated him, hopping and squabbling as they effectively cleared the ground of carrion, their necks suddenly extending from their pale ruffs as the head and sharp curved beak squirmed its way inside the carcase to tear away the juiciest parts, re-appearing stained with gore. Yet when he stared up into the sky and watched them gliding and circling on the thermals, long broad wings extended, primaries widely spread, there was such grace about them, such airborne beauty, that it seemed impossible that they could be so effectively brutish when they landed.

He revelled in each small incident along the way, the wild cattle wandering where they had no right to be, the hunter in his beaded skullcap, bow in hand and poisoned arrows ready to be notched and shot into his prey. But it was the baboons which moved him most. As troupes, running on four legs like canines, a seemingly broken tail behind each one of them, it was as if they were mere grey-green pye-dogs in the bazaars, barking absurdly. But once they noticed he was only watching them, their behaviour and appearance would change entirely. They would suddenly stop, sit up and stare at him, the close-set eyes mournfully thoughtful above the narrow muzzle as though they felt the tug of some vague link between them, and puzzled over it. In those brief moments, as their eyes met and each looked deep into the other, he wondered what the baboon saw, whether he recognised the superiority of the later species, or, as his expression often seemed to imply, contempt for the devious unnatural ways in which his descendant now behaved.

He was relaxing into happiness, letting the life on the plains wash pleasantly over him. But he did not cease to be a realist. He would leave the army soon and so the present overwhelming experiences would be replaced by others that might be more mundane. But he had chosen his path, he had his desert journey still before him and there was no point in being anxious about civilian life. When the time came, he would cope with it.

After weeks of living and working together, he and his platoon became a team, trusting themselves and each other, and providing the speed and precision Johnny asked of them and of himself. By then other battalion mortar platoons had begun to arrive, each allotted their own practice area. Inevitably they spied upon each other and listened to the gossip. His own men assured Johnny that some were late starting, some were slovenly, some were only practising basic firing techniques, and none had an officer as fine as theirs. But he would not let his guard slip. He liked what they told him, but he warned them all, including himself, against over-confidence; and when the brigade exercises started he was glad that he had done so, for it was clear to him that the Kaduna platoon would be a serious rival.

For the first week the battalion mortars learnt to cooperate, working as a brigade on a wide front and using their transport to carry out manoeuvres covering a hundred miles or more. Johnny found it challenging because it was on a far bigger scale than anything he'd done before; but it was also relaxing because he simply followed orders from above and did not have to use his initiative. But the final week was devoted to a series of daily tests that would decide the winner of the Best Platoon Award.

In the early ones, where Land Rovers were permitted, Johnny was happy with the results, certain that his platoon was performing at least as well as the Kaduna platoon and hopefully rather better. But on the last day of the competition, in front of Brigadier Freddy Filer and visiting observers from the Sierra Leone and Gold Coast Regiments, the situation was deliberately made more challenging. As they approached the map reference of the area where mortar support was required, an umpire with a red flag stepped out, halted their transport and informed all the platoon commanders that enemy artillery had knocked out their vehicles and so they must get their men, weapons and ammunition to the rendezvous on foot.

It was the moment Johnny had prayed for, when all their preparation should pay off. He raced back to his men with a big grin on his face and told them to show what they could do. And, delightedly, they did, carrying the mortar parts and boxes of bombs at a steady never-flagging jog trot and reaching the firing area first.

As soon as Johnny saw they were entering a valley between two rock escarpments he told Ator, his fastest runner and clearest speaker, to be ready to carry his field telephone and drum of cable to the best observation post the moment the order came. Half a mile into the valley, still leading, they were directed to their firing point, informed the enemy artillery was in front of them, the other side of the height, and that they should start firing at the blue flags there as soon as they were ready.

Johnny grabbed his field telephone and nodded to Ator who sprinted away, unrolling the cable as he went and racing fearlessly up and over the rocks. Meanwhile the mortars were set up, high explosive bombs stacked in readiness and the field telephone placed on an old termite stack beside Johnny who was watching all the preparations with an eye he hoped was as keen as the vulture's.

Shortly after the loaders had all called "Ready!" the telephone rang. Ator's calm voice told him the targets were straight ahead, estimated range a thousand yards. Dreading the sound of other mortars firing before them, Johnny gave the direction and the range, then ordered No 1 Mortar to fire when ready.

A few seconds later, before any other platoon was ready, the loader let the first bomb slide down the barrel. The base between the vanes of the bomb hit the striker stud at the bottom, firing the propellant cartridge which hurled it up, up into the sky in a glittering arc which turned downward as the weight of the bomb and the gravitational pull caused it to fall. On impact, the striker in the nose ignited the explosive.

They all heard the satisfying *crump,* and still no other mortar was in action.

"Two degrees right," corrected Ator; and shortly afterwards he was able to report the first target flag destroyed, and that the three remaining flags were spaced equally to the right.

Johnny ordered, "No1 two degrees right, No2 four degrees right and No3 six degrees right; fire once when ready."

Just as their salvo got away, other mortars opened up, but Ator triumphantly reported, "All targets destroyed." Johnny stood his crews at ease, winking at them because their team work must surely have put them on the way to victory.

It was twenty minutes before all mortars fell silent. Then they were told that their own infantry were attacking through the destroyed enemy artillery and so they should lay a smoke screen at 1,300 yards.

Without requiring any orders, the bomb handlers moved up the white phosphorous smoke while Johnny increased the barrel elevations, left the transverse variations exactly as they had been, and then gave the order to fire.

Out of the corner of his eye he noticed that Brigadier Filer had moved close to him to watch his platoon in action, and when he saw that the observer accompanying him was Ralph Okoro, now wearing the uniform of a captain, his inward emotional reaction was intense.

Two of his mortars fired normally, but the propellant in the one closest to the brigadier failed to ignite properly and the bomb plopped out of the barrel and fell on the ground just in front of him.

The brigadier hit the dust, covering his head with his hands, while the platoon crouched anxiously as Johnny walked out, picked up the bomb and placed it very gently behind a large rock. Other platoons, too, had stopped firing and were staring at bombs on the ground as their officers gingerly approached them. Johnny strode back, pretended not to notice the brigadier dusting himself down, and ordered his men to continue firing.

It quickly became apparent they were all using a faulty batch of bombs. By the time the smoke was patchily laid, there were fourteen unexploded phosphorous bombs, together with two HE bombs which had delayed the 5th Battalion in the earlier shoot.

The brigadier, seemingly unembarrassed by his sudden contact with the ground, called the exercise to a halt and asked everyone to gather round him. He then announced that the winner was the Mortar Platoon of the 3rd Battalion, Abeokuta.

Acutely aware that Ralph never took his eyes off him, Johnny marched smartly forward. The brigadier then presented him with the trophy, a silver 3-inch mortar with a frontal plate on which the names of previous winners were engraved. Johnny saluted, avoiding Ralph's gaze and just caught the brigadier's ominous *sotto voce* command to keep his platoon behind when the others left.

All the platoons mingled for a while, chatting, exchanging experiences, congratulating Johnny and quietly enjoying the memory of the brigadier down in the dust. Then the drivers were dispatched to fetch the Land Rovers and gradually the valley emptied.

"Bloody good work, Callin," the brigadier commented, "I haven't seen such a well-trained platoon since I've been out here. But I've two questions for you. As I understand it from the military manual, if a bomb drops out of the barrel, all crew and bystanders are required to throw themselves flat. Is that the correct drill?"

"Absolutely correct, sir." Johnny answered, poker-faced.

"I did it, your platoon only crouched, you remained upright and none of the other platoons followed the full drill. I want to know why, not because I particularly mind making a fool of myself, but I'm curious to know if the manual needs rewriting."

Johnny shook his head, and he saw Ralph's amused glance on him. "You were right and we were wrong, sir. The striker in the nose of the bomb is not meant to ignite the explosive unless the bomb falls from a much greater height than just out of the end of the barrel. But nobody can be absolutely sure, so the safety procedure is right and sensible."

"Then why didn't you follow it?"

"We've had so many faulty bombs on this exercise, not one of which has exploded, that we've all become blasé. But it would be valuable, sir, if you could discover why we receive so many dud batches. It seems the manufacturers may be picking on West Africa as the place to dump faulty ordnance, and that shouldn't be allowed."

"I'll certainly try to put an end to it, Mr Callin. But your mention of ordnance brings me to my second

131

question. Our brigade ordnance officer, who normally deals with the clearance of all unexploded shells after our exercises, went down with malaria this morning. You seem a remarkably experienced officer for your age, I'm aware you were acting adjutant for a time, and I wondered whether you'd done any bomb disposal work?"

"Before I was commissioned I was a lance corporal at the Canterbury barracks, and part of my job was to help supervise grenade throwing and 2-inch mortar firing on the Lydd ranges. Anything that didn't explode had to be detonated by hand, and I was responsible for that, sir."

"Excellent. I've got slabs of gun cotton, rolls of fuse and detonators in my car. Will you act as brigade ordnance officer?"

Johnny saluted. "Of course, sir. I'll send my platoon back, retaining, with your permission, one of the Land Rovers as my transport back to base. Then I'll deal with all the misfires."

The brigadier smiled, clearly relieved. "I felt I could rely on you, Mr Callin, and here's your reward." He unbuttoned his pocket and passed him a sealed envelope. "It's from your CO, Colonel Charrington. Your RHE date has come through, and I understand you're going back the desert way. This'll probably be the last thing you do for the army, though we all hope you'll re-enlist. But you mustn't deal with these bombs on your own, they're far too dangerous and I won't allow you to ignore safety regulations twice in one day. Maybe your sergeant would stay with you, he seems a good man."

"I'll stay with him," said Ralph Okoro who had quietly been drawing closer. "I know Mr Callin, we met in Accra at the mortar course there, and there's much I want to ask him about how he managed to train his men so effectively. I have my own Official Observers vehicle here so he won't need to retain a Land Rover; and when we're finished I'll drop him off on my way back to Brigade HQ."

The brigadier nodded, returned Captain Okoro's salute, and strode off to his car. Johnny could not speak, finding no words, and Ralph smiled.

ELEVEN

Ralph helped Johnny to carry the bombs gently up to a small depression and lay them carefully down. While Ralph went to move his vehicle further away behind an escarpment, Johnny unrolled the fuse, cut off two good lengths, fitted the end of each into a detonator, crimped them securely with his teeth and then slit the other ends at an angle of forty-five degrees to expose the powder train. He took two blocks of guncotton, placed them in the deepest part of the hollow and arranged the bombs over and around them.

"How's it going?" Ralph asked from behind him.

"I'm about to insert the detonators into the guncotton, and then we're ready to blow. Maybe you could look for a safe place well down the slope and make sure the two fuses go straight to it, without any kinks."

When he'd carried out his final checks, Johnny joined Ralph below some massive rocks, took out a match, gripped it so that the head was pressed into the exposed powder, then struck it with the striker-side of the box. The powder ignited immediately and began to fizz while he took another match and did the same to the

134

other slightly shorter fuse. Then he crouched close to Ralph and they both covered their ears.

There was a loud explosion above them, followed almost instantly by another. The ground trembled briefly and they saw the white smoke spiral forcefully into the sky. Once it had cleared, they stood up, listening, smelling the air. Then, close together, they approached the site with caution.

At first it looked as though the task had been successfully completed. Then Johnny spotted two phosphorous bombs that had been cast up against a rock higher on the slope, damaged but not destroyed. Both were leaking smoke, and there was a reddish glow to the metal casing which indicated they were probably burning internally.

"It's my fault," admitted Johnny. "I tried to blow too many at once, and one explosion was fractionally after the other. I'll have to do those two again."

"Those three," corrected Ralph, pointing to the far side of the cleft. Johnny followed his direction and saw the vanes of another bomb peering out from behind a smaller boulder. He walked gingerly over to it. Like the other two, it seemed ominously hot; but in one way it was quite unlike the other two.

"Go down to where we took cover and stay there," he said urgently to Ralph. "I'll deal with the three of them, but I can only do it calmly if I know you're safe."

Ralph stared at him thoughtfully, as if rather more had been expressed in the tone than in the words themselves. "It's a high explosive bomb, isn't it?"

Johnny nodded. "It makes no difference," he said. "If they go off while I'm crouching by them I'd rather be killed immediately by the explosive than die a lingering death disfigured by phosphorus."

"Why should I be saved, not you?"

"Because you have something to live for, a cause, and I don't have that."

"You have your antiques."

"That's all I have, and they're unimportant weighed against your life. So go, please, I have to act immediately."

As soon as Ralph turned away, Johnny fetched another block of guncotton, a detonator and a fuse, and prepared them. Then, using his boot, he rolled the hot HE bomb onto his thick cotton khaki handkerchief and dragged it as swiftly as he dared over to the other two bombs. When he was almost there, he heard a loud metallic click and hurled himself behind a rock. But as nothing happened and it clearly hadn't been the internal striker moving towards the nose to detonate the bomb, he was forced to go out again and pull it close to the others. As he knelt to place the guncotton beside them, his face was so close to the hot smouldering metal that he expected to be overwhelmed with terror. But the knowledge that Ralph was watching him removed all fear. He had three Benin bronzes, he had found somebody special and, despite what he claimed, he had already settled his account with his uncle. All he'd wanted in life had been achieved and, if it had to be, it was a good enough time to die. So he positioned the guncotton with great care, walked back to the fuse, lit it and all three bombs exploded.

"I lied to you in Accra," he confessed to Ralph as they lay in the sun among the rocks, his arm under Ralph's head, Ralph's arm lying comfortingly across his chest. "I don't need the Benin bronzes to get my own back on my uncle, because I've already taken my revenge. If I need the bronzes at all, it's to start me off in a new life somewhere."

"Just now, you could easily have lost that new life."

"That's one of the many things that have changed in me since I saw you here. I feared I would never meet you again and nothing would be resolved. But now you're with me, everything's suddenly clear and I don't mind if I die."

Ralph nodded. "I can understand that in a way. I want my people to be free and independent, and we'll only get it by war. I don't expect to survive the fighting, the odds against us will be overwhelming, but I'll die contented simply because I'll have been more than just a spectator. I'll have been involved in something that really matters to me, setting up a country we've decided to call Biafra."

Johnny touched his hand. "You know I would give up my bronzes if you would let me join you in the struggle."

"I know. But you're white, and at this stage you will be seen only as the enemy. So you must go home, increase your collection, and in the years to come, when we're so desperate we'll take help from anyone, whatever their colour, I'll send for you. I would like to have you by my side."

"Truly?"

"Yes, truly. I feel complete when you are beside me."

"Then the moment I hear from you I'll sell all that I have, bring the money for your cause and die with you if that's the way it has to be."

Ralph laughed. "There is another English saying about jumping in with both feet, and you always seem to do that. But I shan't ever forget this moment. It will be the treasure that I'll carry with me into the uncertain future, like your Benin bronzes, though happily less heavy."

They were silent for a while, and then Ralph asked him about his revenge.

"I had such little confidence when I joined the army that I failed my first WOSB, the officer selection board. But they gave me a second chance, and in the interim I was sent to Canterbury as a lance corporal to help train the recruits who'd just joined. Many were the dregs of London's East End: razor boys, foul-mouthed and violent, though they were fine with me as if they sensed my anger and vengeful thoughts. On a 36-hour pass I took a few of them to a pub near my uncle's house, told them he'd been an air-raid warden in the war, which was true, and that he'd boasted of signalling to the German planes to guide them in, which wasn't."

"And they didn't like it?"

"I imagine most of them had lost family or friends in the Blitz, and they were well tanked-up at my expense. They blocked up his doors and set his house on fire. I thought he'd get out easily enough through the windows, though I hoped he'd be burnt a bit; but he died trying to save his antiques. It was the only time I felt the slightest admiration for him."

"And how did his death affect you?"

"It hardened me in ways I hadn't fully foreseen. I became callous, which I hadn't been before. I didn't care for other people, or for myself, and when I first flew here to Nigeria, I felt freed but empty. It was as though I was starting my life over again, but as an older, toughened man."

"Is that how you still feel?"

Johnny shook his head. "Not since I met you. You were the first person I felt I could look up to since my parents died. I still do bad things, but there's a purpose in them, to enable me to have that new life, at least until I can be with you."

"I feel for you as you feel for me, Johnny, but you must understand that my parents have chosen a bride for me, and before we start our war of independence I shall marry her, and hope to leave a child behind me to carry the struggle into the next generation, if that is what is necessary. But it will not alter how I think of you."

"You know perfectly well there has already been one woman in my life and there may well be more. But what we have is different to all that, a real and a lasting friendship."

"Have you decided where you'll start your drive across the desert, and where you'll aim for?"

"I thought I might cross north of Sokoto, and maybe head for Ouarzazate in Morocco."

Ralph sat up, looking down at him and shaking his head. "You must be careful to avoid any territory that's not French, and that way you might easily stray into Spanish Rio de Oro where I can't help you. Since my visit to Paris I have some influence with the French colonial authorities, and as long as you don't veer off across some border I can probably keep you safe. I suggest you take the main route through French West Africa into Algeria and I'll arrange emergency fuel and water supplies along the way."

"Can you really do that?"

Ralph laughed. "Yes, I can. I'm being promoted so quickly to widen the range of people I must have dealings with that I'll probably be a major shortly."

"Then that's the way I'll go. Is there anything else?"

"Before I leave the north, I'll fix an appointment for you with a close associate of the Emir of Kano, who can provide you with an exit visa. It'll save you a lot of trouble at the border."

"I don't ever remember being taken care of before. It's a pretty special feeling."

"Have you checked those papers the brigadier gave you?"

Johnny smiled. "What with blowing up bombs and being so close to you, I've had other things on my mind."

He took the envelope from the side pocket of his bush jacket and opened it. Inside was his RHE certificate for 31 March, and a form for him to fill in, date, sign and return to Colonel Charrington, making his discharge official. He passed them to Ralph who studied them, then handed them back to him.

"That seems all in order," he commented. "You're almost a civilian again, and once your platoon is on its way back to Abeokuta, trailing clouds of glory as the winners of the competition, you can concentrate on preparing your desert journey. Have you got a Land Rover?"

"Yes. I pick it up in Kachia as soon as I'm free. Suli has arranged everything extremely efficiently."

"And the Benin bronzes?"

"I passed the two I had to Kano Brass to give to Suli who already has the third one. They'll be sewn into the seat cushions of the Land Rover."

"Good luck, then," Ralph said softly, standing up and formally extending his hand. "You can always get in touch with me through the Gold Coast Regimental HQ in Accra, though the letter will be read by others so it should be carefully worded. Nobody is fully trusted as Independence approaches."

Their hands met, gripping hard, reluctant to let go as the pain of separation began to spread through them. Then they broke apart, loaded the car and drove away, sitting side by side but already preparing for different lives in different continents.

A few weeks later, no longer in uniform, Johnny drove to the crowded market in Kachia. Apart from his few possessions, his map and compass, his baggage consisted of tinned military rations, engine oil, filled water containers and jerry cans of petrol. He parked in an isolated corner and wandered among the throng of white-robed Hausas, elegant Fulani cattle drivers wearing wide-brimmed conical straw and leather hats on top of their turbans, and jet-black pagan women with shaven heads and no clothing except a short grass skirt. *Pikins* escaped from their busily-shopping mothers, briefly running wild among the dogs and goats. At one stall he purchased a second-hand military flare pistol, bargaining as he watched Kano Brass come nearer and greet him quietly as the price was settled. The trader led him to a confidential meeting with Suli in the shade of the baked mud wall of the Serahi's compound. Suli detailed some important final arrangements, passed him an exit visa, signed by Muhammadu Sanusi, the Emir of Kano, and then left him with a nonchalant wave of the hand and an enigmatic smile.

Kano Brass had waited for him out of hearing, keeping an eye on Johnny's Land Rover. He indicated where the opening was in the seat and passed him a heavy object wrapped in cloth.

"As you have only seen the photo, I thought you might like to study it before we put it away," he said. "Once you have done so, and are satisfied it is genuine, I will fit it in and sew up the seat."

Johnny sat in the Land Rover and opened the cloth. He sensed the great weight of the divine power the *oba* was bearing, the fish legs bending under the strain, the arms and open hands stretched out for support; and for a moment he identified with him, bearing, as he did, the burden of past sins and his almost insupportable loneliness without Ralph.

When he had finished sewing, Kano Brass bade him a dignified farewell, not hurrying away like the busy Suli but looking genuinely regretful at their parting. Then, scarcely containing his excitement, Johnny drove north, crossed the border into French territory without difficulty, and his great adventure began.

He headed towards the distant Massif de l'Air, keeping a special lookout for Monts Bagzane which, at more than six thousand feet, ought to be visible to him at a considerable distance. The engine, serviced only the day before, was purring happily and he began to feel he'd almost achieved his former Somaliland Scouts dream of roaming the desert wastes, though his driving seat was a lot more comfortable than a camel's riding saddle. That night he slept among the dunes, hoping, but failing, to hear the singing sands as the grains moved.

But in all other ways, he experienced the beginnings of contentment. It was as if the desert sands were scouring him clean of past evil and soon all he would carry within himself was the transforming joy of love and the possibility, years ahead, of being with Ralph again.

Four hours after his dawn start, his happiness was intensified by the sight of his first camels. There were five of them, ridden, or so he guessed, by Bedouin sitting on their saddles with their feet behind them as if they were kneeling in prayer, the ends of their faded cinnamon head-cloths covering their mouths so it was difficult to distinguish their features, their rifles slung beneath the armpit, the muzzle pointing forward. Although the camels seemed to be plodding slowly, they approached more rapidly than he had expected, curving round to either side of his track so that he had to brake, and then stop altogether. The central rider, less than fifty yards from him, gave a signal and all five halted.

Eager to have some contact with them, he got out, and looked up at the riders, noticing as he did so that the rifles were now in their hands, almost as if they were an execution squad about to shoot a traitor at dawn. They were magnificent, fierce and independent, never doubting that other races were inferior to them, whatever the colour of their skin. Only the Bedouin, it seemed, had that special combination of harsh desert existence and unwavering religious faith; and it made them strong. They looked, he decided, just like something out of Lawrence's 'Revolt in the Desert', which had so enthralled him as a boy. Then they opened fire.

When it was over, the camels slowly folded their forelegs and their riders jumped down. Two of them

144

opened the passenger door, drew their silver-mounted *jambiyas*, ripped open the cushions, removed the bronzes and carried them to their saddle-bags. One of them unscrewed a jerry can and poured petrol over the Land Rover, and the final two picked up the bullet-riddled body and threw it into the driving seat. All then remounted and four retired to a safe distance. The fifth lit a fistful of dried palm fronds, raced his camel past the Land Rover, threw the torch into it and twined round with a triumphal yell to join the others.

They watched the bonfire with quiet satisfaction, smiling delightedly when the remaining cans of petrol exploded. Then they turned and disappeared into the desert, leaving the smoking wreckage, the blackened corpse and the first circling vulture.

PART 2

SWEDEN 2012

TWELVE

The sudden pain threw Magnus Trygg forward over his desk with a moan he couldn't suppress. It was not the first time something similar had happened. But the earlier twinges had been much less severe, usually occurring after some sudden burst of bodily exertion, like chasing a suspect up several flights of stairs in a block of flats which he had done six weeks ago. So he'd ignored them, telling himself it must be heartburn, though he'd never suffered from any digestive problems.

Reluctantly his hand reached to his shirt, pressing onto the scar on his chest where the bullet from his own pistol had entered him, not long after he'd started his police career. Mentally he traced its passage past his heart and out through his back, recalling vividly the X-rays the cardiac surgeon Subhan Kaluna had shown him afterwards.

"O what a lucky man!" Kaluna had bellowed cheerfully, his natural exuberance almost deafening Magnus. "You are hit on the head hard enough to render you unconscious and yet there is no damage to the skull. Then the villain takes your pistol and shoots you with it at close range and yet again the gods are kind. He misses the heart, as you can see here, and then the bullet pops out of your back without hitting anything vital on the way. A little rest, some nice healing and you will be as right as rain."

At the time Magnus remembered the X-ray had frightened him more than the actual shooting. The inside of his chest looked a terrible mess and he'd found it hard to believe there would be no lasting harm. But the sheer bulk of a beaming Subhan Kaluna had succeeded in pressing his diagnosis upon him and he'd been thankful to believe it. It relieved Sonja's desperate concern, confirmed the children's belief that their Dad was indestructible and since then there had been no indication that there was anything wrong with him at all. Now he could not help but wonder whether there was in fact a link between that wound and the excruciating spasm he'd just experienced.

Remembering the rashness of many of his decisions as a young policeman, he tried now to take time to assess the seriousness of what had happened. But it was not a long appraisal. He was compelled to accept what he had really known from the intensity of the pain, that he could no longer ignore it; so he rang and made an appointment to see Kaluna. A man who had saved his life then would surely be able to sort out any subsequent little problem. But, anxious not to worry Sonja, he decided he would say nothing to her yet.

It was a quiet time for the Sundsvall police, and though experience had taught him that such periods of relief did not usually last long, every department was using the opportunity to catch up with record-keeping, returns to the central crime bureau and all the other paperwork that always piled up. Homicide had been particularly quiet for several weeks, and Lennart Havendal, their Chief, had commented only the day before that it must be because Magnus was such an effective leader of the team. He'd followed the compliment up by requesting a meeting with him today; and it was while Magnus had been wondering uneasily what it might be about that he'd been struck by the pain.

An hour later, feeling much better, he walked along the corridor to Lennart's office, toying with the thought that the sudden reduction in crime might be due to the weather. It had been the coldest June for twenty years, and maybe criminals, even petty ones who exceeded the speed limit, needed the warmth of the sun to get them out of semi-hibernation. Certainly his own reactions seemed rather sluggish during this calm period. He felt slow on his feet and some of his usual self-assurance had deserted him.

Lennart, smartly-dressed as usual, exuded a vigour and enthusiasm that was a complete contrast to the doubts and hesitations that haunted him when Magnus had first met him; and it was only in the last few years that he'd succeeded in fully regaining his confidence.

"I'm leaving the police force, Magnus. I've talked it over with Annica and we both feel it's time we were a full-time family looking after the twins. I never expected to have children, and as you know I never did in my first marriage. But I've always longed for them and once the miracle happened I knew my days here would be numbered. The girls are very active three-year-olds now, and I really don't want to miss another moment of fatherhood. So, half an hour ago, I phoned the District Commissioner, informed him I wanted to leave by the end of this year, earlier if possible, and he accepted my resignation. In view of everything you've done for me, I wanted to tell you myself."

Magnus stared at him, appalled. "But Lennart, we still need you."

Lennart laughed. "You never really *needed* me, Magnus. It's true Amrén's sudden death was a terrible blow to everyone, especially to you who were so close to him. But you were always the preferred choice to replace him as Police Chief. It was only when you refused the post, and were determined to stay as Head of Homicide, that you dragged me out of early retirement and put me in the chair that was rightfully yours. Well, I've given you six years and to my own amazement I've loved every one of them. It's even enabled me to blot out the failures that forced me into a premature resignation. But it's high time you fulfilled your destiny, Magnus, while I fulfil mine as an elderly adoring Dad."

Magnus had been watching him closely as all that poured out of him. So busy with his own life, he'd failed to fully grasp the changes that had been taking place in Lennart's: the joy, and babies, that his former colleague Annica had brought him, transforming the haggard, desolate widower into an ecstatic father and an effective leader.

"You know I love my present job, Lennart, and I hate administration. But somehow I suspect you're not going to change your mind."

Lennart shook his head, smiling broadly. "You've helped me so much, Magnus. Nobody wanted me in this position, I know that, but somehow you made sure I coped. Selfishly I want to go now, for Annica, for the twins, and especially for myself before I make some awful mistake again. But I want you to believe I'm also doing it for you. You've got a great career ahead of you in the police, the sky's the limit, everybody says that, and I'm not going to let you stick halfway up the ladder just because of Amrén's death."

Two days later, his mind still teeming with the problems and possibilities raised by the resignation, and agitated that Lennart might have noticed the physical problems he was experiencing, he went to his hospital appointment.

As always, the sight of Subhan Kaluna calmed him. A friend now as well as his surgeon, and always a large man in every sense, the loudness of his voice was in no way diminished. He hugged Magnus with one arm at the same time as he vigorously shook his hand.

"A reunion of the two famous brown-skinned citizens of Sundsvall," he roared delightedly, for he was as proud of his Indian origin as Magnus was restrained about his Thai blood. "I hope you haven't come to arrest me for speeding, because it's not my fault; that sports car of mine just won't go any slower."

Magnus smiled. "I'm rather more concerned about my own speed, in my chest. The engine seems to be spluttering a bit." He explained about the pains he'd been experiencing, careful to make light of them; and he was worried when Kaluna instantly became serious and skilfully cross-examined him.

"I thought it might be something to do with that time I was shot," Magnus suggested hesitantly. "Could some damage have been done then that's only giving me twinges now I'm older?"

"Extremely unlikely," Kaluna replied dismissively. "There'll be scarring, of course, but that won't be the cause of this. And you're not old. At thirty-nine you're in the prime of life. It's more likely that long hours, rushed meals and sleepless nights are taking their toll. Your heart's probably complaining, and I don't blame it. It may well be giving you a warning, telling you not to push it too hard, to give it a break. I'll talk to the heart specialist, Östholm, who's a fine physician, and arrange for you to have some tests as soon as possible."

"What sort of tests?"

"Blood pressure, chest X-ray and ECG."

"You really think that's necessary?"

Kaluna gave him an old-fashioned look. "To find out what's wrong I'm going to use my influence to get those tests done on Saturday. That's a lot earlier than you've any right to expect and because nobody likes weekend work it'll use up all the goodwill I've so painstakingly built up in this hospital. I can assure you I would not do that if I did not consider it necessary. Am I right in thinking you are involved in stressful situations, when your life, or other people's, may be in danger? "

"Quite a lot of the time, yes."

"And that you get into physical confrontations where you have to pursue people, struggle with them, handcuff them?"

"Yes, of course."

"Then don't ask any more foolish questions. Once we've got the results, Östholm and I will see you together. Meanwhile you should try to take it easy."

The tests, carried out three days later, forced him to consider that his situation might be more serious than he'd thought. Thankful that there was no murder to be investigated, he decided that until he got the results, promised within a week, he would try to spend a little more time at home where he could relax. But when he reached his house late that afternoon the atmosphere was not as peaceful as he had expected. Sonja, just back from the nursery school where she'd recently been appointed Head, was simmering with indignation.

"As if I hadn't got enough grief with Angelica, who thinks she's grown-up at sixteen, sees nothing except her own problems and considers me a cross between a cleaner and a cook, now Johan's suddenly showing signs of adolescent rebellion at the age of fourteen, for God's sake! With you working such long and antisocial hours that you're hardly ever around, I really can't cope with pubescent grumpiness *and* a hormonal hurricane."

He put his arms round her, and felt her relax a little against him, "At least I'm home early today," he said soothingly.

She snatched herself out of his embrace. "Then sort him out. You're his great idol, you do manly things together like hunting and fishing, so see if you can discover why he bunked off school early today, completely forgot to buy the milk, eggs, bacon and mushrooms for our evening meal, failed to tidy his room in any visible way at all despite yesterday's promise, and doesn't seem to be able to give me any sort of explanation."

Magnus adored both his children, and until now he'd always felt completely at ease with Johan. But he realised it was probably true that he'd left most of the potentially confrontational aspects of home discipline to Sonja, who had always been so much better at it. Now, wishing he felt less lethargic, he marched Johan off to the local *Konsum* to buy the food, explained to him the facts of life about tired working mothers and avoiding upsetting them, and exacted a reluctant but seemingly genuine guarantee that his room would be tidied while supper was being prepared. But, having won those battles, he felt he had to accept Johan's word that he had not bunked off school, but just left for home when he'd completed his studies early.

"What's bugging Mum?" Johan asked him as they carried the food home. "You guys having difficulties or something?"

Magnus stopped dead in his tracks, staring at his son in disbelief and preparing a crushing retort. Then he saw the funny side and burst out laughing.

"Doesn't it ever occur to you that it might be *you* who's difficult to live with at the moment; that it's nothing to do with Mum, or me, but just you? Didn't you hear anything I said to you about Mum finding it hard work being a head, and you ought to be doing everything you can to make her life easier?"

"Yeah, yeah, but that's not totally fair. Angelica does nothing to help Mum at all, just paints her face and does dumb stuff to her hair and nails, and spends an eternity in the shower. And, come on, Dad, you're not around to help Mum much, because you're so busy chasing criminals and making the world safe for everybody."

"Is that a bad thing to do?"

"No, I guess not, but then I've got things to do that are important to me, and some of them are about saving the world, too. I'm with a group online protesting about overreliance on fossil fuels, and the failure to put enough money into encouraging alternative methods of power generation."

By the time they had almost reached home, they were so deep in a discussion of Sweden's hydroelectric policy and the relatively small reliance on nuclear power, that Magnus realised he had been completely diverted from the matter at issue. So he stopped, put his hand on Johan's arm, and said quietly, "I'm trying to make changes to my life so that I'll be able to help Mum more, and I'll talk to Angelica, too. But you've got to support me. Please, Johan, will you do that?"

Johan shrugged, giving him a diffident smile. "No need to get heavy on me, Dad. I love Mum too, you know."

And with that Magnus had to be satisfied; though he made it sound a trifle more acceptable when he presented a progress report to Sonja, undeservedly receiving a hug for his pains.

"I don't know what's got into me recently," she said confidingly. "Since I became Head I've changed. I used to be so patient with our children, but now I'm all over the place. I'm really scared that one day I'm going to blow with one of them, probably Angelica who's utterly impossible at the moment, and the damage might be irreparable."

"It's because you've got a lot more responsibility now, and until you get used to it, as you will, the kids will just have to go easy with you. But it may also be because they're *not* children any longer. We really ought to be like primitive societies and maroon them on an island or turn them out to do walkabout in the bush until they reach adulthood."

"If only..." Sonja snorted, but then she laughed. "It's nice having you home early. It makes life a lot easier."

"I've been thinking about rescheduling a few things at work," he said cautiously. "I've been feeling as though the job's getting on top of me a bit, and I'm certainly more tired than I used to be. Perhaps I'm getting old."

"Not you," Sonja reassured him. "But you'd better have an early night tonight."

"I think perhaps I will," Magnus answered, feeling exhaustion overwhelming him now that he no longer had to keep it at bay, and fearful that if he talked any longer Sonja would soon have his guilty secret out of him.

The results were ready in four days, more quickly than he'd dared hope, and he knew he had Kaluna to thank for that, as for so much else. But when he entered the room he was confronted by Dr. Östholm, so pale and gaunt beside the plump and genial Kaluna that it almost seemed he was in the presence of the representatives of life and death, and he hoped Kaluna would speak first. But he did not.

"The tests reveal early ischaemic changes," Dr. Östholm stated baldly. "If you go on as you are, you will have a heart attack and it may kill you." He had a thin face and a thin drooping moustache and he did not seem to be the sort of man who smiled often. He was certainly not smiling as he made his pronouncement, and Magnus felt numb with shock as he absorbed the immediate implication of the words. It was left to Kaluna to add a note of good cheer.

"Don't look so glum, Magnus, it's not as if you've *had* a coronary. And looking on the bright side, which you know I always do, you may never have one. Your body has just rung an alarm bell, 'a warning shot across the bows' as my English teacher in India used to say before he punished me, though it was my stern he hit with his stick rather than my bows. All you have to do is change your present life style and all may be well."

"You'll have to change it a great deal," Östholm put in tetchily.

Kaluna laughed loudly. "No more Action Man cop, Magnus, that's what he means."

"Are you telling me I have to leave the police?"

"No, no, we needn't go to those extremes, not yet anyway. It's time for you to move upwards, take promotion, to become our revered Chief of Police so we can sleep even more safely in our beds."

As he left the hospital, Magnus felt yet again that he was involved in a conspiracy, with Lennart leaving because he'd spotted the signs of heart problems in Magnus, and Kaluna knowing that Lennart was leaving and pushing Magnus into the vacancy. He realised it probably wasn't at all true, it was just coincidence; but it bothered him for a while until he understood he was using it as a way of avoiding the truth about the condition of his heart and, for him, the awful implications. He went for a walk, not ready yet to face his police colleagues and certainly not ready to lay the truth out in front of Sonja. But as he walked in the hospital grounds, meeting patients so much worse than he was, lulled by the beauty of the trees, the hugeness of the sky that made him feel small and unimportant, he gradually grasped the essence of what he'd heard. He wasn't ill yet, he might never have a heart attack and he didn't even have to leave the police. He just had to mature, to move away from direct contact with crime, to take the post that anybody else would be desperate to have: Head of the Sundsvall Police.

He suddenly felt a great calmness, and realised that he'd accepted the inevitable. It wasn't even an immediate change. Lennart would stay on while Magnus looked around for his replacement and prepared for an orderly succession. He began to think about the possibilities among his colleagues, regretting that Annica had left to marry Lennart, and that Lars Svedlund had lost the sight in one eye when the woman he'd come to save had shot him. Then he began to consider officers he'd worked with from neighbouring forces, and by the time he reached his car again he was so immersed in planning the change that he'd almost forgotten he hadn't wanted it to happen.

Relieved that he could finally tell Sonja all about it, he drove home as soon as school finished. He thought of what he'd say, the convincing arguments he'd use to persuade Sonja it was all for the best, the moving discussion he'd have with Angelica and Johan who would grasp his medical difficulties and become co-operative and helpful. But as soon as he opened the front door and heard the angry clamour he realised that Sonja's fear of finally losing it with Angelica had been realised.

"I will *not* allow it, not now, not tomorrow, not while you're in this house," Sonja was yelling, "and that's that!"

"I'm old enough to make my own decisions," Angelica stormed back at her. "You always treat me like a baby; you have no respect for me or for my views. I'm sixteen, for God's sake."

"And that's too young to have a tattoo, and while you're under this roof, and that's until you're eighteen, we, your parents, will be involved in all such discussions and we have the final say."

159

"Discussion," screeched Angelica, "what discussion? I say I want a tattoo, you say no way. That's not a discussion, that's an order!"

Neither had noticed his arrival and he decided it might be time to intervene.

"I thought I'd reached home," he said mildly, "but now it seems I'm in the state penitentiary."

Angelica immediately appealed to him.

"You don't mind me getting a tattoo, do you, Dad?"

"Where's it going to be?"

This question, which seemed a perfectly natural one to him, appeared to upset both his daughter and his wife.

"What's that got to do with anything?" retorted the outraged Angelica. "That's nobody's business but mine."

"It doesn't matter where it is," snapped Sonja indignantly. "You're missing the whole point. She can't have one wherever it is, and that's final."

"What sort of tattoo were you hoping to have, then?" he countered, somewhat less confidently. "A motto, a design of some sort, a picture of a vampire or a werewolf?"

"You don't trust me either, you're as bad as Mum," whimpered Angelica, squeezing out some tears. "You just think it'll be something rude or violent and you'll be ashamed of me."

"For heaven's sake, Magnus," Sonja hissed in exasperation. "What it is or where it goes doesn't matter. She is not having any tattoo at all."

Magnus recalled what Kaluna had said about reducing his stress levels, and it occurred to him it might be better to leave home than Homicide. And as he thought of that meeting with the two medical experts the full implications of what they'd been trying to tell him, which he had been restricting to its effect on his work, suddenly spread out to encompass his family life. He stared unbelievingly at Sonja's face, flushed with anger; at Angelica's, so full of sullen resentment, and he noticed that Johan's door was ajar and so he was probably learning the art of confrontation from this too. It was all too much for him, and he suddenly raised his hand to halt the verbal traffic. His expression must have changed remarkably, too, for suddenly they were all staring at him and there was a deathly silence.

"I have something to tell you," he said. "And since both our children suddenly seem to believe that they should be free of parental control, you'd both better come and listen to what I have to say, for it will affect you too. Then, when you have heard it, I would like you to go to your rooms to get on with your studies, so that Mum and I can have some time together."

He held Sonja's hand tightly while he explained the pains he had been experiencing, the tests and the result, and how it was to be confidential until an official announcement had been made. At the end of it Johan gave him an anxious hug, Angelica threw herself at him and wet him with her tears, and then they both dutifully went to their rooms.

"Why didn't you tell me you were having these chest pains?" Sonja said "I'd noticed you were a bit edgy, but I thought that was work as usual."

"I was afraid of making a fuss about nothing," he admitted, "and I didn't want to worry you unless it was absolutely necessary. Coping with Angelica and Johan at their present stage is quite hard enough, especially when I'm busy with a case and can't be around to shoulder some of the burden, so I wasn't going to add to your load until I knew the full facts. Compared to Angelica in a sulk, I'll take a serial killer any day."

She tried to smile, but it wasn't successful. "How do you really feel about it, giving up Homicide?"

He thought about it, and was comforted by his reaction to such a direct question. "I'm getting used to it, I think. It seemed like a death sentence at first, but already I'm looking to the future. I don't have any choice, so I'll just get on with it."

"And you'll take Lennart's job if it's offered to you?"

"In a way it's been mine for the asking, Lennart's always known that. I don't like administration, as you know, but I'd rather do that than die an early death. So, yes, at the end of this year I'll be the boss."

"You'll have come a long way in a short time, and when I see you on civic occasions as Sundsvall's Chief of Police, I'll be very proud of you. And Angelica and Johan aren't really so bad, they're just growing up, and in their own way they'll be proud of you, too."

"Johan actually told me he loved you the other day, so I suppose we haven't really got so much to grumble about. I'm sure the promotion will mean a bit more money too, and considering what Angelica costs us in clothes and shampoos, and Johan in electronic gadgets, it'll come in handy."

"I just wish you could take over from Lennart straight away. I'm worried you're going to overdo it in the next six months."

Not wanting to admit that he could have done but was reluctant to act so quickly, he tried to reassure her. "We seem to have caught most of the murderers round here, or frightened them away from the area. Things have never been so quiet, so I'll probably just be sitting around twiddling my thumbs."

But the next morning, as he was finishing his breakfast, those glib words came back to bite him. Not only had he felt satisfied with the dramatic drop in homicides, he'd been especially proud that the racially motivated gang violence depressingly common in the large southern cities had never reached Sundsvall. Now the worried voice of Inspector Lars Svedlund informed him that the body of a boy who was probably African had just been discovered beside an isolated lake. The evidence suggested that he had been deliberately burnt to death.

THIRTEEN

Lars jumped into the car beside him and they set off at speed north-east out of Sundsvall towards Ljustorp, though the lake was some distance from there. It was, in fact, some distance from anywhere, and that made Magnus curious.

He always relaxed a little whenever Lars was with him, for they'd started their police careers together up in Jämtland. Magnus had been the serious one of the two, already married, ambitious and a trifle touchy about his colour, whereas Lars had been irreverent, anti-establishment and a serial womaniser. They had worked closely together on the case of the executed Kurdish girl, and even when Magnus was whisked away to Sundsvall by Ragnar Amrén they'd stayed in touch. Finally Magnus had persuaded him to switch forces as well, he'd joined Homicide, and it was while working under Lennart on the complicated case of the Sundsvall Hammer Killer, as the newspapers dubbed him, that he'd been partially blinded. But after a longish spell in hospital, he'd surprised everybody, probably including himself, by marrying Antonia, the daughter of one of the victims in the case, and returned to Homicide as sharp and inquisitive as ever. He was quickly promoted to Inspector and Magnus, who nowadays tended to be a cautious investigator, had come to appreciate his restless and unorthodox questioning of apparently obvious aspects of any case.

"By the way, I alerted Forensics while I was waiting for you, so they should be there by the time we arrive."

"I'll be glad of Sanfridsson's help," Magnus muttered absently, his mind on his heart and when it might play up again.

Lars looked at him oddly. "What the hell's wrong with you, Magnus? Sanfridsson retired last month. It's Sofia Grönberg now."

Magnus groaned, "Sorry, we've been having sleepless nights over Angelica and Johan who've suddenly become teenagers from hell, and I'm not coping particularly well."

"Jesus! You're not telling me kids can be difficult, are you? Because Antonia's pregnant and I thought that was good news."

"It is," Magnus reassured him "You'll have twelve great years, and then you should leave home and come back when they're eighteen and human again."

"Thanks for nothing," Lars said sombrely. "Now I come to think of it, I was a real pain to my parents, absolutely wild, so it's lucky the baby's going to be a girl. I bet Antonia was as good as gold."

"You'll lose that bet, but congratulations anyway. It's the most cheering thing I've heard for some time. Now you'd better fill me in on the details."

"The body was found by a local hunter, and he rang the police," Lars said, taking out his notebook, "The nearest patrolman, Per Björholm, drove out to investigate. He's still there, taping off the area, but I got some information from him when he was put through to me to make his report. He told me the boy might be black, but what the hell does that mean? Are you black because you're half-Thai? And if he was burnt to death he would be black anyway."

"It just means he wasn't white European like you or Asian like me and therefore he was of African descent," replied Magnus with a smile. "Didn't you pay any attention at all at that recent Norms of Racial Language course?"

Lars shook his head. "I slept through most of it," he confessed. "I'm a policeman for God's sake, not a student of anthropophagy, which was the sort of long word the lecturer lost me with."

"I think that's cannibalism, so let's hope we don't see that when we get there. Maybe this Sofia Grönberg will be helpful, though I wasn't terribly impressed with her when she was introduced. Perhaps that's why I forgot her."

"We know we've got a blackened body," went on Lars, still pursuing his thoughts, "so surely a crucial question is why. Why would anyone burn a boy to death?"

"And why would it be done at an isolated lake?"

"Is it really isolated? Per said it was beside the road, but I've never driven here before and I don't even know where Ljustorp is, let alone Slättmon which is apparently the closest village."

"Not many people do drive along this road, that's what makes it isolated. It runs beside the Lögdö Vildmark, a nature reserve now, and it's pretty wild in parts. When I was living in Jämtland I sometimes used to drive to Sundsvall by turning off the 86 at Liden and driving along this road. Sonja's got a cousin in Mellberg and I could always get a cup of coffee there. I vaguely remember a small stretch of water, Black Creek tarn or something like that, and it's likely to be where the body was found."

"But if it's beside any sort of road, it isn't isolated," Lars persisted.

"That's a good point," Magnus replied thoughtfully. "It's a long way from any habitation, and I think there's only one family left in Slättmon, so it's isolated enough to be a good place for a killing. But, as you've made me realise, the road makes it easy to get to and quick to get away from, and that could be an important pointer when we consider who might have done it, and why."

Lars thought about that, and Magnus was distracted by the sudden blaze of lupins among the more restrained tones of the Swedish wild flowers at the road edge. It seemed to him that each year the colourful intruders marched further and further along the country roads, splashing them with shades of pink and blue. Though he enjoyed the cheerfulness of their colouring he slightly resented them, fearful their invasion would soon take over the roadsides he had known and loved as a child, surprising in spring and comfortably constant year after year. He wondered if he felt the same about human immigration, but that was more complicated because his mother had been an immigrant.

The car climbed higher and higher and by the small clearing that was Slättmon he felt he was on top of the immediate world around him. There was a freshness in the air that made his blood pound, and shortly afterwards he caught his first glimpse of the tarn glittering between the trees, the red, yellow and gold of the surrounding mire framing the silver sliver of the water. He saw a 4x4 beside the water, and a police patrol vehicle correctly parked on the other side of the road where it would be less likely to obliterate any other tyre marks. A Volkswagen stood beside it, and Magnus pulled up just beyond them, where he had a complete view of the stretch of water.

"Grönberg's already here, checking the body," Officer Björholm reported, jerking his thumb at a white clad figure on the far side of the tarn. Magnus looked at her with interest, wondering if they would work well together, or whether it would be one of those relationships which moved at a slow speed as if grit was constantly impeding the wheels. But he could see almost nothing of her, for she was crouching over something, studying it and either ignoring his arrival or concentrating so hard she hadn't noticed it. Some distance from her a tent had been erected, so she had not wasted any time getting to the crime scene.

The patrolman was still by his side, his eyes shining with excitement and obviously eager to say more. As he was an experienced officer, who would have attended murder scenes before, Magnus guessed that this one had affected him in some startling way. This was confirmed when he continued his report and couldn't resist adding his own views about what might have happened. "I've taped off a path for you, avoiding any tracks there may be, but it means you have to walk a bit further on to the end of the tarn and then you can circle it completely without being too close to where the body was found. It looks as though the young lad escaped when the car pulled up, and was then pursued by two men who killed him when he was two thirds of the way round. Do you want me to show you?"

Magnus shook his head. He liked to be alone when he took his first look at a murder scene, and he certainly did not wish to be accompanied by someone who appeared to have made up his mind on a number of points already.

"Who's that?" he asked, pointing to the lanky fair-haired man in a hunting jacket waiting patiently by the cars.

"Tove Claesson. He was out early this morning, going to repair an elk hide on the far side of the tarn, and he came across the body."

"Inspector Svedlund will want to talk to him," he said, glancing at Lars, who nodded. "Then you can work with him, taking his detailed statement."

As Björholm moved away, he turned to Lars. "I want you to do the questioning. Björholm seems to have formed his own judgement about what happened and I don't want him leading the witness. He can listen and write it down, but he mustn't interrupt. While you do that, I'm going to talk to Sofia."

He walked slowly towards the figure beyond the tent. He didn't attempt to direct his thoughts, letting them flit from impressions of the tarn to its proximity to the road, which Lars had been so insistent about; then to the tracks he could see occasionally in the boggy waterside areas beyond the tape, and from there to the boy himself. If he *was* black, why would anybody wish to kill him, and why here in Västernorrland where relatively few black immigrants had settled?

That last thought took him by surprise, and he wondered why it had floated into his mind. He did not pursue it now, but made a mental note to do so at a later stage, for it had been marked by the tiny shiver of anticipation that experience had taught him to respect.

The body was recognisably human, but that was all. It lay face downward beside the tarn, pushed up by arms piteously raised as though in supplication. But no mercy had been shown. It was horribly burned, leaving no clothes, no hair and little flesh, no obvious indication of skin colour, no sense of age or sex from where he was standing. It looked small and black, but that was the work of what had burned him up, turning him from whatever he had been to a frizzled carcase. With some relief he switched his gaze to the girl kneeling there immobile, masked and in white protective clothing, very close to the corpse, her concentration so intense it was almost tangible, as though she prayed as well as studied every aspect of the body, trying to soothe its journey to

170

eternity while searching for any clue that might suggest the motivation for an act of such inexplicable cruelty.

"I've seen so much," she said, turning her head slightly so that he realised she had been conscious of his arrival and his scrutiny, "but I've never come across anything as apparently pointless as this brutal way of killing someone so young. It's as though the Vietnam War had come to Norrland."

She got to her feet, struggling painfully to do so. Then she limped towards him, ungainly, one leg so weak it scarcely supported her. But she made nothing of it, as though it was something long-endured, a leftover from childhood polio perhaps. He thought of her walking round the tarn to the body, the boggy ground creating physical difficulties he'd never had to face, and wondered how she'd ever been able to get the tent up.

"You are Detective Inspector Trygg," she said, as though reminding herself of his name. She indicated the tent and walked towards it, taking off her mask and gloves. Outside the entrance flap she turned and said, "I'm Sofia Grönberg. And now you are here, I should like to commend Officer Björholm. He carried the tent for me and helped me to erect it."

She'd spoken stiffly as if she'd been determined to say it whether he wanted to hear it or not, and now she placidly awaited his reaction.

"Per's a good man," he agreed gravely, trying to show that he was taking her seriously and approved of her praise for another policeman. "And please call me Magnus, because we're going to be working closely

171

together as colleagues and we shouldn't stand on ceremony."

"I would prefer that," she said, and her sudden smile seemed to enlarge the brown intelligent eyes behind the heavy-framed spectacles and make them sparkle. She held out her hand and he liked her firm grip, her quietness as she waited for him to take the next step without feeling the need to fill the silence with casual chatter. He began to be more optimistic that her high academic qualifications, which he'd noticed on her application, might be balanced by the common sense and imagination he considered almost as important.

"Can you tell me anything yet?" he asked cautiously, remembering how Sanfridsson had hated to be hurried.

"Several things," she replied with assurance. "But I only brought you here away from the body so I could remove my mask and gloves and greet you properly. The body, as you will have noticed, is in a fragile state and as soon as you have studied it enough I want to get it in here where I can appraise it in more sterile conditions, keeping the curious away from it until I can transport it to the lab. Would you be insulted, as the chief investigating officer, if I asked you to put on a set of protective clothing before you accompany me back to the body? Then you can examine everything for as long as you need, and, if you will allow it, I could raise one or two matters with you."

"Your predecessor always insisted on protective clothing," Magnus said reassuringly, touched by her old-fashioned courtesy. "He often refused to tell me anything at this early stage, and he wasn't nearly as polite about it as you've been."

Sofia pointed to a neat pile of white clothing and then went back to the body, working on it until he joined her, properly dressed.

"I'm taking samples of flesh to test," she explained, "but I need hair samples, and there's none left on this side of him. I'm expecting a technician who will assist me, but I don't want to wait any longer. Would you mind helping me turn him over now you have gloves and a mask on, or should I call the patrolman?"

Although she didn't smile he suspected she was teasing him, and he knelt down by the body without comment.

"We shall have to do this very carefully," Sofia warned him, "because the front of him took the full force of the first blast. It will not be a pleasant sight."

He nodded, they turned the body, and it was certainly not nice at all. The eyes seemed to have melted and so had much of the rest of the face. The remaining flesh all over his body was ridged and crisped, and although he could still just see that he was male, no prints would be available from the finger tips.

Sofia noticed where he was looking, and she nodded. "If we ever identify him, it will be through dental records."

"Do you think this is why they burnt him, to remove the possibility of fingerprints?"

Sofia shook her head. "Lean down and smell him, Magnus."

Magnus did, and recognised the stench. "Petrol?" he asked.

"It is petrol, yes, but with an added fuel thickener. It's from a flamethrower. It's the military forerunner of napalm which was a jelly-like form of petrol which adhered to the body, resulting in such horrifying deaths that it was subsequently banned by the US army. That accounts for my earlier and entirely unprofessional reference to the Vietnam War when I was still in a state of shock at what I had discovered." She paused, and Magnus realised she was deeply affected by what was before her. "But, to answer your question, no, the purpose of this was not to remove the possibility of finger prints. A flamethrower's a pretty crude weapon, and I would guess that it's almost impossible to control the fire it belches out. The terrible burns on this side prove that he was facing them when they fired, and the destruction of the finger tips was probably just an inevitable consequence. But the choice of such an extravagant weapon may, partially at least, have been influenced by such a consideration."

"Now I can see him properly it seems even more as though he's raising his hands in prayer, begging them to stop."

Sofia looked at him with interest. "I had never before thought the attitude was supplicatory, though you're right, it does suggest praying for mercy. But it isn't a deliberate gesture, it was much too late for that. Technically it's meant to look like a boxer defending

174

himself, and so it's called the pugilistic position. The body reacts unconsciously to the intense heat, the sinews shorten and the arms are thrown up. It's actually very difficult to get them down again."

"It reminds me of the casts of bodies in the museum at Pompeii, where I took the family one summer."

"Lava flow will have the same effect, and firemen are used to seeing it on bodies in burnt out buildings."

"When was he killed?

"Sometime yesterday, late afternoon or early evening."

Magnus had been watching her closely. At first her rather pedantic manner of speech had suggested she was in her late thirties, but now, as she'd relaxed, there had been something much more youthful in her quick responses, the fluid movements of her head and hands; and he realised she was probably still in her twenties. That meant she'd been very young to secure such a responsible post and so she must have been well-recommended.

"Have you seen enough of him *in situ*?" she went on. "My technician has just arrived, so if you give your permission she can help me move the body. I've taken photographs and a short video, so you can always refer to it again."

He nodded, suddenly longing to stand there quite alone, to reflect upon what had happened, and attempt to make some sort of sense of it.

"I'll need to talk you again, after your lab tests, but I've a few more questions now. I was told the boy was black. Is that so?"

"I'm not an anthropologist, Magnus, but I shall consult one. Meanwhile I have the skin samples which will reveal the pigmentation, and I've just spotted a remaining pubic hair which I shall test. I'm confident those will confirm he's African, and will probably pinpoint the area he is from. The hair also shows he'd reached adolescence, so he was more a young man than a boy."

"Have you been able to form any idea of what might have precipitated his death at that particular moment?"

Sofia studied him carefully, assessing him as though previous experience had taught her to be cautious.

"If you look closely," she said lowering her voice, "you will see there is a chain padlocked round his throat. Apart from the obvious slavery implications, I'm fairly certain an object would have been suspended from it. When I've finished my laboratory tests I'll be able to tell you definitely whether something was there, and whether it was recently wrenched off from the chain. If so, it's possible that might have been what killed him."

For a moment she stood with him as he looked down at the charred corpse of a youngster probably much the same age as Johan. He couldn't fully control a shudder of horror at what the flames had done to face and fingers, genitals and toes. Beside him Sofia sighed, a mournful sigh; and he respected her all the more for such an instinctive reaction. Then, seeing the technician

176

approaching, he straightened up, turned away from the body, and stared out at the peaceful tarn beyond.

"There's something all wrong about this killing," he said. "The wild place, the absurd weapon that was used, two men to kill one boy, it makes no sense at all."

Sofia looked at him oddly. "I was struck by a similar thought. It's as though the whole thing was somehow staged, as if we were dealing with theatre, not murder."

"Perhaps the chain was part of a costume? Or maybe what was on it had some personal importance?"

"Or was it simply a key, literally a key, but also a key to something else?" Sofia suggested.

"A key to something else need not literally be a key. It could be a tool like a computer memory stick."

Sofia nodded, and he almost smiled at her likeness to a fastidious professor acknowledging some value in a student's comment. But he was glad he hadn't done so when he heard her next chilling statement. "When I discovered the chain and realised something might have been attached to it, my immediate thought was of a fire bomb, built as a copy of a hand grenade and attached by its pin to the chain. That would make it a sort of a suicide belt, and when he pulled it off, for whatever reason, he died a horrible death."

Magnus took the thought very seriously, though in his mind he broadened its implication. Was it possible that it was the act of pulling something off the chain that triggered his death by flamethrower?

"I think you've made a very important point," he said gratefully. "If it had been something of value to the two men, they would have taken it when they were together in the car. So its removal has different implications which I must think about."

He walked off towards Lars who was coming to find him.

"How was Claesson's statement?"

"Straightforward. He's very much a countryman and he doesn't waste words. He'd been circling the tarn at six this morning, heading towards one of his hides beyond that grove of trees on the far side. He saw the body, phoned the police, waited here, told us the facts and now he wants to go."

"Maybe not quite yet," Magnus said thoughtfully. "A hunter knows about tracks and it would be a pity not to use his expertise."

He went across, introduced himself and asked his question.

Claesson thought about it, sighed and then agreed. "While I was waiting for Per to arrive I poked about a bit along the road. I wasn't going to say anything in case you thought I was interfering in police work, but now you've asked me to assist it may be worth showing you what I found."

He led the way along the road back towards Slättmon, stopping at a wooded area that obscured the view of most of the tarn.

"They stopped their car well before the usual place where I parked mine," Tore said, his bright blue eyes beneath the thinning blond hair fixing themselves on Magnus as if to compel his attention. "They pulled up here, and they must have stayed on the road as there are no tyre tracks. But it's here that the footprints start, just beside the road. So it could have been an unplanned halt, perhaps because the driver wanted a pee or the boy felt sick. That would make this tarn a chance location, not a planned one."

Magnus, thankful he'd asked him to help, gave him his full attention, and even Lars kept silent.

"I think the two men, and the size of the tracks shows they were men, were taken by surprise when the boy jumped out and tried to make his escape along the edge of the tarn and then round it. But they had a secret weapon, the flamethrower. Now nobody carries a weapon like that for emergencies, so perhaps they were collectors of militaria and had just bought it in a country auction or, more likely, from a private collector. Maybe they thought it would be a good opportunity to try it out, give the boy a fright. Anyway, the boy got a start while they took it from the boot. But the men obviously weren't too worried about that because they never broke into a run. I'll show you."

He pointed to the men's tracks in a boggy part of the ground. "The second man is carrying the weapon, that's why his tracks are deeper. But the leading man, a few metres ahead of him, is definitely walking, not running."

He waited while the two policeman studied the footprints and Lars photographed them. Magnus made a

179

few notes, then looked up at Claesson. "I know we've kept you waiting, and now we're taking up even more of your time, but all this is really very helpful."

The hunter looked pleased at their appreciation, and pointed to the tracks again. "I expect they didn't want to spook him, letting him think he was safe as long as they couldn't literally get their hands on him. So he only bothered to stay out of reach, saving his energy for a last sprint away from them and out of sight."

He spat reflectively. "That's the only explanation I can come up with for the fact that the men weren't running, and once he was well ahead the boy stopped running too."

"He was three-quarters of the way round before they burnt him up," commented Magnus. "So why did they wait?"

"I don't know much about flamethrowers, but I imagine you have a pack on your back containing the flammable liquid, and it could have taken that long to get it ready to fire, to prime it or whatever you have to do. Perhaps the distance between them and the boy was crucial as well. If you look very carefully where they stood, you can see drops of petroleum in the water that would have oozed up around their feet, and the rear tracks are deeper than before, so the one with the weapon stood quite still for a while. When the boy turned at bay, he was probably warned he couldn't get away and urged to come back to them, perhaps to a life of slavery or, heaven help us, prostitution. When he refused, they may have tried to give him a fright and ended up killing him."

180

At a sign from Magnus, Lars busied himself photographing those tracks too, and the nearby pools. Then Magnus thanked Tore for his help, shook his hand warmly and stood, deep in thought, watching him hurry away to his 4x4 and drive off. It was pretty clear he'd talked a lot to Per Björholm, while waiting for Magnus to arrive, and it was perfectly possible they already knew each other, probably through hunting. He reflected that hunters and police had much in common, and they were almost certain to influence each other. Both tended to have a mindset that encouraged them to think in terms of pursuit, of hunting the quarry, and, if they were lucky, the prey turning at bay, to be captured, or, in the case of an elk or an armed criminal, shot. That would have been the most obvious picture to form in Tore's mind when he found the body; and, talking to Per when he drove up in answer to his call, they probably helped to convince each other that escape, pursuit and death when the quarry turned at bay was precisely what *had* happened at the tarn.

Magnus, though a hunter of both elk and humans, felt instinctively that it wasn't what had occurred. The truth, when they finally discovered it, would, he was sure, be very different. Yet he did not regret having asked for Tore's help. However faulty his conclusion might be, he had drawn their attention to possible meanings in the tracks that deserved the most careful consideration. It wasn't Tore's fault that he was a hunter, not a detective.

But all the jumbled information he'd picked up on that walk, what he'd heard and seen, and the very different pictures it conjured up in his mind, were now

181

pressing in on him in a way he'd never experienced before the chest pains began. He felt an overpowering need to get away for a while, to be quite alone until his heart stopped beating so rapidly and those pictures formed a more rational narrative. So he asked Lars to represent him at the crime scene while he went off to do a bit of pondering to try to clear his mind.

"Be very tactful about it, but check that Sofia is going to take a sample of that water with the petroleum in it and make casts of the tracks, if she hasn't in fact already done it. And if I'm not back by then, you'll have to oversee the removal of the body."

Lars nodded cheerfully, enjoying being left in charge, and Magnus drove back a short way towards Sundsvall. He turned off up a forest track he'd noticed on the way in, parked out of sight of the road, switched off the engine and prepared himself to review all he'd been told. He settled himself comfortably in the driving seat, closed his eyes, and conjured up an image of the whole tarn, its narrowness, the mire all round it, its proximity to the road, the grove of trees on the far side, the pools where the boggy ground was especially wet. Then he took out his notebook, drew an outline plan of it and marked where the boy was found, where the men had stood when he was killed and where the car had stopped when they first arrived.

Staring at it, he mentally walked over the ground several times, then listed the various scenarios arising from the comments of Sofia, Lars, Tore and Per, and adding a few from his own observations. He realised he'd been especially struck by Sofia's observation that the whole episode looked as though it had been staged, that the participants had behaved like characters in a theatre or on a film set, somehow following a script. At the climax, even the victim seemed to have turned to the audience of the two men, not at all like an animal at bay, but like an actor expecting to receive rapturous applause.

A number of points seemed clear to him now. The car had not stopped by chance at the lake. These people were almost certainly from some large southern city like Göteborg or Stockholm, places where there were Nigerian gangs which might conceivably have a weapon like a flamethrower. It had not been bought along the way, for it was illegal to sell such an item and it had been in working order. So it had been brought with them, and that meant the murder had been planned in advance and the venue pre-arranged.

Magnus made more notes, trying to imagine what might have occurred. The boy had not escaped from the car, nor had he run away. A teenager, with a head start, would quickly have outdistanced his pursuers, especially as they'd had to get the bulky weapon from wherever in the car it had been hidden from the boy. For he was increasingly convinced there had been two different scripts. The boy had been following one which was based on what he thought they had come to the lake to do. But the script used by the two men contained the scenario of what, from the very beginning, was really intended to happen.

Magnus felt much of the tension drain out of him. It had to be the answer, for nothing else fitted. It would account for the sense of theatre, where the men acted the good guys until they killed him, and the boy unsuspectingly acted the part they'd prepared him for, believing there was no danger at all from what was behind him.

Why had he run from the car then? He thought of the times he and Sonja had taken the children on outings by car to a new lake or stretch of forest. Cooped up in a confined space, excitement rising as they got nearer and nearer to their destination, they always burst from the car as soon as they arrived, rushing down to the water, the camp site, the beach, stretching their legs, expending their pent-up energy, exploring the immediate area. It was the adults who stayed by the car, unloading the tent, the boat or the fishing rods, though in this case it had been a flamethrower.

He put down the notebook and relaxed even more, feeling his heart relax as well, resuming the steady beat he never normally noticed. He felt he had a much clearer picture of the whole situation now. There had been two separate plays, one starring the boy, the other starring the two men. The boy was being given a treat, an exciting trip north, and his performance was entirely genuine, full of exuberance and delight. But the men, in their drama, were carefully following their own script, avoiding any sense of threat until the particular moment when they burnt the boy up.

Magnus could scarcely contain his excitement. He almost sprang out of the car, paced about, punched the air, then drank some coffee from his thermos. He did not yet know why the men had killed the boy, just as he could not conceive why they had come so far north, to this particular tarn, when there would have been so many equally isolated places much further south in Dalarna or Hälsingland. Those two points, which might subsequently be of vital importance, could be put on one side for the moment. For if it proved that there had been something suspended from the chain around the youngster's neck, he thought he knew what had triggered the actual execution.

The boy, skipping ahead of the men so light-heartedly, running at first and falling into a walk, was making for a particular location, and Magnus was certain it was a place where he'd been instructed to do something. That was why he'd ignored the men behind him, and they hadn't hurried, because the place where they would meet up was the same in both scripts, and it had been pre-arranged. One man had hung back behind the other, so that what he was carrying was obscured. Then they'd waited until the boy had carried out his task, which might have been discarding something hanging from his neck, probably some mark of servitude. It was delightful to be rid of it, so he wasn't fearful at all, and he turned to them to receive their applause or even some gift. But the men weren't interested in what was round the boy's neck. That was just the distraction so that he would not notice what his reward was going to be.

FOURTEEN

It seemed to Magnus that he'd reached his conclusions comparatively quickly. But when he returned to the lake he found that Sofia had taken the boy's body to the Sundsvall Forensics Laboratory and that Per, having taped off all entrances to the tarn, had driven back to Sundsvall to report for any further duty.

"I hope your pondering was productive," Lars said teasingly. "I was beginning to get the creeps here by myself, so I'm glad to see you, especially if you've got some coffee left."

Magnus poured him a cup, staring out at the tarn with fresh eyes now that he had a much clearer idea of what had probably happened there.

"Sofia left a message for you," Lars told him as he drained his coffee. "She'd done a further study of the chain once she'd got the body into her tent, and I was to tell you there *had* been something suspended from it, and it had been wrenched off."

Magnus felt relief flood through him and recklessly took a swift decision. "Then we've got work to do," he said excitedly. "We're going on a treasure hunt. I'll tell you more shortly, but for the moment I want you to walk behind me round the tarn, following the boy's tracks but not going too near them. Forget what anybody else has said, take no notice of the men's tracks at this stage, just form your own impressions of the boy's state of mind. We'll stop where he stopped."

The start of July had brought warmth at last; the sun was high in the sky and the wind over the tarn was no longer bitter. They set off, Magnus busy imagining he was the boy, free for some reason and heading towards the reedy end of the water. He was pleased to find that after that initial rush, the footprints were obviously not too hurried, and they certainly raised no spectre of fear or the need to escape. If anything, they were placid steps, moving towards some particular goal, not pausing to look over his shoulder because he knew the men would be following and it didn't worry him.

"There was no sign that he was running away," Lars said perplexedly when they stopped. "No sign of a chase at all."

"You may be blind in one eye," Magnus said with a grin, "but you've already seen more clearly than Claesson did. His problem was that he'd talked a lot to Per and they'd both persuaded themselves that if it was a killing it must have been preceded by a chase. Once that theory had been supported by the fact the boy ran from the car, the later tracks were almost meaningless."

He told Lars what he'd worked out in the car, about the parallel plays, the boy believing he was having a treat, an outing from the city to the country, with a reward at the end of it if he performed a particular task.

"You believe he had to pull something off the chain round his neck?"

"Yes. And as nothing was found near the body, he probably threw it away from him."

"Casting off slavery?"

"It's as good as any other answer at the moment, maybe better. It would account for his eager running at the start, as if he couldn't wait to get it done."

"But why did they then kill him, in such a horrible way, and with such an extraordinary weapon?"

Magnus sighed. "We don't know, because they were in a different play, following a different script; and so far we know nothing about that. But if you and I can find whatever it was he threw away, maybe we'll have our first clue."

"Shouldn't we wait for a proper fingertip search team, with someone from Forensics present throughout, and an underwater team on standby?"

"Yes, we should," replied Magnus. "But the sun's out to help our search, and with only two of us there's less chance of whatever it is being inadvertently pushed into the bog or nudged into the water. Apart from anything else, I feel lucky and I want to move fast. Can you imagine how long it would take to get a team like that together in the holiday season? So we're going to break the rules and try our luck. Are you with me?"

Lars laughed. "I may be one-eyed, but I'm not missing the fun. Where do we start?"

Magnus studied the footprints close to the reeds, the common *vass* so often found at the edges of boggy stretches of water. Here the boy had stopped, and the blurring of the rear footmark did suggest that he might have hurled something.

"Right here," he replied. "First of all we'll search the immediate area, in case he just chucked it a short distance."

"If it was bad magic of some sort, he'd have wanted to throw it as far away as he could," objected Lars. "And I doubt if the men wanted it found, so he'd probably been told to toss it into the tarn."

"I agree. But we ought to do the search of the immediate land area first, just to eliminate every other possibility."

Lars nodded, but after half an hour they'd found nothing.

"It looks as though it's going to be a job for the underwater team, after all," Magnus muttered disappointedly.

Gloomily they stood together near the boy's last tracks, staring out over the water and reluctant to give up the prize.

"He was a teenager, right?" Lars said suddenly.

"Yes, maybe fifteen or sixteen."

"Then it's just possible he would be able to throw it over the water to the other side there, not too far from the road. Don't get your hopes up too high yet, because if it was something like a little metal devil mask it wouldn't have the weight to go so far. But if it was something heavier I think I could have done it at that age."

"Or if it was a circular charm he could have skimmed it over the surface of the water. That's something all boys like doing."

Lars laughed. "You want to go and look on the other side as much as I do; so let's do it. I spotted you'd brought the thermos with you, so if we don't find anything we can drown our sorrows in the last of the coffee."

He walked away from the immediate crime scene area, cut through the stem of a dwarf pine and pushed it upright into the bog as close as he dared to where the boy's tracks were. "That'll help us to get exactly opposite, and concentrate the search there."

"And since they say two pairs of eyes are better than one, maybe we'll strike lucky."

"Your arithmetic is up the spout, Magnus. I haven't got a pair any longer."

"The eye you have got is a bloody good one, though. You're like my old aunt who couldn't read a book any longer, but she could spot a dropped needle on the carpet quicker than any of us." He stooped, picking up a pebble. "He was so badly burnt, it wasn't easy to be sure of the boy's size and strength, but he could have been quite tall and muscular. So I want you to stay here, just

190

back from the footprints, and when I reach the other side, hurl this as far as you can. It should give us a rough idea of the area we need to cover."

Magnus set off back the way he'd come, and when he was in position he signalled to Lars. The stone arched through the air and landed only just beyond the water's edge. Magnus marked the spot; and as soon as Lars joined him they began a painstaking search.

It was a damp and messy business, and in the watery areas they were compelled to crawl and feel below the surface to discover if there was anything lying in the gloomy murk. After two hours, despite using their torches in an attempt to get an answering metallic glimmer from the reed bed, they'd discovered nothing. They rested, and Magnus, experiencing the now more accustomed thumping from his heart, produced his thermos again. He poured some of the remaining coffee into the cap and passed it to Lars, putting the stainless steel thermos down carefully in the reeds. As he did so, Lars pointed to it excitedly.

"I heard something when you put it down," he whispered, as though a raised voice might change the situation. "Since I lost the sight of that eye, my hearing seems to have become more acute, and I also thought I saw a reddish colour reflected in the polished steel."

Very cautiously, Magnus lifted the thermos, passed it to Lars, and then felt among the base of the reeds. His fingers touched a small solid object, and he lifted it up so that they could examine it. Both groaned in disappointment, for it was just a piece of the local red granite. The optimism that had filled Magnus until then drained out of him. He took the empty cap from Lars, filled it with the last of the coffee and swallowed it.

"Are you OK, Magnus?" Lars asked, with some concern. "You don't seem to have been yourself since you picked me up in the car this morning, more like a bear disturbed during winter hibernation. You'd forgotten Sanfridsson had taken early retirement, you were unusually critical of Per, and after Claesson had talked us through the tracks you just went off by yourself, which is the first time I can ever remember you needing to do that. Now you seem to have suddenly lost all enthusiasm for this treasure hunt. Is there something you should be telling me?"

Magnus looked at him carefully, realising the change in him was bound to be noticed by a man who had been with him since the start of his police career.

"If I do tell you, it must be in absolute confidence until this case is over. Nobody must know until then, nobody at all; and that means not even Annette. Can you cope with that?"

"Yes," said Lars. "I don't like leaving Annette out of things, but you know I'd never let you down, Magnus, not in any serious matter. And it sounds so serious that you've got me really worried."

"I've got a bad heart, Lars. I've been warned to avoid all sorts of stress if I'm to dodge a heart attack that might be fatal, so this will be my last case."

"You're not leaving the police?"

"No, but I won't be Head of Homicide any longer, and I can tell you now that if you and I bring this to a successful conclusion, I have every hope you'll succeed me. Even though you're a cocky little bastard who doesn't even let me have a secret about my internal organs, I shall certainly recommend you."

"I've often dreamed of that, but after I was shot in the face I never thought it would be possible. Was it the chest wound you got that's done the damage?"

"The specialist says no, though I still think it might be a contributory factor. Anyway, I feel much better for telling you, so we'd better get on with the treasure hunt."

"Fair enough," said Lars, "but first things first." He pointed to some reddish-orange seedy berries growing in the bog. "There are quite a few cloudberries growing here and I think I'll go and pick a few for Annette while I've got the chance. They seem to be ripening in the sudden sunshine, and that plump one over there is yellow enough to eat already." He winked at Magnus. "It'll give you a chance to have an extra rest, now that you're uncomfortably past your prime."

"You're the one who's likely to be uncomfortable, not me. I always get stuck in the bog picking *hjortron* and you'll end up with wet feet at the very least."

He watched Lars incautiously extend his hand for the yellow berry, stretching out his body and his arm and shifting his weight away from his already sinking feet. Then, with infinite caution, he reached down and let his fingers slip through the water raised by the pressure of his feet, and then come up with what he'd grasped. But it was not the berry, which he ignored at the last moment. It was a small leather pouch.

"There's a broken metal ring in the top," he announced triumphantly, still not quite believing it had really happened, "And there's a metal figure attached to the front which looks African to me. I really think it's what we've been searching for, but you'll have to pull me upright and get me onto firm ground, because I'm stuck, just as you said I would be."

Magnus scrambled over, seized the free hand Lars extended and heaved him into a vertical position. Then he took the object reverently from his fingers and splashed back to firm ground, leaving Lars to extricate himself.

It was a roll of rawhide, carefully stitched at the sides and along the top to form a secure container. Sewn on to the front of it was a flat cast brass male figure with arms outstretched which added to its weight and explained why it had been found further inland than the thrown pebble. He felt pretty sure the water would not have penetrated the leather and so there was a good chance that whatever was inside would not be damaged.

"What do you think?" Lars asked excitedly, squelching towards him.

"I think I was so right to choose you as my fellow treasure hunter," Magnus answered soberly. "You had the devil's own luck when a girl like Annette agreed to take you on, and you've shown the same luck now."

"Then you do think it's what we're looking for."

"Oh yes, there's no doubt about that. Empty out your shoe and let's get this safely back to Sundsvall."

"What do you suppose is inside?"

"We'll know soon enough when Sofia's opened it."

"If the boy was so keen to get rid of it, it might have been a curse of some sort."

Magnus shivered, as though a bat's wing had brushed his cheek. "I know you're just being an overgrown schoolboy, eager to find something to do with witchcraft. But it's just possible you've raised an issue we need to keep in mind, because it backfired on him, didn't it? When he threw that pouch away, he wasn't freed from anything. If it did contain an evil omen, it may have come true in the horrible death he died."

Lars thought about that, but finally he just shook his head in puzzlement. "I can see it might be important, but I can't grasp the point you're trying to make."

"Nor can I," admitted Magnus, setting off towards the car. "We'll just have to be patient until we get Sofia's report, and then the answer may leap out at us. But once we've dropped this off, I'll buy you a big meal because you've proved there's more to you than a lot of charm and a big mouth."

The next day he and Lars called in on Sofia, and found she was still working on the pouch. She'd opened it and was about to test the blackish amalgam which was all she'd found inside.

"I don't mind if you both stay," she said in answer to the offer Magnus had made to leave her in peace, which was what Sanfridsson would have demanded. "But this may well be made up of a mixture of substances, and in that case the separation and testing of each one could take several hours. In view of what I've already discovered, which will all be in my final report, you might be better occupied getting background knowledge from some expert on African magic, specifically West African, and, even more specifically, Nigerian."

Magnus, grateful she'd given him valuable advance information from her ethnicity tests on the hair and skin samples, watched her settle again to her work as Lars hurried back to the car to ring Annette. He noted her rapt attention, the nimble fingers as she prepared slides for the electronic microscope, so out of keeping with the clumsy dragging leg he had seen at the tarn. As if she felt his gaze on her, Sofia raised her head, pausing in her study, and said in the gentler, less official tone she seemed to reserve for him, "I've checked my list of experts, and, as it happens, there's one living in Sundsvall who knows about Nigerian customs. I've photographed the pouch and the figure on it for you to show him, and he'll certainly be able to tell you more about it than I can. His name is Gustav Carlsson, and I've clipped to the photo a note of his address and phone number. I rang him earlier to check that he could see you, and he'll be there for the next few hours. But for personal reasons he made it clear he would be glad if you would agree to see him on your own."

It felt almost like an order and Magnus didn't entirely like it. "You know him then?" he asked stiffly, feeling he should have been asked before she rang and put out that Lars had been so casually excluded.

Sofia went rather red, and shook her head. "My father knows him slightly," she explained.

"Is he really much of an expert?" Magnus queried doubtfully.

Sofia smiled, as though, after the sting of his implied rebuke, she was about to be gloriously vindicated.

"He's worked successfully with many other police forensic teams in Sweden, and that's why he's on our register. He has one of the finest collections of Nigerian art in Sweden and I'm sure he'll enjoy showing it to you while he tells you about the various forms of magic in Nigeria. The customs and traditions of that country are his particular speciality."

FIFTEEN

Magnus worried that something fundamental might have changed in him since he'd heard the medical diagnosis. He'd quite lost his happy, carefree attitude that had got him through every problem and, hopefully, had made him an easy colleague to work with. Now, unless he was with somebody close to him, like Sonja, his children and Lars, he felt a general irritability entirely unlike his previous self. The hunter had rubbed him up the wrong way because he'd made more out of the tracks than was actually there. He'd inwardly criticised the patrolman because he's discussed the case with Tore. He'd been abrupt with Sofia because she'd rung Carlsson without getting his prior permission; and now, as he walked up the rising road towards the impressive building where this so-called expert lived, he knew he was preparing himself to dislike a man who had told him to come alone.

Normally he shrugged off any such tiny irritations. Life had always been good to him. He adored Sonja and the children, was in love with his job, felt he was successful and woke each morning eager for the day ahead. Now, so suddenly, nothing was quite the same. It was as though Death was sitting on his shoulder, threatening him unless he changed his ways; and it was the changing of those ways that was altering him as a person. It was not logical, it was not necessary, and now that he'd spotted what was happening to him, he was determined to mend his ways. That was why he was walking from the police station to Gustav Carlsson's apartment block, up to the high point of the hill which flanked Sundsvall on the north. He'd decided exercise would drive the nonsense out of him; and to an extent it had. Already he could smile at his peevishness, and he made a resolution to recover his usual serenity.

But as those aggravations had been swept out, the space was immediately filled by vaguely suspicious thoughts about Carlsson, a man he'd never even met. He had a feeling there was something pertinent in the Bible about driving out devils, but his mind was so obsessed with the art collector he couldn't even turn it to reviewing Holy Scripture. That did make him smile briefly, but it didn't alter the negative impressions he'd already formed. Before he'd left his office he'd trawled the internet, and everything he'd discovered about Carlsson and his magnificent collection had indicated wealth, and so probably power and influence. But there was a suggestion of caution, too, in what it carefully didn't reveal about his personal details. These two indications seemed to underline what he'd been told already: that Carlsson would see him if he came within a few hours, but he did not wish to be outnumbered nor, perhaps, have a witness to what was said between them.

He pretended to listen on his mobile as his eyes focussed on the high-rise white cube that was now only a hundred metres distant. Instinctively Magnus had kept to the shady side of the road where he was less likely to be conspicuous to anyone watching out for him. He'd quickly noted that the top balcony seemed to encircle the whole building, giving the resident fine views, good light for his display of Nigerian art, and the ability, should he wish to do so, to watch the approach of visitors, especially those who might not be as welcome as others. Of course, with such a valuable collection, he would be right to be vigilant. But Magnus could not rid himself of the nagging suspicion that for some reason he, a policeman, might be numbered among the not so very welcome.

But when Magnus stepped out of the hissingly-swift lift, and faced the man who was awaiting him in his open doorway, he was unprepared for what occurred. Immediately, at first sight, he liked him. He was neither puffed up with self-importance nor secretive or suspicious. He was just an unexpectedly old man, eighty perhaps, but wearing his years lightly and without complaint. He disarmed Magnus with his swift, matter-of-fact handshake and warm approving gaze. There was still a sense of vigour in the youthfully upright bearing though the close-cropped hair and thick moustache were unashamedly silver and, when he turned briskly and ushered Magnus in there was no attempt to mask the liver spots on the back of his hands, the neck wrinkles and the slight sag to the chin. He seemed entirely at ease with himself, just as Magnus always had been until his heart intervened; and Magnus admired the fact that he felt no necessity to pour out words of greeting as he led him into a vast white room and pointed him to a pale goatskin armchair. Nor did he make any attempt to draw his attention to the masks, bronzes and standing ebony figure carvings discreetly decorating the room. This is a special man, thought Magnus. He has lived a long time, he knows what he wants and doesn't have to pretend; and Magnus was as happy to meet him as Gustav seemed glad to have him in his house.

He sensed it was the living room of someone who loved art rather than an exhibition gallery; and, ignoring the chair as he gazed about him, that was exactly what he said to his host.

Gustav nodded. "I know that you are here on police business, but feel free at any time to wander round as you talk, if that would please you."

It was a graceful welcome, but Magnus was certain he caught the slightest foreign intonation in some of the words, and decided to keep the conversation general to see if he could nail down his suspicion that Swedish was not this man's first language.

"It must have taken you a long time to acquire such a collection," he said, sinking into the comfortable chair.

"Almost a lifetime," answered Gustav, relaxed now in a matching Norwegian chair. "I fell in love with Nigerian art at an early age and I've been collecting it ever since. Most collectors begin with pieces of rather ordinary quality; and then, as we learn, exchange them for something better until finally you have a smaller but more worthwhile collection."

Magnus nodded, but it wasn't just in response to what Gustav had said. He was acknowledging to himself the certainty now that Swedish was not Gustav's natural language. He was very aware that sitting where he was, in such surroundings, in the presence of such a man, there was a danger that he might be subtly drawn into Gustav's orbit, a student respectfully reticent at the feet of the expert. There was a quiet authority about Gustav which, though it did not faze him, instinctively suggested that the most effective way to mine the information he required about Nigeria would be to use dynamite rather than a pick.

"Were you born in Sweden?" he asked, interested to discover if it was difficult to upset his equilibrium.

"I was," replied Gustav.

Magnus tucked away the information that he lied smoothly and easily, and he then gave a non-committal grunt that nonetheless conveyed some scepticism.

Gustav smiled.

"You have a quick ear, Inspector. I was born in Sweden, but, when still quite young, I was taken to England. I was educated there during the Second World War and didn't return to Sweden until I was a grown man. As a result I expect I have a slight English intonation. Perhaps you are quicker than most to notice it because you are conscious of such things, not being fully Swedish yourself."

Magnus nodded, pleased that Gustav seemed prepared to be honest with him and provisionally deleting the earlier information about his ability to lie. "I'm half-Thai and though I've never spoken anything but Swedish, my mother's accent may well have made me especially alert to such details in other people."

They stared at each other, frankly assessing one another in the light of confirmed knowledge. Then Gustav made a fractional move forward in his chair.

"I am not a young man any longer, Inspector, which is why I'm at my best in the one-to-one situation I took the liberty of suggesting. But I am still rather a busy one. I believe you wished to consult me on some matter."

Magnus felt the gentle pressure of the reins turning him in a new direction, but there was none of the resentment he'd experienced earlier, before he'd met Gustav. That had been replaced by a sense of excitement, as though he was involved in some sort of intellectual duel that was nevertheless enabling him to uncover clues about a man he still liked, but who triggered the suspicion that there was either much more to him than met the eye, or, less likely, was not in fact at all the man he seemed on first acquaintance.

"I'm investigating a crime that seems to have a Nigerian connection," Magnus explained, careful not to reveal too much, deliberately leaving it to Gustav to seek further clarification. But, when no questions were forthcoming, he added, "I believe you've helped other police forces in matters like this."

"Yes, I have, in Stockholm, Göteborg and Malmö," Gustav confirmed. "There are problems of people trafficking there, and Nigerian gangs are involved. But to the best of my knowledge there have been no such problems further north, and certainly not in Sundsvall."

"It may have reached us now. A body was found beside a lake yesterday, and there were indications it might be a Nigerian."

Magnus was watching him very carefully as he said this, but Gustav revealed neither shock nor surprise, merely interest. But, and this intrigued Magnus, he did not ask any of the obvious questions: whether it was adult or child, male or female, the cause of death or what in particular made them think the body was Nigerian. Years of interviewing suspects had taught Magnus that the cleverer and guiltier ones never asked any questions at all, reducing the chance of an incriminating answer. But Gustav was not a suspect and he certainly was not guilty. So Magnus had acquired a further titbit of information, that, for some reason he didn't understand at the moment. Gustav was being cautious.

"It was a teenager, a boy, and he'd been burned to death, though that is confidential information until my press conference in a couple of hours."

Magnus had deliberately thrown all those facts at him at the same time, but again there was no obvious reaction except heightened interest.

"There is no doubt it was murder?" Gustav asked, and his voice was harsher, as if the horror of it had reached him.

"None."

"Then you are right, city gang methods may well have come north. It sounds like a punishment killing."

"In what way?"

"The use of fire. You're certain it wasn't self-immolation?"

"That seems unlikely, though of course I can't at this stage give you many details."

"You may have to, if I'm to be much use to you."

It was there again, that quiet but assured authority, an order masquerading as a suggestion. Magnus felt surer now. The ramrod posture that defied his age, the set of the shoulders, the brisk movements, unflinching gaze, and the moustache that was so out of place for an aesthete but would perfectly fit a colonel, it all pointed in one direction. At some formative time in his life this man had been a soldier. He'd been someone in command, someone whose apparent requests were backed by weapons even though he himself was either unarmed or had not drawn his revolver.

"Why would the use of fire mean a punishment killing?"

"Nigerian gangs are ruthless. If it was an execution he would have been shot or knifed and the body would not be found. That's how they like it, quick, efficient and leaving no clues. But burning takes time, and the body was left for you to find. There will be publicity, in newspapers and on TV, and normally they would avoid that. But sometimes they use such publicity to spread the word of what happens to those who fail to cooperate."

"Even if they are only sixteen or so?"

Gustav paused, seemingly sunk in thought. Then he raised his head and said, "It's hard for me to comment on that without more detail."

Magnus, aware that he was taking a risk in not waiting even longer before revealing it, placed the photo of the pouch on the padded leather arm of Gustav's chair. He leant forward to study it for a long time, and then he sank back again. "The figure is definitely Nigerian, cast brass, simple, rather crude work, circa 1950. It originally formed the top section of a spinning toy, and if you look closely you can see that his feet are small, close together and upturned at the toes so that he would spin smoothly on the metal base. Beneath his outstretched arms you can see the remains of thick copper wire which would have extended downwards on each side attached to weights to balance him."

Magnus waited for Gustav to pass the photo back, but, when he didn't do so, he reached forward and took it, seeing at once what Gustav had pointed out though he himself had not noticed it before.

"What about the pouch?

"It's common to many parts of Africa, but with that figure on it one can safely assume it's Nigerian too. What was in it?"

Normally, so early in a case, Magnus would never have revealed such information. But Gustav had already demonstrated he knew far more about these matters than Magnus had ever expected, and he was afraid a refusal over this might dry him up.

"There was nothing very much at all. I'd expected a holy scroll, a charm or talisman, but there was just a blackish mess."

"Have you had it tested?" Gustav's voice was sharper, more urgent. He had risen to his feet and, deliberately or not, he was towering over Magnus who felt, momentarily, as though he was being questioned by a superior officer.

"I can't tell you that," he replied quietly.

"You don't have to," Gustav said, and he walked about the room in an agitated manner, passing works of art without even glancing at them. "It was the boy's own blood, mixed with hair taken from his armpit and clippings from his finger and toe nails." He gave an exasperated sigh. "You're a country policeman, Magnus; you just don't understand what you're involved in."

Magnus stayed very calm. "That's precisely why I'm here, Gustav. And now we seem to have got onto first name terms, perhaps you would be so good as to tell me what I certainly do not understand."

Gustav stared at him for a moment, and then he smiled. "I am properly rebuked. I hope you will forgive my outburst." Then he sat down again, but remained leaning forward. "But I do feel at a disadvantage in that you expect me to tell you all you want to know, but you only give me information as and when you see fit."

"I have already given you more information than I normally would. But your point is a fair one and I will keep it very much in mind. What more can you tell me about what was in the pouch?"

"At least that tells me you haven't received the forensic test results yet, or you would know there is nothing else to learn about the contents. But, when you get the chance to look at the body again, you'll find a small straight scar on his chest or shoulder, darkened with black powder put into the flesh after it was opened and blood extracted. The boy was allowed to keep part of his body essence in this pouch which was never to be parted from him; but most of it was retained by his master so that he could control him however far away he was."

Magnus stood up and came closer to him. "How do you know that sort of thing?"

Impatiently Gustav waved his hand at the walls around them. "If you collect Nigerian art you research everything, and you not only become an expert in tribal history and customs, you learn about more hidden areas of the culture, witchcraft, magic, *juju*, superstition."

"And that's what this is?"

Gustav nodded. "It's using deeply ingrained traditional beliefs in a modern and much more evil context. It's a very powerful way to control people, especially if they are from groups like the Yoruba and the Edo which have a long tradition of such beliefs. In a solemn ceremony the masters of these migrants take the blood, hair and nails which represent each owner's body. They then have to swear a solemn oath to obey whatever instructions are given to them, never to run away and never to betray their master. This may be forever or until the money they owe for getting them into a wealthy country like Sweden has been paid off."

"Is it ever paid off?"

"Never. But they don't know that, so they retain some hope."

"It's a form of slavery?"

Gustav stood up again, coming close to Magnus, his expression unable to hide the anger and disgust he felt. "It *is* slavery. Instead of the bright future they are promised, they work as prostitutes or labourers."

"And if they break their oath?"

"Their body parts are used to find them and they die, horribly."

"By magic?"

Gustav turned away. "There's no magic in it. It's deliberate murder."

SIXTEEN

Gustav fetched some strong coffee, and when they'd both drunk some, Magnus expressed his thanks.

"You've helped me a great deal. I'm beginning to see what this might be about."

"I doubt that very much," Gustav replied dismissively. "Policeman like you, upcountry you might say, have no conception of what this is like. You need to talk to your big city colleagues. They'll tell you stories that will stop you sleeping at night."

"I'm still grateful to you."

Gustav hesitated, looking curiously at Magnus and for once seeming unsure.

"I could help you a lot more," he said after a time. "But you'd have to let me see the crime scene and the body, and you may not wish to do that."

Magnus considered this, knowing it would be against all precedent. "Do you think they're moving into the Sundsvall area?"

"That's very unlikely. But they may have discovered how useful your wild areas are for killing or torture. That is my worry, and I believe I could help you stop a repetition."

Though Magnus had considerable reservations, not least about Gustav himself, he made an immediate decision. "I'll accept your help. Are you free now?"

"Yes."

"Then I'll take you to the lake first, the body afterwards."

Gustav nodded, apparently forgetful of the fact that he'd told Magnus earlier he was so very busy. But as they left the apartment he turned to Magnus with a slight smile. "You didn't seem very interested in my collection?"

"At the moment I'm only interested in catching the killer of this boy," Magnus replied bluntly; and he noticed that Gustav did not seem displeased with the reply.

The power of the sun was increasing as the morning passed, and by the time they reached the lake the day was glorious. Magnus was aware he was acting uncharacteristically. He could remember no other case where he had returned to the crime scene for a third time. He was thorough, he had a retentive memory and so it had been unnecessary. But all those crimes had been local, attached to the area for which he was responsible through the victim, the perpetrator or, at the very least, through the witnesses who'd been present when the crime was committed. But this was not a Sundsvall crime. The victim was not from the locality, he was certain the killers were not, and there had been no witnesses. He had never felt close to the crime, strangely uninvolved, and increasingly the only question in his mind was an irritating WHY? Why had it been committed here, on his patch? If he could solve that he might begin to understand what he was looking for; and he sensed Gustav might throw some light on it.

But Gustav himself was a secondary lurking shadow. Usually he would have discovered him himself, following a trail of some sort. But on this occasion he had been pushed in his direction, ostensibly by Sofia, though she might have been used. If so, it was possible he was being used as well. It made him uneasy, even though his unwarranted action in taking Gustav to the crime scene might merely be the result of his own medical condition, the consciousness that it was his last case and so had to be a success. Such possibilities should have made him very cautious. But, instead, he was simply following his instinct because, at this early stage, it was all he had.

The bright sunshine and the beauty of the tarn made it hard to accept that they were visiting the site of a gruesome killing. Yet something of it must have been discernible to Gustav, for he seemed busy with his own thoughts, asking no questions as Magnus explained about the padlocked chain round the boy's neck, the broken attachment link and the way in which the two men had come after him, at a distance, not hurrying, not pursuing.

They followed the line of footmarks and Magnus, watching Gustav carefully, did not interrupt the gloomy reverie into which he'd fallen until they reached a particular spot.

"You can see here that one pair of footmarks is deeper than the other pair. We think it's because that man was weighed down by a flamethrower pack on his back, though where on earth they managed to get hold of such a horrible weapon I can't imagine."

"Probably the IRA," Gustav said, finally rousing himself from his thoughts. "They were supplied originally by Libya, but, once the Irish troubles were over, the republicans were happy to raise funds by selling them to any group or gang that wanted to acquire one."

Magnus wondered how he knew about such matters and spoke so casually about them, but he was careful to show no surprise as he walked on. "Here both men seemed to stop and stand still, and there are no indications that they went any further forward. There were some drops of petroleum in a pool, and we wondered whether they'd been preparing the flamethrower?"

"One of them might have been, but I'm afraid flamethrowers are not my area of expertise," Gustav replied brusquely. "But I do know what the other man was doing. He was filming what the boy did, and what the result was."

Magnus stared at in him horror, recalling Sofia's intuitive assumption of something theatrical.

"Filming him?"

"Yes, of course. He probably filmed it on his mobile, which would have been an expensive one if he was quite high in the gang hierarchy. That would mean the images would be very clear when the film was distributed and shown."

"You're either going too fast for me or I just don't want to understand what you're trying to tell me," Magnus said sharply. "Are you really suggesting he filmed the boy breaking off the pouch and throwing it away?"

"Yes. He would certainly have filmed that. But then he would have kept on filming, probably in close-up, as the boy was burnt up."

"But why burn him to death, and why film it?"

"Because the film won't show a flamethrower or any other people," Gustav explained patiently. "It will just show the boy breaking his oath by tearing off the *juju* pouch, his body bursting into flames as the direct result of his action and then, in graphic detail, his horrific death."

"Then why did the boy do it?" asked Magnus, pretty sure he already knew the answer but interested to hear what Gustav would say. "And why did he show no fear?"

"The boy would have been told an entirely different story," Gustav replied. "Probably he was given the happy news that he'd done enough to pay off his debt and he could go on an outing to a lake where he would

214

perform the ceremony of breaking off the pouch and casting it away. Then he would be free to go back home to Nigeria. Even if he noticed the flamethrower he would just assume it was some instrument of magic, and by the time he discovered its real purpose, it would be much too late."

"And the film would be shown to all the others they control, to make it clear what happens if they break the rules?"

"Perhaps to all, perhaps just to any who showed resistance or disbelief. However they used it, the word would quickly get around and the power of the gang would be strengthened. After seeing that, no one would run away, betray them to the police or refuse to work."

"And you said the work is labouring or prostitution?"

"Yes. If they're men, they'll be labouring for a gang master. If they're women or boys they'll be in the sex trade."

"And what might this boy have done that could have made him believe he'd earned his freedom?"

Gustav stared at him, and Magnus noticed that for the first time he looked his proper age.

"He may have been offered to some very important man, a politician perhaps, even a policeman. In such circumstances he might have been told that if he gave full satisfaction he would be freed. As you will understand, once you've embroiled a really influential person in that sort of sex – which was probably filmed too – he's in your power. But it may not suit you to

215

retain the most involved witness to it. So the boy becomes dispensable and is used, in death, to provide a warning to others."

"Do you think it's possible the boy might not have been offered to trap somebody, but as a reward for services already rendered?"

The suggestion lay between them in the silence, and neither dropped his eyes from the other's face. The mournful cry of the loon could be heard with sudden clarity, the splash of a diving duck and the high plaintive mew of a buzzard overhead.

"Yes," Gustav answered finally, "that's a perfectly possible scenario, though it would seem to be a less plausible reason for killing the boy."

"Then I think it's time you saw the body," Magnus said. "You did say you wanted to do that."

It was a statement, not a question, but Gustav still nodded. "Yes," he said slowly, "I did say that."

SEVENTEEN

Later that afternoon Magnus went to see Lennart to tell him that he'd flouted police regulations by allowing Gustav to visit the crime scene and see the body. He wanted to be honest with him, but he was only too conscious that he'd already withheld from him the state of his health. Not only that, he'd never told Sonja that he could in fact leave Homicide immediately, which was what she was increasingly pressurising him to do. Usually straightforward, and prizing honesty in relationships at work and at home, he felt not only uncomfortable about what he was hiding but diminished. Yet this was overridden by the unchangeable fact that he could not give up the case until it was completed. He supposed it was his form of drug. Whatever the circumstances, whatever the effect it might have on others, he was addicted to solving the puzzle of the crime, especially now he sensed he was close to a breakthrough.

But just before he reached the door to Lennart's office, he took a decision. He would tell him about the danger of a heart attack; and then he would not wait until the end of the year to leave Homicide, he would go as soon as this case was concluded even if it meant being on sick leave until Lennart retired and he succeeded him.

He hoped that decision would alleviate Sonja's increasing worries and he did not feel he needed to do more than that. The children, in his opinion, were not a real worry. After their immediate sympathy, treading softly around him, bringing him cups of coffee when they remembered, and even presenting him with the occasional bar of chocolate or some flower from the garden, they had quickly resumed their own intense lives. Johan mooched about his room listening to music, playing computer games online with his mates and speaking secretively into his mobile, for what seemed like hours on end, to his best friend Lucas. Angelica again spent an excessive amount of time in the shower and was devoted to varying the colour of her nails and altering her hair style. Her shy and less precocious boyfriend, Alex, got some of her time but rather less, it seemed, than her closest friends Emilia and Tindra, who lived nearby, and Pernilla, the apparent leader of the pack, whose startling purple hair and black lipstick had persuaded Sonja that she might be a bad influence. Magnus refused to allow himself to be affected by it, even getting a laugh out of Sonja when he claimed that it might be construed as colour prejudice. But the fact was that he could not believe that any girl would ever be able to dominate Angelica, who gave every indication that she would unflinchingly die at the stake for her frequently repeated principles: that she was grown up, she would take her own decisions, she could look after herself, it was *her* life and nobody should tell her what to do.

Lennart reacted reasonably to the news that Gustav had been given special access.

"You never do anything without a good reason, Magnus. Are you going to tell me what that reason was?"

"It was a hunch rather than a reason," Magnus answered slowly, clearing his own mind as he gave the explanation. "Gustav Carlsson's a remarkable man, I saw that straight away. Despite his age, and he must be almost eighty, he's alert, very sure of himself and something of a commanding figure. That aroused my curiosity, and so did a number of other things. But, alongside those concerns about him, I became sure he could give us valuable information about this case. No, it was more than that. I was convinced that deep down he *wanted* to help us; and, so far, to be fair to him, he has given us a great deal of important background information."

"So what were those 'other things' that made you curious?"

"They were nothing much at all, but they all built up to a sense of unease that we weren't getting the full picture. I was surprised that as an art expert he had such a deep knowledge of how Nigerian gangs operate. And when I held out the photo of the pouch he was careful not to touch it, almost as though he didn't want his finger prints on it. So I put it on the arm of his chair, but even then he never leant forward to look at it closely. It was as if it troubled him emotionally and he didn't want it too close to him. And though he said the figure on it was just a simple everyday object, I noticed he kept his eyes fixed on it for much longer than seemed necessary and he made no move to push it back towards me, almost as though he was reluctant to part with it."

"How did he react when he saw the boy's body?"

"That was interesting. He was deeply shaken, as I think anyone with a gram of humanity must have been. The body's not a pleasant sight."

"But...?"

"I sensed he was upset in some almost personal way."

"Do you think he recognised the boy?"

Magnus raised his eyebrows. "Do you think he's involved in all this?"

Lennart laughed. "You know I wasn't a great success at homicide, so I don't have thoughts like that. But I do think that you believe he's involved."

Magnus considered this. "Yes, I suppose I do. But I don't think he's involved in any obvious way; and, whatever way it is, I get this strong feeling he wants to assist us, possibly as a means of easing his conscience over something or even as a means of freeing himself from whatever hold somebody, or conceivably some group, might have on him."

"Follow your hunch, then," said Lennart. "I wouldn't have dared let a possible suspect so near the case, but you've never lacked courage and you're not a worrier. Is there any way in which I can help?"

"I want him investigated," Magnus said. "There's something false there. He claims his parents were Swedish, but he was brought up in England and only came back here when he was an adult. And that's another point that aroused my curiosity – he never uses dates, just vague timings like 'when I was a child' and 'when I was grown-up' which are less easy to check. So I want to know about his parents, his time in England which was presumably during the Second World War, and on what date precisely did he come back to Sweden? Given his age, I think it may have been in the late 'fifties, but I need to find out if there's a record of it and whether any checks were run on him at the time. I'm pretty certain he was a soldier before he was a specialist collector, probably an officer because he speaks as though he's used to being in command. I was especially struck that when I asked him about the flamethrower he said it wasn't his area of expertise, as though he did have military expertise in some other weapon; and, with the dates we're guessing at, that might have been acquired in the British Army. Lars could probably do most of the research, he's good at that, but it would be a huge help if he could use your authority as police chief if he hits any opposition."

Lennart frowned. "Why do you think he might encounter such difficulties?"

Magnus looked surprised. "I don't really know, but confidentiality is such a big thing nowadays, and the whole human rights issue; so finding out facts about people is less easy than it used to be."

"Something just occurred to me, Magnus, and I have to ask you this. Who suggested you should get in touch with this Gustav Carlsson?"

221

"Sofia Grönberg. She said his name was on the Forensics list of experts, as someone who knew about Nigerian art, witchcraft, that sort of thing."

"Did she know him personally?"

"No. But she mentioned her father knew him."

Lennart put his head in his hands, and as a man who rarely swore his comment was particularly expressive. "Shit!" he said.

Magnus looked at him, crestfallen. "I've missed something, haven't I?"

"You really don't know who her father is?"

Magnus shook his head. "I've no idea. Why should I?"

"There was a lot of talk about it when she was appointed."

Magnus took a deep breath, aware that the moment of confession had arrived. "I wish I could be sure I refused to listen because I don't like gossip. But it's more than likely I just wasn't paying attention. The fact is, Lennart, I've had other things on my mind for the last few months and I've not been as alert as I should have been. Who is her father?"

"He's a big noise in SAPO, Detective Superintendent I think. A few people expressed concern that he, or the Security Service itself, might have influenced her appointment, though in fact he had nothing to do with it at all and she got the post entirely on her own merit. But

Security does have a particular interest in people trafficking, drugs and prostitution, and a senior officer like him will certainly use anyone he can to infiltrate such gangs if an opportunity arises."

Magnus shook his head in disbelief at his own stupidity. "I walked straight into that one, didn't I? Gustav Carlsson probably cooperates with SAPO, so a stop will automatically be put on any background checks we try to run on him. But, far worse than that, and I really can't forgive myself for it, SAPO now know, through him, every detail of our case and will be able to step in and take it over on the grounds of national security."

"Would that be such a bad thing?" asked Lennart. "They have all the facilities, they understand urban crime far better than we do, and you're meant to be concentrating on taking over from me, not charging around after Nigerian gangsters."

Magnus stiffened, wondering whether Lennart had already heard something about his heart problem, and the truth burst out of him.

"I've been keeping something secret from you, Lennart, from almost everybody but the family. I told myself I wanted to fight it on my own, but the truth is that I was ashamed to admit it. I've never worried about myself before, just basked in the glow of good health and supreme fitness. I never felt the slightest fear of any criminal I came across for I knew I could always overcome him. If he wanted to fight, I'd win; if he wanted to shoot, I was a better shot. Now all that has been stripped away from me because I've got a bad

223

heart, and any sudden exertion or physically stressful situation could kill me. I can't outrun anybody, out-shoot them, or throw them down and arrest them whatever their size, strength or weapon of choice. That's shrunk my self-esteem, and it's why I couldn't bring myself to speak of it. I'm sorry."

"How's Sonja taken it?"

"Not well."

"Which is hardly surprising, Magnus. She's suddenly told the man she loves, the father of her children, might drop dead at any moment, and she's upset! She must be half out of her mind with worry."

"She goes on and on about my dropping this case immediately. But I can't do that, Lennart, not now, not when we're just getting somewhere. Yet however certain I am about that, I'm haunted by the fear that Sonja's instinct may be right, as it usually is, and by staying on I'm making a terrible mistake. So, just before I came to see you, I decided to compromise. I'll leave Homicide the moment the case is over, and I'll tell Sonja this evening. But you must let me stay on the case until I've cracked it. It'll be my last case."

Lennart looked at him doubtfully. "You realise that if you insist on seeing it through, it may indeed be your last case because you'll be dead. I assume the specialist told you that?"

"Yes, he did. But I believe I can do it and stay alive."

Lennart raised his hands in surrender. "You know that morally I have no real authority over you, Magnus.

You refused this post, and I'm just keeping it warm for you. All I can do is urge you to reconsider and tell you again that the moment you leave Homicide, this job is yours. I can't wait to be full time with the twins. But I still don't see why you won't let SAPO take some of the burden."

"I don't like SAPO," Magnus said frankly. "And they won't ease my burden; they'll push me aside and do it their way, in their own interest and regardless of justice. I came across them when they muscled in on an earlier case, and their methods were almost as dishonest as those of the criminals. They don't seem to have to follow the rules that apply to us, and they'll use any tactic to get results, turning a blind eye to corruption or wrecking the career of anyone who gets in their way. This boy was horribly murdered on our patch, and I don't want any interference from them."

"Don't close the door completely, Magnus," Lennart urged him. "If this has its roots in a city like Stockholm, which is very probable, we can't cope on our own. Ring Sofia's father, discuss everything, and I'm sure they'll let you get on with it until it is beyond us. He may even tell you some of the things you want to know about Gustav." He saw that Magnus looked doubtful, and so he added, "You don't seem to realise what a reputation you've built up. After all that happened with Amrén you can call in a lot of favours, and SAPO will know that and step carefully around you."

Magnus nodded, though he did not look convinced. "I'll call him," he conceded, "But, please, I don't want them allowed in unless I personally request it."

When Magnus phoned him, Detective Superintendent Grönberg was cautious at first. But once it must have occurred to him that Magnus was working closely with his daughter, though neither mentioned her, he opened up a little.

"Nigerian gangs are a particular problem for us at the moment, especially now we're beginning to suspect a tie-up with drug barons from Columbia. Anything you can uncover in your case may well be useful to us, so we must certainly stay in touch. But one question strikes me immediately. Why was the execution staged near Sundsvall?"

"The same question's been nagging me as well. They could have killed that boy at a wilderness lake much closer to whichever city they operate in, but they came to our patch."

"I agree. You certainly don't need to travel three hundred and eighty kilometres north to find enough emptiness to use a flamethrower and film the proceedings. So why did they do it?"

"There's one possible link, a very vague one," Magnus replied in a deliberately diffident tone. "There's an old man here in Sundsvall who's an expert on Nigerian art and he's been helping us with our enquiries. But it did strike me that he seems to know a great deal about everything Nigerian, and it occurred to me that he probably lived there for a time."

"Who put you on to him?" Grönberg asked, and there was a new incisiveness to his voice.

"Our Head of Forensics."

"I see."

"Apparently his name was on the Forensic list of experts."

There was a pause, then Grönberg, reluctantly or so it seemed to Magnus, asked for the man's name.

"Carlsson. Gustav Carlsson."

"I know him," Grönberg conceded. "I've used him occasionally when we're involved with Nigerians."

"Was he helpful?"

"Yes and no. Vast knowledge, excellent background material, but there was never anything so specific that it led to an immediate arrest."

"Did you feel he was diverting you from the truth?"

"No, he wasn't doing that, not directly anyway. He's proud of his reputation as an expert, and I suspect he likes to increase that reputation."

"But...?"

"But it has occurred to me once or twice that he may be protecting himself in some way, probably from the terrible revenge that would be taken on him if he was involved on the edges of a gang and it was thought that he'd betrayed them. I can't blame him for that, and so far we haven't needed anything more than he has given us.

If we did, then of course we'd have to lean on him a lot harder."

"Have you looked into his past?"

Grönberg sounded offended. "That's a very direct question, and I ought to warn you that you're close to crossing a line. I'm trying to help you but, as you know perfectly well, we are not answerable to local forces."

"But you imply I haven't crossed that line yet, so I'd appreciate an answer to my question."

For a moment Magnus feared Grönberg had cut him off, but then he got a careful, and probably untrue, response. "Quite deliberately, we have not looked into his background very deeply. He is helpful to us and we don't want to spook him. We need to get our hands on somebody from the inside of these gangs and force him to sing, and on our way to that goal we're looking after a minor fish in the hope he'll eventually lead us to a bigger one. End of story."

"I understand that, of course," replied Magnus, trying to keep the distaste out of his voice at the use of 'get our hands on' instead of 'arrest' and 'force him to sing' instead of 'question him'. "But is it all right if we do some digging?"

"I'm fairly familiar with your record," Grönberg commented tartly, "and I would be surprised if you weren't already doing just that."

"Do you mind?"

"Not as long as you share the information with me. He'll expect you to poke around a little, but it's a very different matter if we do. However, it's only fair to warn you that you may very quickly come up against restricted material."

He rang off then, leaving Magnus more than ever convinced that SAPO knew all about Carlsson's past and had made sure nobody else would get to know it until Gustav ceased to be useful to them. Then they would probably throw him to the wolves. But what interested him most was the way Grönberg had carefully avoided the deliberately diffident suggestion that the crime had been committed near Sundsvall because Gustav lived there. The implication must have been perfectly clear to him. The killing was a warning to Gustav who was getting too cosy with SAPO; and that in its turn implied that Gustav was somehow implicated in the gang's activities. The superintendent could so easily have ridiculed the idea, or he could have taken it seriously. But, when Magnus had not pursued it, he'd simply let it drop.

He called in on Lars and explained his problem about trawling Gustav's early life. Lars immediately said he'd use a different path, get some information on British regiments in Nigeria in the 1950's, and then see what that threw up.

"It's possible Gustav will be receiving a piece of film on his computer or iPhone, something that will upset him and perhaps leave him open to an approach. Is there any way we can check that?"

Lars laughed. "We're not SAPO, Magnus, and even they would find that difficult unless they were already secretly monitoring all his electronic equipment. But there is one way you could find out."

"What's that?" Magnus asked eagerly.

"Watch his face, and then you'll probably see when he's upset. It's called old-fashioned policing."

Magnus acknowledged the hit with a pretended scowl. Then, filled with a strange impatience as though his time was beginning to run out, he went to see Sofia in case her report was ready.

She was at her computer, still busy working on it. But she seemed pleased to see him and, as if she sensed his poorly-controlled eagerness, she took pity on him.

"He was just out of adolescence, probably sixteen, though it might be a year either side of that. He was Nigerian, an Igbo, and he died of a combination of the burning and the shock it caused to his system. There is some evidence that before death occurred he was healthy and cared-for."

"Had he been used for sex?"

Sofia frowned, "It wasn't easy to ascertain, his body being so destroyed. But, though I cannot be certain, I would say it's probable."

"Recently?"

"In the last month perhaps, though again I cannot be accurate about it."

"Any semen traces we can check?"

"No. The high body heat at death removed any traces that might have been left."

"The chain round the neck?"

"Cheap but effective, certainly not intended to be jewellery. As you already know, something had been wrenched off it with some force. The broken ring that was still attached to the pouch is a perfect fit, so that is unquestionably what had been discarded."

"What about the contents?"

"Finger and toe nail clippings, hair and blood, the DNA all matching that of the victim."

"Did you by any chance discover where the hair was taken from? Head or groin?"

Sofia looked at him quizzically. "I think you're testing me, Inspector. I think you already know the answer. It came from the victim's armpit."

Magnus nodded. "I believed I knew and you confirmed it. But I was testing somebody else, not you. I've already had ample proof that you know your job."

Sofia looked awkward but pleased, as though she was not used to such direct compliments. "Is there anything else?"

"Was there a sort of darkened scar on his chest or neck?"

"On his chest, yes. An incision had been made there. The state of his skin made it difficult to spot but, and I can only posit this as a theory, it's likely to have been a cut from a sharp knife or razor."

"To extract the blood?"

"You can assume that if you want. I have no evidence to support it."

Magnus pretended to look suitably chastened and Sofia, surprisingly childlike when she relaxed, giggled.

"If I may make an assumption in my turn, you obviously found Gustav Carlsson helpful."

"I did."

"Was it you who felt it necessary to enquire about sexual activity, or was it Carlsson?"

"It was my idea. Why, does that surprise you?"

She shook her head. "No. It doesn't surprise me."

Magnus looked at her thoughtfully, reflecting yet again that she was, beneath her girlishness, extraordinarily sharp. He was also feeling a sense of relief, for both her giggle and her last comment finally convinced him that although her father might be trying to use him, as perhaps Gustav himself was, Sofia was not involved in any such conspiracy. For the first time he felt completely confident that the investigation was now a team effort. The double act of Magnus & Lars had become a triple turn, with Sofia playing a vital role; and it gave him so much confidence that he felt he could finally venture a personal question.

"Was it polio?" he asked gently, pointing to her leg and prepared to withdraw the question if she showed the slightest discomfort. But once again she surprised him.

"It was much more romantic than that," she answered delightedly, "though I can't actually remember anything about it. It was snakebite, when I was a baby in Indonesia where my parents were working. A small but particularly venomous snake crawled into my basket and bit my ankle. Perhaps I'd frightened it when I was kicking my legs and it reacted instinctively to such an attack, so I don't blame it. But we were out in the wilds, there was no hospital or doctor, and my life was saved by the local medicine man. My leg, though, was pretty useless from then on, so I just had to learn to cope with its infuriating feebleness."

"That's quite a story."

"That's why I'm glad you asked me. Most people are too embarrassed to draw attention to my leg, so I don't have the opportunity to tell my tale."

He left her to her report and walked out of the building thinking about her courage and the possible implication of her comment that she would not have expected Gustav to suggest an enquiry about the boy's sexual activity. His talk with Lennart and the prospect of telling Sonja that this was to be his last case had brought him considerable relief, and he felt confidence seeping back into him. He even began to wonder whether, with what he'd learnt from Sofia and what he might discover from the research Lars was undertaking, the end of the case could be closer than he had dared to hope.

EIGHTEEN

The next morning Lars, whose feelings were always reflected in his expression of the moment, was clearly very pleased with himself. Magnus, still glowing with the joyful relief his announcement had given Sonja, approached him cautiously, hardly daring to believe that he might have found something helpful in Gustav's background. But before he could even speak, Lars was ahead of him.

"I think I've got something," he burst out. "I went in through the back door, investigating National Service officers who served in Nigeria in 1953, using official British army sources which SAPO can't control. The major British unit in the area was the Royal West African Frontier Force, and within that there were three regiments, one for Sierra Leone, one for the Gold Coast and one, bingo, the Nigeria Regiment."

Magnus shook his head bemusedly, "Colonialism must have been big business in those days," he commented. "That sounds like a hell of a lot of soldiers for one little bit of Africa. But how could you get any further without knowing what his name was when he was in England?"

Lars gave a great grin which lit up his whole face. "You may remember I'm interested in ships, naval and civilian. I think I helped you once when you were investigating a case in the High Coast, some boating accident you wanted to know about."

"I remember all right," Magnus said nostalgically. "You put me onto something that opened the whole case up."

"Well, being interested, I know that there are published histories of most parts of the English Royal Navy. So I guessed the same would be true of regimental histories and, via abebooks.com, I got this in the post this morning."

He reached into a drawer, flourished 'A History of the Nigeria Regiment' and made triumphal trumpeting sounds.

"OK, you're amazing," acknowledged Magnus, laughing, "But does it get us any further forward?"

"I wasn't hopeful because junior officers don't usually get much of a mention. But then my one good eye was suddenly caught by this footnote."

He passed the book to Magnus and showed him where to read. It was in a chapter entitled 'Returning Home' and the footnote was short and to the point. "Until 1954, some adventurous subalterns received permission to return home by making their own way across the Sahara Desert. This was forbidden after the tragic death of Lt. Johnny Callin, Mortar Officer of the

3rd Battalion, who was attacked, killed and burnt in his car by desert marauders."

Magnus felt the same surge of excitement Lars must have felt. "If you need to disappear, and then re-appear as a different person, with a new nationality, faking your death in the desert is a perfect way of doing it. And when I wondered why he said his specialism was not flamethrowers, it was because he was an expert in mortars."

Lars nodded. "There's one thing more. As soon as I'd got a name, I googled it. There was nothing more about Johnny, but an officer with the same surname was killed at the battle of El Alamein in October 1942. He was posthumously awarded the Military Cross for gallantry, and I printed out for you the short article about it, together with the photo of his Swedish widow receiving it at a military ceremony where she was accompanied by her young son, John."

With a final flourish he handed the print-out to Magnus and sat back, very pleased with himself.

"It could be him," muttered Magnus. "And it all fits together. You've done so much, Lars, but please now try to get a copy of the original photo sent to your computer so we can enlarge it and be sure."

When Magnus drove to Gustav's apartment he was prepared to confront him and get at the truth. But as soon as Gustav opened the door to him, Magnus realised something had happened, and he was pretty certain it was what he had expected. Gustav seemed to have sagged into his actual age. His eyes were haunted, the shoulders had rounded, his voice was throaty as though he'd been going through some terrible experience and, when he stood aside to let Magnus in, his movements were stiff and slow.

"They sent you the film they took of the boy's death, didn't they?"

Gustav nodded wearily. "You'd think I'd be prepared for it after you'd shown me the body. But nothing could have prepared me for the horror of the close-ups, the melting flesh, the agony."

He sank into a chair and stared into space, as if he still saw the images before his eyes.

"It must be so much worse when it's somebody you love," Magnus said gently, but Gustav made no reply, just nodding over and over again.

"Did you love him?" Magnus asked, more insistently this time.

"He had a name," Gustav snapped back bitterly, "He wasn't just 'him' or 'the boy'. He was called Arthur, after Lieutenant Colonel Arthur Unegbe, the first martyr of the Biafran war, a heroic name for an Igbo."

"Did you love him?"

"Yes."

"Was he supplied to you as a reward for your services to the gang over many years? Since 1954, perhaps, when Johnny Callin became Gustav Carlsson?"

Gustav gave a sour smile. "You've certainly moved fast, Magnus, and you must have dug deeply to find Callin's name. But he's dead, killed in the Sahara."

"How did you arrange that?"

"It was arranged for me. I knew no details, so, when I was surrounded and the rifles were pointing at me, I thought my last moment had probably come. Then one of the Bedouin threw down what looked like an old bundle of clothes that had been lying across the front of his saddle. It lay like a broken puppet on the sand in front of the Land Rover and I saw it was the corpse of a white man they'd either dug up or killed. They all fired their rifles into him and then tossed him into the driver's seat. I was settled onto a spare camel that was brought up from behind one of the dunes. I remember it was made to kneel for me before lurching to its feet. My possessions were removed from the car and all were honourably put into its saddle bags. Then the vehicle was set on fire, a break from their usual routine which they thoroughly enjoyed, especially the final explosion. They set off northwards after that, taking me with them to the coast. It provided an unforgettable education in hardship and stoicism which enabled me to cope with the disorientation of becoming a new man in a new country now that Johnny Callin was no more."

"You crossed into Europe, settled in your mother's country and took the name of Carlsson, which just happens to be the commonest name here?"

"That helped, though it was actually the name of a nineteen year Gustav on a gravestone in Värmland. You must remember it was only nine years after the Allies won the war in Europe. There were still displaced persons everywhere, all needing to be resettled, so it wasn't difficult to put together a partly invented back-history about my mother to get a passport issued, and an identity card. But, though you've found out so much, Magnus, faster than I ever expected, you haven't grasped the full picture, not about me anyway. You've forced together the pieces of your jigsaw well enough, but you've missed the vital point that people are often more complicated than jigsaw pieces. What you think you see, even what it suits you to see, is not always the truth."

His words jolted Magnus, for the suicide of his friend and mentor Ragnar Amrén was still a raw memory. He'd judged him superficially, not bothering to look below the surface to the suffering that was there. Sonja had understood so much more about him, which still made him feel guilty; and he wondered now whether Sonja would have seen more in Gustav than he had taken the trouble to look for.

"Can you explain the correct picture to me?"

"I have no real interest in doing that, and I doubt if we have the time for such an indulgence. You probably know enough to be able to act, and the fact that you understand little about me or my motives doesn't really worry me. I'm sure you've already discovered that I cooperate with your security people. I give them information that helps them in their battle against people trafficking, prostitution and drugs and in return they protect me from my own dim and distant past. Being the good detective that you are, you will have already deduced that Arthur's burning took place near Sundsvall because it was a message to me. They were punishing me for my treachery in co-operating in any way at all with SAPO, which must have become known; and they were warning me that what happened to Arthur will be my fate if I ever betray them again."

"How do you think they discovered you were helping SAPO?"

Gustav shook his head sadly. "I find it hard to believe you are such an innocent, Magnus. In order to protect myself against these ruthless new-style gangs, I was careful never to give the security boys enough to arrest the leaders. So I assume SAPO let the gang know that I was thinking of betraying them so that I would be pushed into exactly the corner I'm in now. Ruthlessness is not reserved to Nigerian gangs, Magnus. Your own people are quite capable of it too."

"They're not my people," Magnus said sharply. "Ordinary police do have some rotten apples, that is inevitable; but I like to believe we have an overall code which doesn't include betraying those who help us just to get a bit more out of them."

"Are you saying I can trust you?"

"Yes."

"So I can do a deal with you and know you'll stick by it, come what may?"

"I can't make blind deals. But if you tell me what you're offering, and what I have to give you in return, you'll get an honest response. If I have to turn you down, nobody else will hear about it unless you choose to make it public."

241

Gustav studied his face for a while and then he slowly nodded.

"I'll trust you, Magnus. I've prepared exactly the sort of declaration SAPO want. It's a written, signed and dated statement chronicling my occasional arrangements with the gang and stating what information, support or endorsement I gave them in return for certain art world favours. I name names, including those at the very top, and provide addresses. It will enable this gang, and probably other similar gangs, to be broken open. The big fish will be arrested and imprisoned for long terms, and the smaller fry will be used to provide evidence as witnesses in those trials. As for the slaves and prostitutes, I hope they will be rescued and rehabilitated."

"They will be, "Magnus assured him. "I shall keep a special eye on that."

"It may interest you to know that I wrote the whole document after watching the film of what they did to Arthur, which just demonstrates that sometimes threats don't work in the way you expect. Far from frightening me, it made me vengeful and entirely careless of my own life. I won't survive, but I'll take all the important ones with me."

"Where is this declaration?"

"You'll get it at the proper moment, probably when I'm dead. Here's the name of the lawyer who's holding it, but she won't let you have it until then. I'm trusting you, Magnus, but you're going to have to trust me, too."

"That's fair enough. It's a document we in the police will want as well as SAPO. What are you asking in return?"

Gustav waved his hand around the room. "This collection is my life's work. I want you to give me your word you'll do everything in your power to fulfil the conditions laid down in this legal document which forms part of my will. SAPO already has a copy, which I gave them as the price of my cooperation at the very beginning of our association. They guaranteed the conditions would be carried out if I served them well, but of course I don't trust them. I would feel much more confident if you were peering over their shoulders."

"I think you exaggerate my influence," Magnus said, accepting the document "In essence what does it say?"

"Everything is to be bequeathed to the Stockholm National Museum, because I want it recognised as important world art, not just something to be tucked away in an Ethnographic Department. It is to be called the Ralph Okori Memorial Collection."

"I'll contact Grönberg later today and I'm pretty confident that once he hears what you're offering he'll get the whole thing set up immediately. In fact I'll make sure he does. Don't you want your name attached to the collection as well?"

"I have no wish to be remembered. Arthur brought such joy into my life, my first real emotional delight since a brief period in Nigeria when I was a young man. So I tried to buy him out of his slavery so that I could perhaps become his legal guardian, or at least keep him safe and provide for his future. But, as I ought to have foreseen, the gang had only ever considered him as a sex object and so my special interest in him was misconstrued. It simply convinced them that he could be used as a weapon against me; and, as a warning, they cremated him alive."

Magnus heard the bitterness, the terrible hatred. "You want revenge. That's why you're helping us."

"Revenge is all I have to live for now. Keep that in mind, Magnus, for desperate men sometimes do desperate things, and innocent bystanders can get hurt."

NINETEEN

As soon as Magnus left, Gustav threw himself down on his bed and began to wrestle with the memories the conversation had stirred up in him. He saw Ralph on the warm rocks after they'd finally disposed of the mortar bombs, heard his own offer to give up everything to stay with him and heard Ralph turn the offer down. Of course it hadn't been for ever, just until the moment came when a white man's help would be acceptable. But by then a homeland for the Igbos had been declared, the proudly named Republic of Biafra, and independence was proclaimed. But attempting to break away from Nigeria led to a brutal civil war; and by the time Gustav could have joined the fighting because Biafra was desperate enough to take help from any quarter, any skin colour, it was too late. Ralph was already dead.

He'd died in battle, as was to be expected, and probably bravely, though that was not confirmed except in Gustav's mind. It had happened in 1967, in one of the many futile struggles against overwhelming odds when, after the mutiny of the Hausa troops at the Abeokuta barracks, the northern General Yakabu Gowon invaded Biafra on behalf of the Nigerian government.

Numbed by the news, not caring whether he lived or died, Gustav did what he could. He raised money, borrowing against his art collection, then went to Nigeria in the forlorn hope of finding Ralph's body among the million and more dead. He failed; and he was equally unsuccessful in finding any trace of his family, for Ralph had written in one of his letters that, understanding the probability of death, he had fathered a son.

Desolate, not wanting to return home but with no purpose to keep him in the war zone, he stumbled across a Swedish acquaintance, Count Carl Gustav von Rosen, who was also a sympathiser with the Biafran cause. Talking over a beer, it turned out that he was now a mercenary fighting against the Nigerian government forces, and Gustav helped him to finance the Biafran Air Force which the Count commanded. It sounded a great deal grander than it was, for it was only a tiny squadron consisting of five Malmö MFI-9 MiniCOIN piston-engined aircraft, armed with rocket pods and machine guns. But, with Gustav's money, the Count optimistically predicted it would punch above its weight; and he was proved right. The four pilots, Gunnar Haglund and Martin Lang from Sweden, Augustus Opke and Willy Murray Bruce from Biafra, ignored the odds and flew sorties against Nigerian military airfields in Port Harcourt, Enugu, Benin City and Ughelli. To the consternation of the other side, they managed to destroy a number of Mig-17's and three out of Nigeria's six Ilyushin Il-28 bombers. It was a time of mad courage and heady triumph, bringing some comfort to Gustav and postponing for a while the grief that was threatening to overwhelm him. But, glorious as their exploits were, it only delayed the inevitable; and on 13th January 1970 Biafra was compelled to surrender.

The next day Gustav had a memorial plaque cast in bronze, took it to the church nearest the battlefield where Ralph died and persuaded the priest to place it on the wall, He gave him a sum of money for its installation and upkeep, and a few hours later he was able to mumble an incoherent prayer while kneeling before it. Beneath the half sun that was the emblem of Biafra was inscribed: 'In loving memory of Ralph Okori who died for what he believed in.' Gustav was already ill by that time, and a few hours later he collapsed with malaria and dysentery. He did not want to live, and he nearly died. But once the local doctor had done what he could for him, von Rosen arranged for him to be placed in a grass hut on an island off Lagos, with a boy to mind him. There he struggled with the awful visions of his delirium, drank what was poured into his throat and finally woke to the reality that he would live, he would gradually grow stronger and somehow he would have to face a life in which he would never see Ralph again.

Hardening himself, forcing himself to recover his strength and in danger of returning to the man he had been before he'd met Ralph, he set about building upon those earlier Benin bronzes. But there was one difference. This time his motive was not to attract fame to himself, as the collector, but to provide a form of immortality for Ralph after whom the collection would be named. Where once he had been filled with hate, he was driven now by love. But it was a stern love that considered nobody's good but Ralph's. Before returning eventually to Sweden, he ruthlessly exploited the post-

Biafra years to acquire every good piece he could. As he had foreseen, a considerable number of art works suddenly became available after the Civil War, at exceptionally low prices. He avoided those that had clearly been looted, knowing they would eventually cause him trouble. But many others he bought even though he knew he was taking advantage of post-war poverty, especially among the very Igbos he'd been trying to help. But as what he purchased would one day be a memorial to Ralph and the Biafran struggle, he did not hesitate to use the situation; and his collection grew and grew. Inevitably it meant associating with dangerous people who would later have their eyes on an expansion of their crime empires into Europe; and then they did not forget that Gustav, wealthy and respected, would be in a position to vouch for them if they wished to settle in Sweden. What he had not foreseen was their desire to be introduced to powerful people there who might protect them in return for certain services.

As the years rolled by and their requests turned into scarcely-veiled demands, he took the precaution of approaching SAPO and was put in touch with Grönberg. It was a lengthy courtship in which they danced around each other. Gustav maintained that he knew very little but wished to stay on the right side of the law after he had inadvertently become involved in a few transactions that, with hindsight, he ought to have avoided. Grönberg, as his mentor, seemed sympathetic, understanding his wish to protect his art legacy, though initially vague about how they might be able to help. Gradually Gustav fed him titbits of information, then a few larger mouthfuls. Olle Grönberg became warmer, and assurances of a general nature were forthcoming. And so

248

it had continued until the present, by which time he'd provided some hard information in return for a statement of support filed with the appropriate authorities, and read to him, though a printed copy was unavailable.

More time passed, a lot of time, without any problems, and he almost believed he had got away with his particular variation of the double-cross. Then Arthur entered his life.

Gabriel, his own special intermediary with the gang which had expanded its interests into money laundering and now styled itself The Group, suddenly sent some photos to his computer telling him he deserved a reward for all his help over so many years. Perhaps, Gabriel suggested, he would like to select one of the attached for his own personal and possibly exclusive use. Gustav had never been blind to the likenesses between SAPO and The Group, the use of a single intercessor, the stately language masking the ruthlessness, and the desire to involve him more and more deeply so that he would never be able to extricate himself. He was only too well aware, therefore, that he should not even glance at the pictures, deleting them unseen. But he had lived alone in Sweden for forty years, without love, and he did look.

Five were girls and five were boys. He did not expect to be stirred but he told himself it would be useful to have visual evidence that he might be able to pass on productively to Grönberg. But one picture struck him instantly. It was of a Nigerian boy who had the same amused look as Ralph when he'd lain beside him on the sand outside Accra, a kindly amusement, understanding, open, almost welcoming. His heart raced as he stared and stared. The likeness was uncanny. It was Ralph as he would have been as a teenager; it was how Ralph's son would have looked at sixteen; and, after the ruin the conflict had brought to so many Igbo families, it might so easily be Ralph's grandson, now in the hands of The Group, trafficked and ripe for prostitution.

It was this thought that swept all other speculation aside, and he did not hesitate. He chose, and delivery was made.

He was an old man now, and he often dreamed that he and Ralph had been able to live together in Sweden, and Ralph's son had become their son whom they watched grow up, marry and propagate a child, who might well have been named after a Biafran hero. So as soon as he saw this Arthur in the flesh, and welcomed him into his home for the three days he had been permitted to keep the gift, he instantly became that grandchild. Gustav let him roam around his apartment and stare out from the balcony, which Arthur said was like being at the top of a white palace. He cooked him special meals, and he gave him the presents he had bought for him, inwardly predicting his delighted reaction to each as he unwrapped them. He showed him the guest bedroom, explaining carefully that it was now Arthur's room, personal and private, set aside for him whenever he came to stay. Remembering the troubles of his own childhood, he gave him the only key to the room's door; and he assured him he would always be secure there, because he wanted nothing from him except the chance to be like a grandfather to him and to keep him safe.

That first night, when the slightly bewildered boy had fallen into a deep sleep, he contacted Gabriel and explained that he wished to purchase Arthur, to buy him out of slavery, and he would not quibble about the price. Gabriel had not demurred but said that the transfer would take a while. As was customary in these matters when the time limit was up, Arthur would be collected by the armed couriers so essential in case any client attempted to retain goods owned exclusively by The Group. But he was assured Arthur would not be offered elsewhere and Gustav eased his own suffering now by imagining the boy's joyfulness at the lake when he was freed from his slavery in a little ceremony, his mind full of excited anticipation of his return to that white palace and to Gustav. He prayed the death that followed was swift enough to leave that happy optimism unalloyed.

But that did not in any way take the edge off his hunger for revenge. The man who had burned Arthur to death must pay for it with his life; and he, Gustav Carlsson, formerly Johnny Callin, would kill him. As soon as Magnus had told him what weapon had been used, he'd known the perpetrator. Benjamin was one of a number of executioners, all with fearsome reputations and mostly high on dope; but Benjamin was the only one who liked to use a flamethrower. He would have to be exceptionally cunning to set up another meeting where he could execute him as justice required. Now The Group knew he'd been touch with SAPO he could, he supposed, threaten to give them more information unless he got that meeting; and, since visiting the crime scene with Magnus, he knew exactly how to show up Benjamin as a liability who had to be eliminated. It might even suit The Group to bring the two of them together at the lake so that both problems could be resolved when they slew each other, suggesting that all three killings there were no more than a personal vendetta.

But these were just fancies in his mind and none of it was enough. The bait had to be much, much bigger, and the prize one that only he could offer them. It must be something that required a local solution; and above all, it had to be something that would permanently disrupt the police investigation before it reached a conclusion.

But though he used 'something' in his thoughts, the reality was 'someone'. It would just be collateral damage, he told himself in an attempt to ease his conscience. An American statesman he'd always despised once said, "Stuff happens"; and that was how he would have to try to look at it. As if he'd foreseen what would be necessary, he'd even given fair warning about desperate measures and innocent bystanders. Now it was the only solution.

Once the guarantee about his art collection was confirmed, he would betray Magnus Trygg.

TWENTY

Magnus was exhausted by the ever more frequent pains in his chest, but he remained determined to complete the investigation. He'd already spoken to Grönberg about the price of Gustav's cooperation and at first his response had been typically cautious. But once Magnus gave him the name of the Sundsvall lawyer to whom the art collection transfer papers had been sent and explained that, as they knew each other, the lawyer had felt able to confirm the arrival of such a document marked for the Head of Homicide, Sundsvall Police, Grönberg grudgingly admitted that the arrangements with the National Museum were in fact already in place. Gustav had not been aware of this certainty as they hadn't wanted him to feel too comfortable; but he hoped Magnus would take his word for it. He was clearly irritated when Magnus insisted he could only proceed after receiving written confirmation of the arrangement from the museum itself. But the acquisition of so much inside information was just too tempting, and it finally overpowered Grönberg. He agreed, without much grace, that a letter from the Museum Director would be in the post within the hour; and when Magnus received it the next morning he immediately forwarded a copy to Gustav.

Walking to his car in the late afternoon, tired and eager to get home, he saw a tall, broad-shouldered man in front of him, walking slowly and swaying occasionally. As he passed him, the man asked him how he was. Certain he did not know him, and suspecting he might be one of the drinkers who spent much of the day sprawled on the sloping grass bank beside the Selånger waterway, he answered briefly though untruthfully, that he was doing fine. The man enquired his name, but Magnus pretended not to hear him.

"I only wanted to shake your hand," the man said, rather plaintively, and Magnus suddenly felt ashamed. There was no smell of alcohol and as a young policeman he'd dealt with enough drunks to realise this was something different. This was a very lonely man, in some agony of spirit, who needed human contact, however brief. He wondered whether he, too, had just been examined in the hospital and told that he might die, and the anguish of such a diagnosis would be much worse for someone who lived alone. So he turned, said he was Magnus and shook his hand.

"Thank you, Magnus," the man said quietly, studying his face as though he recognised some need in Magnus, too. "If you're ever in trouble with any people, tell them you've shaken hands with Big Björn and they'll leave you alone."

Magnus nodded gratefully and went to his car. But as he drove home he couldn't put the man out of his thoughts. He compared Big Björn's sense of isolation, when a word with someone in the street was such a pressing need, with his own good fortune where a united and loving family awaited his return. Since he'd dropped his bombshell the children had been less self-centred, and Sonja seemed to have discovered a fount of patient good humour that amazed him. But inevitably there were still occasional confrontations, and shortly after the kindly welcomes-home and two offered-and-accepted cups of coffee, a storm did blow up.

As so often, it was the state of the youngsters' rooms that caused the trouble. Johan, as he passed Magnus in the hall, raised his eyebrows in expressive masculine disdain and loudly shut himself inside his room which had just about passed Sonja's inspection. But it was clear from the suddenly raised voices that Angelica had been less diligent in the last-minute clear-up.

"You may *not* go out tonight, and that's final," he heard Sonja declare in her most peremptory immoveable-Mum voice. "You promised me faithfully you'd sort out that tip you call a room, and you haven't. You were going to gather up all your dirty washing, remove the used cups, glasses and plates of half-eaten snacks, and then clean and tidy everywhere. You promised, but you've scarcely even begun. So you'll stay in and do it now, this instant."

"But can I go out then, Mum?" Angelica demanded in an injured tone. "Emilia wants me to do a night-time photoshoot with her, and the weather's perfect for it."

"By the time your room is done, and done to my satisfaction, not yours, it'll be far too late for something like that. You can do it tomorrow."

"That's so unfair, Mum. Emilia's expecting me, we've planned it for a long time, and I can't let her down just because my room's not as perfect as *you* want. I'll do it now, immediately, and you know I can move fast when I have to. But it's *my* room, I'll do it to *my* satisfaction and then I'll run across to her place, do the shots and be back before eleven. I promise, okay?"

"You know perfectly well ten is your deadline, you agreed that with both Dad and me, and there's no chance you'll get anything worthwhile done by then. Concentrate on your room, get that out of the way, and then you can relax and really enjoy yourself tomorrow."

"But it's summer, Mum, it's not dark at night. And think how childish it's going to sound when I tell Emilia I can't come out because my Mum won't let me. None of my friends have this problem and they're going to think I'm super lame. Someone might even post it on Facebook and my life won't be worth living."

Magnus sighed, waiting for the final 'NO', the slammed door and being nearly knocked down by Sonja storming back to the kitchen, muttering furiously. He opened his arms ready to hug her comfortingly and hold her until she relaxed against him. But it wasn't necessary. To his astonishment he heard a United Nations peacekeeping force in action.

"Is this photoshoot really that important to you?"

"Yes, Mum, for Emilia *and* me. We both love art, you know that, and you and Dad have always encouraged me to specialise in it. Now we're really into photography, we've told everyone we're going to do a shoot tonight, and they'll be waiting to see the results on their iPhones."

"Let's do a deal, then. You text Emilia saying you're coming straight away, and I'll sort your room out. You've been so good recently, and nice to Dad, you probably do deserve a break. But this is a one-off. I'll expect you to keep your room decent from now on, and you'll be back tonight before ten, not letting the deadline overrun as you usually do."

"You're amazing, Mum!" he heard Angelica say joyfully. "And you needn't worry, I'll be back early tonight and I'll never let you down again."

"I imagine you heard all that and don't you dare smirk," Sonja warned Magnus as she joined him in the living room; but then she couldn't help laughing, "You're just as useless at controlling that girl as I am, and you spoil her rotten as well. Now I'm going to put something in the oven, and after we've eaten I'm going to have a long shower, go to bed early and read my book."

She kissed him and then bustled off eagerly, leaving Magnus regretful that he was just too worn out to join her when she went in to the shower. He thought he'd stretch himself out on the sofa to watch athletics on the TV. But when Sonja called out that the food was ready he woke with a jolt, realising he must have been asleep for some time.

"You're sure you're not overdoing it?" Sonja asked him as they ate. "You seem more tired recently."

"It's just the case, I think. It's hotting up, possibly nearing the end, and that's always a busy time."

257

"So it may be over soon and it's your last case. Are you finding that hard?"

"Not nearly as hard as I thought I would, and that's surprised me. Where's Johan?"

"He loaded up his plate and took it to his room because he's in the middle of some computer game with Lucas and the others. You were asleep, so I thought it would be all right for once."

"It's certainly peaceful without either of our children and I like having you to myself. Do you think Angelica will really be back at ten?"

Sonja nodded. "Funnily enough, I think she will, this time. She was so shocked when I let her have her own way that she'll want to surprise us by sticking to the bargain we made. That's partly why I'm going off to bed early, so she doesn't find me standing in the hall looking at my watch when she does come back. I want to show her that I trust her."

"Thank you very much. That means you're leaving me to do the checking."

"But you don't get in a panic like I do. You'll be in front of TV, not by the front door looking worried. You'll probably have forgotten all about her until she actually arrives." She stuck her tongue out at him, blew him a kiss, and, once they'd finished the meal and cleared up, she hurried away to her shower and a long read in bed.

Magnus slumped in front of the TV with the sound off and began to review everything he'd discovered in the case. He thought about the horrific nature of the murder and what he really knew about Gustav, brooding on his involvement and his intentions. He was so deep in his thoughts that the sudden ringing of his mobile made him jump.

"Did I disturb you?" Grönberg asked him, not as if he cared but because, or so it sounded, he felt it was something you were expected to say.

"It's lucky you did," Magnus replied feelingly. "I'd almost fallen asleep in front of the TV."

"Ah," said Grönberg awkwardly, as though he could not comprehend that a protector of the peace would be capable of doing such a thing. "I just felt obliged to put a thought in your mind because I know you're not used to dealing with Nigerian gangs."

"It's my first experience of them," said Magnus encouragingly to fill the pause that had been left for some sort of reply, and again he was surprised by the stiffness of Grönberg's social intercourse.

"Gustav's got you mixed up with really nasty people, Magnus, and of course we listen in to them whenever we have the chance. We haven't been very successful with this lot, they move houses quite often so our bugs don't work, and they regularly change their mobiles. But we still hear some things and just now they seem worried about you, not liking the speed and success of your investigation. I hope you're taking sensible precautions."

"I'm probably not," admitted Magnus, suddenly realising that Grönberg was trying to help him, but was embarrassed in case it annoyed him. Relations between local police and the security service were often marked by mutual hostility, and Magnus decided to put that right without further delay.

"Just tell me straight out what I ought to be doing. I really do need some advice."

At once the voice at the other end became more fluent. "We've reached a stage now where you may be in personal danger, Magnus. If it ever becomes known to this particular group that Gustav has produced a dossier on them, and there was a possibility he might have passed it to you, they'd kill you instantly as well as him. I know them, they don't wait on facts, they react on instinct. That's why they often get ahead of us, not just killing witnesses but people who might be witnesses as well. I know you're a police marksman, but these people don't just use flamethrowers or guns, they use bombs – and your police pistol won't be much use to you then. They might think a beating would persuade you to suppress evidence, and again I happen to know you're top in unarmed combat. But they won't send one man to work you over, they'll play safe and despatch ten. They've done it here, in Stockholm and in Göteborg, and they won't change their tactics just because they think you're a country bumpkin. Are you listening to me, Magnus?"

"Yes," said Magnus soberly.

"Then keep on listening. Down here, when they want to influence a policeman, they use bribery even more than beatings. But it's possible your reputation as an honest cop is known to them, and in that case they won't bother to attempt it."

"I can't believe that many policemen take bribes, even in the cities."

"Then you're a bloody fool, and it's time you opened your eyes. The combination of people trafficking, prostitution and drugs is a multimillion *kronor* business and so bribes aren't any longer the odd crumpled hundred *kronor* note. Nowadays, from people like this, it gets you a better house, a bigger pension, several nice holidays or a lot of sex in whatever style you fancy."

Magnus sighed. "I don't want to believe the picture you're painting, but you've just about convinced me."

"There's more to come, and I don't think you'll hesitate after I tell you this. For somebody like you, senior, honest, unafraid and ready for a fight, they'll use a different method; and I know about it because we've had a few Magnus Tryggs down here, and it's how they've been dealt with. They don't go directly for the police officer; they go for the officer's family."

Magnus felt the panic strike him, and he only just heard Grönberg's final words before he rang off: "Act as if they may be watching your house already and take every precaution. Don't trust anybody, not even somebody who may seem to be on your side."

Magnus glanced at his watch and saw it was a quarter to ten. Without saying a word to Sonja, he left the house and ran down the road towards Monica and Henrik's house, careful to follow the return route he knew Angelica would take. He was there in a few minutes, pressing the bell insistently.

"I thought I'd get some fresh air and collect Angelica," he explained when Emilia's mother opened the door, looking slightly puzzled.

"But, Magnus, she left for home ten minutes ago. You must have missed her somehow on the way."

Magnus forced a smile, though he felt sick inside. "I'll run back and maybe catch up with her," he said, and with a wave he was gone, leaving Monica staring worriedly after him.

As Magnus raced home peering in every direction but not seeing a soul, he began to panic. He could no longer put off the dreadful moment when he had to tell Sonja, and he was starting up the stairs towards their bedroom when his mobile rang.

Certain it would be Angelica he answered joyfully. "Darling, where are you?" But the voice that replied had the unmistakeable military briskness of Gustav Carlsson.

"They've got your daughter, Magnus," he said without emotion. "It's the same ones who killed Arthur. They want to talk to you, on the road beside the lake where he was killed, and she's the hostage to ensure they get your full cooperation. She won't be harmed, though I'm afraid she's bound to be pretty terrified. They're probably watching your house at this very moment, so get over to me as quickly as you can so they realise you're following their instructions. Above all, don't use your mobile for any other calls, don't carry it with you, remove the SIM card and make no attempt to contact police or security. I'm the trusted go-between, guaranteeing your obedience, and we'll have her home safe and sound in no time."

"I can't move that fast, Gustav. I have to talk to my wife and reassure her so that she doesn't ring the police herself. It won't be easy, but I'll be with you as soon as I can."

He rang off, went in to Sonja, and it wasn't easy. She was already half-asleep, and the moment she heard Angelica was missing she assumed she'd broken her word about coming back early and became angry. He had to lie on top of her, wrap his arms round her and tell her that Angelica had done nothing wrong; she'd been on her way home well before time when she'd been caught up in his murder case and taken hostage as a warning to him. The gang would release her as soon as he'd given them certain assurances.

She stared at him, facing the new situation more calmly than he'd expected.

"Did you know this might happen?"

"It had never even occurred to me until SAPO rang tonight, maybe ten minutes ago, to warn me the gang might target my family and me. I went out immediately to fetch Angelica, but she'd already left for home. Then Gustav phoned to say she'd been snatched and I must meet the gang leaders tonight in order to save her."

"Will you give them the assurances they want?"

"Of course. I'll do anything to keep her safe, you know that."

She began to tremble. "Will they have done anything to her?"

"No. That wouldn't help them. They know it's the fear of what they may do to her that will force me to cooperate with them."

He felt her shudder as a new thought came to her. "Are they the ones who burnt the African boy?"

"Yes. But they want something from me, and so they won't risk antagonising me."

His instant admission of who they were, the very worst news for her, seemed to steady her, convincing her he was not trying to shield her from the truth.

"Are you certain, really certain, that you'll get her back unharmed?"

She was looking at him so searchingly, so beseechingly, that he might easily have quailed. But he didn't.

"Yes, I'm certain."

"Will it be safe for you?"

"I shall make certain arrangements, so yes, I'll be quite safe. But I have to go now and I want you and Johan to come with me. You're no longer secure here; they may be watching the house so I'll take you both to

Bodil. Now you must get dressed and I'll wake Johan. We have to leave in five minutes."

The sense of being part of some sort of police procedure, and the prospect of being with her cousin, calmed her slightly. With a sleepy, grumbling Johan in tow, they were away shortly afterwards.

He watched his mirror carefully and he made a few sudden detours. When he was convinced no one was following him, he turned a last corner and pulled up at Bodil's recently purchased house in central Sundsvall. There he quickly handed them over to an anxious Bodil, and took her quiet but burly partner Leif aside. He told him to make sure each door and window was securely locked, and that nobody was to be allowed into the flat until he rang to say he'd got Angelica. He stressed that this included friends or relatives who might be forced by a gang member to try to get the door opened. Then he borrowed Leif's mobile, made three short calls, handed the phone back, hugged Sonja reassuringly, and left.

He felt the anger growing in him as he drove to Gustav's apartment, but he knew he must control it, at least until the right moment. Someone had shopped him. Though he wouldn't put it past SAPO to pull such a trick if it helped them grab The Group, Gustav, in his lust for revenge, was a more likely suspect. However far he might pretend to go along with him, whatever Gustav said when they met, he knew he could not trust him. Gustav had got what he'd wanted from Magnus when the deal over his collection had been confirmed; now he could use him as a staked-out kid to bring the tiger near enough to wreak his vengeance.

TWENTY-ONE

The prospect of the forthcoming confrontation had transformed Gustav into an army officer again. He moved with youthful eagerness and his eyes were shining with excitement. Magnus spotted immediately the tell-tale bulge beneath his jacket when he stretched out his arm to greet him.

"We have much to plan before we go if we are to keep Angelica safe whatever develops," he said in the trenchant tone of a senior officer greeting a subordinate. "But we'll get her back, you may be sure of that, and she won't have been harmed. The Group is worried about all you seem to have discovered, and this is just a warning."

"How did they know what I'd discovered?"

"I was shooting a bit of a line, trying to get them rattled so they'd come down here and walk into a trap when they confronted me. I'd assumed you and Grönberg would be happy to spring that trap if I could get them here. So I told Gabriel, a senior contact in the gang, that whoever had been carrying the flamethrower and pack would have been sweating by the time he waited for the moment to fire, and you would find his DNA in the bog water beneath his feet."

"The forensic team tested that water and no DNA was found."

"You know that, and I assumed it. But they don't know it, and the possibility worried Gabriel a great deal. The man with the flamethrower was Benjamin, who sweats profusely when he's excited at the prospect of killing someone and as he's done time in prison his DNA's on record. If The Group believe there's the slightest chance his DNA might be discovered I knew they'd be delighted to have him eliminated."

He deliberately betrayed me, Magnus thought bitterly. He wanted to get a reaction from Gabriel that would show Benjamin was the killer, and then he made sure they'd come down here to try to eliminate me. And I'll have to look after myself and Angelica because all he really wants is the opportunity to take revenge on Benjamin. Maybe he even suggested kidnapping one of my children to render me helpless.

"Taking Angelica is just a means of persuading you that you're in their power," Gustav went on glibly, as if he'd guessed the furious thoughts circulating inside Magnus. "It demonstrates how easy it is to take a member of your family and so, to protect them, you'll agree to stop looking for DNA and let the case fade away through lack of evidence. It's a technique they often use, and always successfully."

"If they're as bad as that, why should they trust my word? I can agree, get Angelica back, put the family in a safe house and then go after them as if nothing had happened."

"Because they don't know you, that's why. These are city people, they get away with this sort of thing with city police and they're too stupid to realise you might be an exception. They may even offer you a bribe as well, just to be certain."

It was so unconvincing he was surprised Gustav had even tried it on. It would be foolish for any of the gang to return to the scene of the crime and they would have agreed to it for one reason only - a clean sweep of all potential problems. They would kill Gustav as soon as he'd eliminated Benjamin for them, then they'd kill him and probably Angelica as well. Out loud he said, "I'm going to have to play this very carefully."

Gustav stared at him, puzzled. "You don't seem to be taking this seriously enough, Magnus. I hope you aren't relying on any arrangements you've made on your own. SAPO will do anything to smash this group, but you can be sure their operation will take priority over saving Angelica, whatever the circumstances. And if you're banking on your own local force, then frankly I doubt their ability to stay hidden from these people who are probably watching the area of the lake already. If they feel you've betrayed the conditions I accepted on your behalf, Angelica won't survive. I'm your trump card, because they've trusted me longer than they've suspected me, and they don't know we've become sufficiently close that I might actually risk my life to save you and Angelica."

Magnus stared at him dully, compelling himself not to trust him, refusing to commit his feelings to words and so forcing Gustav to go on talking and perhaps reveal a little of the truth that lay beneath his posturing.

"For God's sake, Magnus, Listen to me. I've tried to tell you this before, and it's vital you grasp it. This Group doesn't mind what it does. Most gangs don't like killing policemen or their families, because the consequences are bad for them. But these new Nigerian gangs don't think like that. Think Boko Haram, now in the northern Nigeria I used to love, it's just mindless violence, and that filters down to the gangs here because they see it works. There's nothing sacred about a policeman to them, and they have so many underlings who can be cannon fodder when the police take their revenge. They have no compunction in sacrificing them as long as The Group, and the top bosses, survive. Fear is what they live on, and only one thing frightens people more than hearing a policeman's been killed, and that's hearing that one's been killed and nobody serious has been punished for it. That's when the general public finally realises who runs the streets, and that it's every man for himself. When policemen and their families can be hurt or killed with impunity, society as we know it is at an end."

Magnus, busy sifting truth from deception, looked at Gustav, and merely commented that he thought it was time he knew the details of the meeting and the agreement Gustav had made on his behalf.

"We meet at the lake at five tomorrow morning. I will bring you there, in my car. I shall appear to have your pistol and holster in my hand, held up to show them, and you will have your jacket open to show your gun's gone. There will two of them, spaced out at the lakeside, and Angelica will be standing alone, in full view, at least twenty metres distant from them. If she isn't, or there are more than two men there, we could in theory just drive away, though I know you'd never abandon Angelica. In the same way, of course, the conditions they've agreed would be nullified if more than two of us arrive, if any police or security personnel are seen in the area, if a helicopter is spotted or you're armed. Then Angelica would pay the price."

The bitter anger that had been building up in Magnus finally boiled over. "You betrayed me to them, Gustav, just to get the opportunity for your revenge. If they were genuinely interested in negotiation, they'd have insisted you brought me to them handcuffed, but they simply want the chance to eliminate me. Angelica probably will be at a distance, but since you don't give a fuck about anything except killing Benjamin, you'll end up dead, and so will I. That means there will be nobody left to protect Angelica, so you can stuff your plan and come up with a better one. And before you do that, I have to know whether you told them to take Angelica, because that's something I could never forgive."

Gustav laughed. "I'm glad I'm working with you, Magnus. You see straight through me, and you tell me so to my face. Yes, I did betray you to make my revenge possible. But I never intentionally put your family in any danger. That was Gabriel's own particular twist, and it's why, before they kill me, I'll do everything in my power to save her and, if possible, you as well. I give you my word on that, Magnus. And, whatever happens, this will be a last stand to rival Custer's, though considering what a big-headed incompetent windbag he was it's really not claiming much. But The Group has no idea of my military experience or my shooting skills; they did, of

270

course, insist that your hands were secured behind your back, though not with handcuffs, which they never use, but with a cable-tie." He held one up, thin and black. "I made this while I was waiting for you, and I'm rather proud of it. It will hold your hands over your police automatic in the back of your waistband; and as the tie is made of black paper you'll be able to snap it whenever you need to draw your weapon. Does that seem to level the odds a little?"

"A little," Magnus replied cautiously.

"And I know you well enough to believe that you have one or two tricks up your sleeve which you're not going to tell me, and I confess that I do, too, which I'm not going to tell you about either, not yet, anyway. But as Angelica is more important than my life and, I suspect, your life too, let's at least try to trust each other enough to discuss how best to protect her."

Tentatively he held out his hand, and Magnus, against his better judgement, took it. Then they talked, about the lake, the areas of firm ground, the cover, the weapons they might be up against, where the rays of the rising sun would strike the eyes, how best to divide between them the firepower of their two weapons: a 1950 vintage English military revolver shrouded in a Swedish official holster and a concealed standard police automatic. Then they considered all the possible dangers their opponents might try to spring on them, and how to react to every eventuality.

"After all," said Gustav, "if *we* can't be trusted to play to the rules, how can we possibly expect them to?

And if we can't outplay them, then we're not the experienced military and police pair we think we are."

"How did they get hold of Angelica?" Magnus asked him bluntly.

"Your house has been under surveillance for some time. Last night the snatch mob moved closer, behind the large birch at the beginning of your *cul-de-sac*. Angelica, hurrying home, walked straight into their arms. I think they were as surprised as she was, but they had the presence of mind to bundle her into their car and drive off with her."

"How many armed men will we really be facing?"

"Six. They'll be in the big black Mercedes, with Gabriel at the wheel. Benjamin will be beside him, already high, as usual, on something that will make him careless of injury or death. I'm afraid Angelica will be in the boot, but at least it's a big and airy one with nice carpeting. The back seat can take four. One will be dropped off to the north to put out warning signs stating 'road temporarily closed', another to the south to do the same; and fortunately both will be too far away to trouble us. Another one will be concealed near Angelica ready to shoot her if we don't behave ourselves, and the last one, probably armed with a sniper's rifle, will be watching us from quite a distance in order to take us out if we try any funny business when we 're confronted by Gabriel and Benjamin."

"Six to two. That's not very good odds."

Gustav laughed happily. "But what a magnificent pair we'll be, Magnus."

He looked at his watch, yawned and announced that if he was to be at his best so early in the morning he needed to sleep for an hour. "When I'm awake again, we'll have some coffee and open sandwiches to fortify us, and then we'll be ready for anything. Meanwhile, you'd better have this." He passed Magnus a wrapped mobile and, noting his raised eyebrows, he added, "It's never been used, so it's secure."

Alone in the room, surrounded by Nigerian bronzes, masks and weapons, Magnus found it hard to relax. He'd made himself sound so confident when he'd assured Sonja he'd save Angelica; but now he was assailed by doubts. His chest was hurting even more than usual, his heart seemed to be beating too fast and he felt little confidence that his body would be up to the fighting ahead. He pushed the mobile he had been given down the back of the sofa, not trusting Gustav enough to be convinced that it wasn't set up so that any call could be intercepted and that his location could be monitored. The odds were not even as good as he'd stated because he would be unable to do anything until he knew Angelica was safe. That reduced them to 6-1, which gave him no comfort. He muttered a hasty, desperate prayer, wishing he'd inherited his mother's unquestioning Buddhist faith or his farmer father's dogged acceptance of whatever God sent in the way of weather or anything else. But, by simply remembering his parents, so ill-assorted and yet so happy together, a sense of calm did begin to flood through him. They had at least bequeathed their ability to bond powerfully with their children, and perhaps in a

273

way they had passed on something of their simple faith as well.

He even felt a rekindled spark of confidence because Gustav, normally so perceptive, had not noticed any physical deterioration in him. He had spoken of them as a magnificent pair; and in an odd way that had lifted a burden from his shoulders. Maybe he'd been unnecessarily concerned about his heart and any weakening in his general condition. Maybe his determination to save Angelica would more than compensate for any slight imperfection. Maybe, whatever the odds, they might pull it off.

He woke with a start when Gustav touched his shoulder. "Battle will soon commence, Magnus. Food and coffee is on the table."

TWENTY-TWO

It was just getting light as they passed through Slättmon and approached the tarn. The cloud cover was so thick the rays of the rising sun could not penetrate it, so there were still shadowy areas at the forest edge which could be used to advantage by both sides in the forthcoming confrontation. Magnus comforted himself that being an experienced woodsman might just give him an edge. He was relieved to see that Gustav seemed very calm, driving slowly and steadily, studying the ground as a good soldier should and whistling gently between his teeth in a way that could have been irritating had it not revealed a certain enjoyment of their parlous situation.

Then Gustav's mobile rang, and he stopped to answer it. He listened briefly, said, "We're on our way," and rang off.

"Bastards!" he muttered bitterly, and when he turned to Magnus his face looked drained of the hope that had rejuvenated it.

"You'd better tell me," Magnus said, though he dreaded hearing it.

"They've outmanoeuvred us," Gustav admitted bluntly. "They didn't trust us, obviously thought you

275

might have arranged some support troops, and so they've changed the meeting place."

Magnus, stricken, realising the slight hope of help had disappeared and that he would be on his own, unconsciously massaged his chest, though he still managed to speak calmly. "Where are they?"

"Gabriel wouldn't give a new location. He just said I was to drive past the lake and on along the road until we saw them."

"It won't be too far beyond the tarn then or they'll be getting near the area around Liden where a number of people live. Strangers would be noticed there, gunshots would be investigated and they won't risk having witnesses to the massacre they're planning."

"Do you know the area well enough to guess where they might be?"

"They'll want to be just off the road where they won't be noticed if a car does happen to pass, but they'll still want to be able to make a quick getaway if that becomes necessary. So I think they'll probably stop two or three kilometres beyond the tarn where there's a wide track going into the forest that leads eventually to the Nature Reserve."

"But your people, thinking it's going to be at the tarn, won't be able to get there in time?"

"I know nothing about *my people*," Magnus replied curtly, though inwardly he felt crushed by the turn of events. "What I do know is that even after this alteration they'll still be worried about some sort of trap, so they'll act quickly, maybe open fire at once, and we'll have to be ready for that."

"I'll make sure I park well back, then, and when we make our approach I'll go ahead of you just in case. But Gabriel's not a hothead and it would be unlike him to rush things or make more changes to the plan than absolutely necessary. I'll put that cable-tie on you now so that we're absolutely ready for them, seeming to obey their instructions but prepared to give them a few nasty surprises."

Once that was done, Gustav drove slowly past the tarn, and Magnus called out the moment he spotted the black Mercedes backed up the track on the right, just where he'd expected it to be. The car's speed reduced to a crawl.

"They've placed someone on the left of the road," Gustav said quietly. "I saw movement."

Magnus nodded. "He's in the trees there, with a good view of the track, and he's got what looks like a Kalashnikov."

"There are a couple of men by the Mercedes, but Angelica's not with them. So she's staked out somewhere beyond them, as agreed, and another man will be guarding her."

"Go a bit closer, very slowly, and we'll check if we can see her. Keep the engine running and be ready to drive straight at the Kalashnikov man if he opens fire at us. I'll try and shoot him as we're hurtling forward."

He eased his pistol in the broad elk skin loop attached to his belt at the back of his waistband and peered between the sparse and spindly birch trees that lined the side track.

"She's there," he muttered, relief making his voice husky. "They've gagged her and tied her to a tree at the left side of the track about thirty metres beyond them, so we won't be able to make a quick dash to get her."

"Can you see the man who's guarding her?"

"No. But there's a large pine tree several metres beyond, at forty-five degrees to her, and he might be behind that."

"At least it looks as though they're going to proceed with the farce of negotiation, initially anyway," commented Gustav. "I'll park here, and then we'll get out and stroll down the right-hand edge of the road towards the track, trying to keep what trees we can between us and the Kalashnikov. At least it'll allow Angelica to see you coming to her rescue and that should cheer her up."

"I'll keep to the left of you so I'm closer to Angelica in case some opportunity to free her comes up. I'll also stay well away from you, so they can't get us both with a single burst. You volunteered to go first, and I'm very happy to let you be the leader."

Gustav grinned. "I enjoyed leading my troops in Nigeria" he said, "and it'll be the proper way to end my life. If at some stage I toss a hand grenade at the enemy and also close to you, it's a diversionary tactic to give you the chance to snap the tie, get your gun out and start shooting while they're shitting themselves or running for their lives."

Magnus relaxed his caution enough to smile in his turn. "Thanks," he said. "I hope I can assume you've removed the detonator."

Gustav winked at him. "My memory's not reliable now I'm so old, but I think I did, yes. Now let's go to war."

He switched off the engine and stepped out, holding up in the air his army revolver crammed into Magnus's empty police holster, his hand and the black leather hiding the tell-tale cylinder and curved butt that would have revealed it was not a police automatic. Magnus noticed the hammer was already cocked and he braced himself, understanding that battle would commence the moment they were at close quarters.

It was eerily silent, no traffic and no sound of human habitation: no wood being chopped, no clatter of a tractor engine, no children's laughter which usually carried quite a distance. He listened to the forest itself, anxious to note what the sounds told him. But it was silent too. No solitary raven croaked in the sky above him, there was no scratching of the red squirrel racing up a tree and jumping from branch to branch, the greater spotted woodpecker did not drum upon a trunk and no bull elk scraped a branch with his antlers as he lowered his head to uproot blueberry bushes and browse on the glossy leaves. It was as if nature knew what was about to happen and wanted no part in it.

But it was light, even though the sun had so far failed to pierce the clouds. He could see everything very clearly, and he would be able to spot the slightest movement. He felt fresh and relaxed in what had been from earliest childhood his natural environment. So as he turned off the road and onto the track he had a detailed view of Angelica in the background and the two men who awaited them, well in front of her. He called out cheerfully to his daughter, shattering the increasingly oppressive stillness and expressing himself in heavily accented Norrland Swedish which would be incomprehensible to the Nigerians, "I'll have you untied and free in no time at all. I love you, seize any chance to escape."

The two men ahead of them had also positioned themselves with care, well-spaced, not far from their car, and in clear sight of the man with the Kalashnikov poorly concealed across the road. Each was holding an automatic at his side, ready for instant action. As he drew nearer, Magnus noticed that the one who must be Benjamin had a gold-plated pistol and was sweating heavily, grinning in anticipation, sniffing and unable to stay still in his excitement. The older man, Gabriel, was bulkier, smart in an expensive suit, calm and statue-still, his plain weapon hardly visible.

"Benjamin's mine," Gustav said in his commanding officer voice. "Don't be fooled by Gabriel's pleasant manner and measured approach to everything. If he wants you dead he's capable enough and that large calibre pistol would make a big hole in you."

"You know there's nothing I can do until Angelica's safe."

Gustav shrugged. "We're probably fucked then, but I'll kill as many as I can before I go out in a blaze of glory."

Steadily they walked forward until they were within pistol range, though you'd still need to be an excellent shot to hit the target in a vital spot.

"Here he is, then," said Gustav loudly, holding out the filled holster, "I told you I'd bring him to you unarmed, hands secured behind his back, and I have. If you give him back his daughter, he won't test the bog water that will have your DNA in it, Benjamin, and so you'll be quite safe and able to mess up even more of The Group's activities."

Benjamin, who was flaunting a bullet-proof vest, seemed pleased to be singled out for attention and he giggled happily.

"I hear you went to see the body of your little friend Arthur. I hope you took careful note of what my flamethrower did to him?"

Gustav nodded. "Yes, I did," he said, and he fired the army revolver through the holster, straight into Benjamin's forehead. Then he swung round towards Gabriel.

But as he turned, the man on the far side of the road opened fire with his Kalashnikov; and Magnus, as he dropped to the ground and rolled rapidly into the blueberry bushes at the left side of the track, closer to Angelica, saw at least two bullets strike Gustav. But somehow he still stayed upright, removing his left hand from his pocket, lobbing the grenade towards Gabriel and shooting at him as he threw himself down behind a tree in an attempt to avoid the blast. Only then did Gustav, as more bullets struck home, topple over with dignity intact and a smile of satisfaction that Arthur had been avenged and a final military operation successfully completed.

Magnus used the opportunity the grenade provided to snap the paper cable-tie, draw his pistol, slip the safety catch off and run, crouching, towards the pine tree where he'd seen a blur of movement which confirmed that Angelica's guard *was* concealed there. A bullet from Gabriel's pistol passed close to him and at any minute he expected more accurate shots from the Kalashnikov. But he had to get himself between Angelica and her guard, so he ignored all danger.

He heard the high crack of a rifle; and momentarily he wondered if it could be some unknown person coming to his aid and pinning down the Kalashnikov man. But then the horrifying truth dawned on him. He'd tragically underestimated the nervousness of the rifleman behind the pine. Moving in his direction with a drawn pistol had been enough to spook him; and he'd fired at Angelica.

Despairingly he looked at the birch tree to which Angelica was tied and saw her slowly sag, down until she was hidden by the blueberry bushes and the close-packed saplings. A terrible cry was forced out of him. He seemed to feel his heart split, experiencing a pain worse than anything he had ever known and he fell forward on his knees, his head almost touching the ground. He wanted to be dead, to be with Angelica, but such relief was not granted to him. He rocked back onto his knees, wincing at the stabbing twinge, but he was no longer able to raise his arms or lift the pistol towards Gabriel who, assuming now the grenade must be a dud, was moving up on him Bleeding from a wound in his thigh where Gustav's bullet had struck him and glancing inquisitively across the road where everything was uncannily silent, he still seemed largely undaunted.

"What the hell's wrong with you, man?" he asked Magnus as he crossed the track, pointing his pistol at him. But then, quite suddenly, he understood and smiled broadly. "I think you're having a great big heart attack, Inspector, and there's no doctor, ambulance or hospital to help you."

Magnus could not speak, but he gasped and shuddered with the torment in his chest. He stared up the track in the direction of the distant lake in the reserve where he'd caught his largest-ever trout, refusing to look at the triumphant Gabriel and awaiting the shot that would unite him with Angelica. Then, out of the corner of his eye, he saw movement in the tall grasses beyond Gabriel, not far from the birch tree where he'd seen Angelica shot. Deliberately keeping his face blank, refusing to let any hope rise in him yet, he felt he recognised the young, lithe figure speedily bowling in a tight ball over a short piece of open ground, circling round to get completely out of Gabriel's field of vision and moving with the grace and speed he'd seen in his daughter at a recent school sports meeting. When Gabriel turned his head slightly, the figure dropped down into the hazel bushes which then swayed almost imperceptibly as a safe position was attained behind him.

The rush of joy didn't obliterate the pain, didn't free his arms so that he could raise them and defend himself. But instead of meekly waiting for the bullet, he forced himself to keep Gabriel's attention fixed on him.

"You're right," he muttered. "I think I'm dying, you've got to get me help."

Gabriel smiled, took a few steps closer and probingly kicked him twice, first in the ribs which produced a gasp of agony, and then on the hand to dislodge the pistol. Magnus stifled a scream, but his fingers remained locked around the butt. Satisfied there was no pretence, Gabriel looked down at him. "I've never seen a man die from a heart attack before," he said interestedly. "Maybe I'll stay and watch; or I could leave you here until your moment comes. But I guess it's kindest to put you out of your misery." He raised his pistol and stepped even closer, ignoring the blood flowing from his leg and falling onto Magnus.

The two kicks had almost rendered Magnus unconscious. But Angelica was close enough now for him to see the fury and determination in her face and, knowing that at any moment she would be on the open track behind Gabriel, he began to groan and cry out loudly to cover the sound of her approach, praying she'd remember his lessons on how to handle herself when in desperate personal danger.

Gabriel put his pistol to the back of his victim's head and Magnus, knowing he had to gain a few seconds, gasped the first words that floated into his mind.

"You'd better be careful. I've shaken hands with Big Björn."

He heard Gabriel's jeering laugh. "Big Björn! Who the hell is Big Björn! I've never even heard of him. Your mind must be failing as well as your heart." But it had provided the necessary respite. Angelica, shrieking furiously, hurled herself onto Gabriel's back, wound her legs round his waist and dug the vivid green finger nails of both hands into his eyes exactly as her Dad had told her she should do in a real emergency.

Taken totally by surprise, Gabriel staggered forward against Magnus, his wounded leg momentarily giving way under him and causing him such anguish that he almost fell and his heavy automatic slipped out of his grasp as he struggled to regain his balance. But, once recovered, he began to pound Angelica's legs with his fists to try to break her hold on him. His left foot was now below the pistol Magnus could not raise; and as he heard the thump of the blows against his daughter's flesh, and her yells of pain, a primal rage convulsed his whole body and the reflex finger-twitch operated the light trigger action.

The effect was instantaneous. Gabriel's face contorted as the bullet passed through his foot. He hurled Angelica off, couldn't find his automatic which she'd deliberately covered with her falling body, and he ran limping to his car, urged on by shots from another police pistol close-by, one bullet almost clipping him. He threw himself into the Mercedes and the tyres smoked as he drove off at speed.

Magnus felt Angelica's arms round him, her tears moistening his face, "Oh Dad, Dad," she cried disconsolately, "he got away."

"Part of the plan," Magnus gasped into her ear. "There's a SAPO helicopter watching him, high up, and when they've seen where he goes they'll pick him up with the rest of the gang. I didn't want too much action here; I was trying to keep you safe." He began to sob with relief that she was there, hugging him, though he couldn't raise his arms to put them round her. Nothing mattered now, not the intolerable pain in his chest, not his utter helplessness.

"Lars was awesome," Angelica chattered excitedly. "After you rang him last night, he camped out in the forest with his mate Tore, who's a hunter, and they saw the Merc go past the tarn. So they pursued them on foot, running all the time, using a short cut Tore knew and getting here shortly before you. Once he'd seen your car arrive, Lars crawled round to where I was tied and I suddenly saw him at my feet, cutting me loose from the tree; he'd already sorted my guard, bashing him over the head and handcuffing him. Then someone shot that man who'd come with you and I ducked down as Tore, up in a tree with his hunting rifle, took out whoever had done it."

She glanced at Gustav's still body and shuddered, "Is he dead?"

Magnus nodded.

"I'm glad Tore shot him then, though I think he only wounded him because Lars had to dash away through the trees to secure him when he was crawling towards where his gun had fallen. He'd told me to hide in the forest up near the reserve, but I didn't take any notice and legged it as fast as I could to help you. When I saw him kick you I got really, really angry, like I didn't care what I did to him."

Magnus longed to say something about her courage, that she had indeed saved his life, that he loved her and would always love her. But his strength was fading. In the distance he could just make out the sirens of the ambulance and police cars Lars must have called up, and very faintly he heard Angelica's frightened voice begging him to hold on until help came, and that he must stay with her. He thought that odd, because she was hugging him, kissing him, and telling him he was going to be all right. He wished Sonja could be here too, to see that he had kept his word and saved their daughter; and Johan should come as well, though it was rather early in the morning for him to be out of bed. Then he did sense them around him; and for a moment, before they faded, he saw them clearly. He could still feel Angelica holding him, though he couldn't discern her anymore; and, as a gradual darkness enveloped him, he was comforted by the consciousness that though Angelica had gone, and all the others, he did not feel he was alone.

CONCLUSION

Five extracts from the local paper, 'SUNDSVALLS WEEKLY':

SAPO SMASH VICIOUS NIGERIAN GANG

SUNDSVALLS
WEEKLY

Key members of the gang, involved in people trafficking, drugs and prostitution, have been arrested in Stockholm. This follows the successful helicopter-tracking of a car fleeing a shoot-out with Sundsvall police between Slättmon and Bodäcke.

BRAVERY AWARD FOR SUNDSVALL SUPER COP

SUNDSVALLS
WEEKLY

Inspector Lars Svedlund received his second police bravery award for capturing an armed gangster and fearlessly freeing a hostage near Black Creek. At the same ceremony local hunter Tore Claesson, unexpectedly caught up in the confrontation, was presented with a civilian valour scroll for heroically incapacitating a Kalashnikov-wielding killer with a single shot from his elk-hunting rifle.

SUNDSVALL ART COLLECTOR BEQUEATHS COLLECTION TO THE NATION

SUNDSVALLS WEEKLY

The late Gustav Carlsson's world-renowned collection of Nigerian art, which includes many rare Benin bronzes, has been left to the Stockholm National Museum of Fine Arts under the title of "The Ralph Okoro Memorial Collection'. It will form the centrepiece of an exhibition next year.

TEENAGE BEAUTY WANTS TO JOIN THE POLICE

SUNDSVALLS WEEKLY

Angelica Trygg, 16, recently held hostage by murderous gangland thugs, says she's considering a police career in the future, or she may become a fashion photographer.

NEW POLICE CHIEF FOR SUNDSVALL

SUNDSVALLS
WEEKLY

Soon-to-retire Lennart Havendal announced today that his successor will be the popular hero of last month's 'Gunfight at the Black Tarn', Magnus Trygg. Recently discharged from hospital where he underwent successful heart bypass surgery, he is currently recuperating at home. Our special reporter spoke to his wife, Sonja, aged 38, who said, "He's been an action-man for long enough. I'm looking forward to having him safely behind a desk."

Inspector Trygg was unavailable for comment.